Miss Webster and Chérif

PATRICIA DUNCKER

BLOOMSBURY

First published in Great Britain in 2006

Copyright © 2006 by Patricia Duncker

The moral right of the author has been asserted

Bloomsbury Publishing Plc,
36 Soho Square,
London W1D 3QY

A CIP catalogue record for this book
is available from the British Library

'The Way that it Shows' by Richard Thompson. Published by Beeswing Music.
Admin by Bug Music. Used by permission.

ISBN 0 7475 8277 7
ISBN-13 9780747582779

10 9 8 7 6 5 4 3 2 1

Typeset by Hewer Text UK Ltd, Edinburgh
Printed in Great Britain by Clays Ltd, St Ives plc

All papers used by Bloomsbury Publishing are natural,
recyclable products made from wood grown in well-managed
forests. The manufacturing processes conform to the
environmental regulations of the country of origin

For my students 1987–1991
Hassan, Mohammed & Chérif

'Allah removed all surplus human and animal life from the desert so that there might be one place for him to walk in peace . . . and so the great Sahara is called the Garden of Allah.'

(Desert Saying)

Abbas, I wish you were the shirt
On my body, or I your shirt.

Or I wish we were in a glass
You as wine, I as rainwater.

Or I wish we were two love birds,
Who lived alone in the desert.

No people.

Abbas Ibn Al-Ahnaf
(750–809)

You sing about love,
Your very flesh is consumed,
And you look quite ill.

Let me praise friendship,
This candle burns more softly, but it's constant.
Slow heat – that's the way it shows.

Abbas Ibn Al-Sabah
(?780–843)

I

THE MESSENGER

S he heard an English voice. Rising above the surrounding
babble of security announcements in different languages
and the distant honking taxis, the English accent, harassed and
irritated, yet full of expectant self-assertion, gave her an
immense rush of reassurance. Someone English, close at
hand. She pinpointed the voice.

'I don't think that'll do any good. We've tried all the
main airlines. I'm going to ring the consulate again and
insist. They keep saying that it's a matter for the police.'

He was tall, narrow-shouldered, wearing a white linen
suit that had creased a little in the small of his back. He
sported a cream hat, wedged on the back of his head, which
made him look theatrical, as if he were playing the part of a
colonial inspector. An Arab in a shiny pink shirt with a
neatly clipped moustache was leaning in towards him,
anxious, fidgeting. Was this an airport official? No, insuffi-
ciently dressed. He was wearing sandals, the thongs tight
over his bare toes. An undercover customs officer? Unlikely. Security guard? No uniform. Not armed. There
were guards swaggering through the airport in desert storm
battledress, carrying Kalashnikovs. A guilty travel rep, who
has mislaid one of his flock? In which case I hope you give

him hell. The Englishman turned and brushed against her inquiring hand which was raised to intercept his elbow. She retreated in shock. He was a black man, an old black man in a white linen suit, his coiled hair white at the temples.

'Oh, excuse me,' she murmured, pretending that she had taken him for someone else.

'May I be of any assistance?'

The English voice never faltered, neither did the urbane and knowing confidence. He had registered her recoil, her alarm. He had read her correctly. She was afraid of him. She had thought he was white. The voice coloured with irony, and the gesture, for he actually bowed towards her, gleamed suave and contemptuous. He had the excessive certainty of a gentleman.

'Are you in difficulties?'

This was too much for Elizabeth Webster. Tears flooded her words.

'I've missed my plane. They said I've missed my plane. We were too late leaving Gatwick. I was meant to join my group here. The transfer to Ouarzazate has gone without me. I can't find anyone here who has ever heard of me.'

This came out as an existential declaration. The two men surrounded her with a cloak of courtesy and concern. The Arab man began waving his hands. His glossy shirt shimmered in the dingy lights.

'This is most unfortunate. I am sure that something can be done. Please do not upset yourself.'

She dug about for a handkerchief in her floral carrier bag and withdrew a small plastic bottle of Evian, a sachet of salad dressing and a yellow biro. Unaccountably, the Arab man accepted all these as legitimate offerings.

'Do you have your travel schedules?' The black man took over. 'Or your ticket?'

2

Helplessly convinced by his Englishness, Elizabeth Webster handed over all her vital documents: tickets, passport, insurance, driving licence, faxed confirmations from The Magical Adventures Travel Company, list of medicines and allergies, vaccination certificates and Foreign Office travel advice, downloaded from the Internet, suggesting that North Africa was a highly undesirable holiday destination. The tall black man sorted through them, trying to identify the airline that was responsible for abandoning fragile old ladies in North African airports. He registered her name: Elizabeth Webster; date of birth: 2 June 1933; domicile: some appalling rural backwater where the local shop wouldn't even stock the national press and the vegetables were long past their sell-by date.

'You flew in with Royal Air Maroc?'

She nodded.

'And now you have to change to another airline? Or do you stay with Royal Air Maroc?'

He looked round the sandy marble hall with its huge dome and the fountain dripping recycled water on shining wires. The space rumbled and boomed, full of scurrying Westerners and local boys trying to hustle them into taxis. She had come downstairs and was now outside the security zone.

'Aren't the Magical Travels responsible?' demanded the pink Arab man.

'No, they're not. They have to meet her at the other end. She hasn't arrived yet.'

The Arab man filched all her documents and snatched the tickets. His pink shirt now appeared detestable. Elizabeth Webster discovered that she was not happy watching him clutching her private papers. Ha! He had deciphered the additional computer printout.

'She's been re-registered. She's on the six o'clock flight. Look here. It just hasn't been called yet. I'll go and check.'

And he trotted off to check-in, clutching her passport and tickets. He was a little overweight and his buttocks wobbled. She watched him spiriting away her national identity and expensively purchased holiday rights with a little surge of alarm. She stepped closer to the Englishman and forgave him for being black. He seemed calm, even protective.

'Shall we sit down?'

Two backpackers suddenly liberated a small table by the kiosk selling fresh orange juice and scuttled away. The black man pulled out the chair for her and settled her bags between them.

'An orange juice perhaps? Or a coffee?' She had not yet acquired any foreign currency as the dirham proved to be non-transferable and was therefore worthless outside the country. He brushed her objections aside.

'They accept Euros. At an extortionate rate.' She confronted a small plastic glass of freshly squeezed orange juice.

She ventured a conversation. 'Are you looking for someone? I couldn't help overhearing –'

'Yes,' he replied gloomily, 'and it's hopeless. We've lost all trace.'

He spread out a newspaper cutting on the table, beside her floral carrier bag and plastic glass. The headline read CRIME OF PASSION KILLER GOES FREE. A grainy picture of a sullen street girl in dreadlocks glared back from the middle of the text. Runaway. Jumped bail. Spanish courts. Miss Webster gave up. Why were the Spanish courts bothered? Didn't they let you go with three months suspended sentence and an understanding reprimand from the judge for killing off the women taken in adultery? So was this man her father, mired in grief, hunting down her fleeing passion killer? Perhaps the pink Arab worked as a private detective. She arranged an expression of sympathetic tragedy and held it up in front of her face. To each his own sorrow. The strange hunt faded softly back into the papers on the table. I have my own sadness. This is not my affair. They sat silent, anxious among the booming announcements: Arabic, English, French, Spanish. All unattended luggage will be treated as a security risk and may be removed or destroyed.

'Are you on holiday?' The black man was clearly wondering why she was alone.

'My doctor told me that I should go far away,' she murmured.

Far away from what? She no longer made any sense. The black man in the creased white linen suit nodded his assent, baffled, humouring the mad. She sounded deranged, even to herself. 'You see, I wasn't at all well.'

He bowed. For indeed, she gleamed an unhealthy yellow, unnervingly thin, her head adorned with a curious arrangement of white punk spikes, bobbing at an angle as if she had caught the first whiff of Parkinson's.

'Ah. You have been ill.'

The voice – and he was rapidly dissolving into nothing but the voice – managed to convey respect and concern. She didn't have to go into details if she didn't want to do so. On the other hand the voice made it clear that she could have flung an entire nervous breakdown into the abyss between them. The black man possessed a golden tooth, somewhere up to the left. He smouldered slightly, now that she was close to him, exhaling an interesting perfume. What was it? *Opium pour homme*. She peered at the stitching on the pocket of his suit. The whole thing was handmade, tailored to fit. He smelt of wealth. He would not abandon her until her situation was resolved. He would carry her bags. The cool patrician patina of the English middle classes hit her again like the first wave of a typhoon. Another moment and she would break down and gabble. She blinked. No, the gentleman was still there, still listening, still black. He was a sort of miracle.

'Yes. I have been very ill,' she whispered with relief.

In fact she had come to a full stop; not on the street or on the bus, which would have attracted attention, but in the privacy of her own sitting room, slumped before *Newsnight* on her green striped sofa. The television, still murmuring gently, retreated to a great distance. George Bush was addressing The World. '*States like these, and their terrorist allies, constitute an axis of evil, arming to threaten the peace of the world . . . The United States of America will not permit the world's most dangerous regimes to threaten us with the world's most destructive weapons.*' The scene cut to a stage-managed international conference around a horseshoe table with pink curtains as a backdrop. She could still hear it, far away, as her blood stilled and her eyes became fixed. The flickering blur accompanied her into a dark place of buzzing silence. The midnight serial-killer movie played itself out with no one aware of its terrors and expensive special effects. The lights still burned above the fireplace and in the kitchen, but the curtains upstairs were never drawn that night. Elizabeth Webster sat, silent and rigid, surrounded by all her possessions, magnificent and colossal as the embalmed pharaohs, far embarked upon that journey from which there is usually no return.

Yet when the early spring dawn came, she was still there.

The television hummed to itself, the screen presented a young girl hugging a labrador, surrounded by gaudy radiating colours, the lights dimmed. The jubilant birds in her garden and in the meadow that confronted her house celebrated a new day. They were the first things she heard again in her own flesh. She sat paralysed, confused. She had lost seven hours of time. She could not remember what had happened, or where she had been.

The first person to approach the house was the postman. Sometimes, when she had not spoken to another human being for many days, she apprehended him in the tiny space of the porch and assailed him with conversational clichés. But on that day he slapped down three offers of car insurance, one for MasterCard, and a special reduced subscription offer. Join The Royal Society for the Protection of Birds and receive a free gift – an illustrated pamphlet on migrating species. He had to double this over to get it through the letter box, but as it hit the mat he pushed off back down the lane. He did not notice that the curtains remained closed downstairs and that the lights were still burning. He passed on, moving from house to house.

Elizabeth Webster was unable to stir her limbs or see clearly, but her hearing strengthened as the morning advanced. By nine o'clock she was capable of extending her right hand, crisped like a dead chicken's claw, towards the telephone, which perched beside the sofa. The telephone had a row of numbers, ordered alphabetically and buried in the small computer's brain: Council tax, CPS Gas Supplies, Garage, Gardener, Hairdresser, Shop, Surgery. One button, waveringly disturbed by her clenched knuckles, resulted in a dialling tone and then a voice.

'Great Blessington Medical Group. How can I help you?'

But she could not speak.

A sort of burr, burr, burr, gathering strength and resonance, emerged from her throat.

'Hello? Is anyone there?

'Hello?

'Hello? Who's there, please?'

Click.

But the receptionist at Great Blessington Medical Group was mistrustful of mystery calls. Someone was trying to get through. She rang 1471 and then traced the call, so that when the phone rang and rang in the eerie, illuminated stillness of the sitting room, Elizabeth Webster knew that her muffled yell for help was being slowly heard.

'It's Miss Webster.' The receptionist checked the name back against the computer's list of patients' numbers, carefully ordered by village and doctor in attendance. The practice now boasted a website and on-line services. 'I remember her. She won't come in for check-ups. Aged sixty-nine. Forcibly retired at sixty-four. Ex French teacher at the convent. Lives alone. Very high blood pressure. They must have dragged her out of the classroom. I bet she's had a stroke.'

Behold Dr Humphreys banging on her front door twenty minutes later, thirty-four years old with a young wife and twins. He didn't get much sleep at the best of times and felt as if he too had lost seven hours the previous night. He lurched around the porch as if swimming through soup. He didn't know the retired old lady who lived alone at the end of a rough un-made-up track, the last cottage before the woods, a little brick and flint building facing the meadows, covered all summer in sweet peas and climbing roses. Here it is, the greening process of spring just beginning. Why do I always end up with the tricky home visits? She's one of Dr Brody's patients. The old boy should set the date for his retirement party. Then we can get someone younger for the practice who'll help me out with the rural clean-up jobs.

'Hello? Miss Webster? Hello?'

Curtains still closed, lights on. She's had a fall. Quick, round the back. He could look in through the kitchen window. Behind the garage, down past the dustbins, through the flickering hard sunshine beneath the apple tree. He peered through the uncurtained back window.

There she was, still upright, grey-faced, eyes fixed. She must be dead. She may have been dead for hours. I thought the surgery said she'd phoned in for help. Dear God, she's dead. He attacked the back door in a panic. It was open. Dr Humphreys flung himself though the kitchen, bouncing off the solid wooden table, disturbing every cup hanging on the dresser, across the dining room, and into the warm cluttered space where the morning breakfast show on the television stuttered into the weather forecast and a list of forthcoming programmes to a ludicrous accompaniment of banal music. Out of respect he turned it off. Then he noticed that her eyes had moved. She looked dishevelled, shifty, distressed, as if she had spent the night drinking. He knelt quietly beside her and took her hand. The hand transmitted a rush of glacial cold. She must be dead. But she was looking at him.

'Miss Webster? You are not at all well.'

But she did not reply.

He felt for her pulse and then called the ambulance. She was very much alive, but had come to a dead halt. When the ambulance men lifted her tenderly on to the stretcher a pond of urine rushed down her legs and saturated the red blanket.

9

'Whoops-a-daisy.'

The men were gentle, unperturbed.

'Let's get you to hospital, dear, and make you more comfortable.'

Dr Humphreys locked the back door, shut down the central heating and turned out all the lights.

The lights never seemed to go out in the hospital. Alarmingly, the ward was mixed. Men to the right, women to the left. They were cordoned off in bays of four beds, islands of white separated by green plastic armchairs and yellow screens. She awoke attached to a floating bottle, suspended by invisible wires, three feet above her head. The nurses looked at the clipboard attached to her iron cage, but not at her. NIL BY MOUTH. She saw this sign hanging upside down on the bed next to her and twitched, irrationally pleased that she could still read, albeit like Alice, from the other side of the glass. Somewhere, far away, she heard voices. But on the whole the ward resembled a silent film, played out in unfocused shots with an alarming zoom for close-ups and much repetition. The doctors touched her wrist, her forehead. The nurses issued endearments and instructions.

'I'm just going to take a little bit of blood, dear.'

'Can you hear me, dear? If you can, move your eyes to the left. Ooh yes. Aren't you the clever one? Now to the right.' A pencil torch shone directly into her shrinking pupils.

'Left again.'

She closed her eyes. Someone patted her hand. She felt belittled, patronised. She began to worry about her house. Who would water her plants? Thank God the cat was dead. It had been dead for years. She groaned slightly. The patronising voice was immediately present, as if she had set off a recorded message.

'Are you in pain, dear? Squeeze my hand if you are.'

Elizabeth Webster opened both eyes and glared at the blue mass topped with a blurred white label. Staff Nurse Something or Other. Piss off, she snarled. But all that came out was a burr, burr, burr, deep in her chest.

Another voice said, 'I'll arrange for the brain scan to be brought forward.'

Elizabeth Webster heard someone chanting.

This man hath penance done
And penance more will do.

Then the boat drifted out of reach on to an immense shelf of darkness.

She lay beached on a coral shelf. A huge machine purred all around her, the note changed to a gentle hum, the lights scorched her eyeballs. She saw the reflection of red – red sky, red dunes, red sand. She had crash-landed in a desert. There were no other passengers.

'Is there anyone we can ring, dear? To let them know where you are.'

'Do you have any family?'

They always ask the same fucking questions. *Où est votre mari? Où sont vos enfants?* As if you couldn't conduct your life without assistance from either one or the other. A small fast car, driven by a youth convinced of his immortality, had smashed into her on a hill in Normandy. They were all scraped up by the *pompiers*, who had asked exactly the same questions, over and over again. *Où habitez-vous? Où est votre mari? Où sont vos enfants?* She was always in the dock, always being cross-examined.

But I ask the questions. I have the right to ask the questions.

I'm not timid.

I'm not scared.

They see a little old lady, bird bones collapsed together in a fragile heap. I'm inside. I have a voice.

But she didn't. Burr, burr, burr.

Do you have any family, dear? *Où est votre mari? Où sont vos enfants?*

She heard the slow lap of water. The keel shuddered and rose into the air. She was sailing back from X-ray.

Repeat after me: I am not helpless. I am not a victim. I am an old woman. But I am still here.

'Move your eyes if you can hear me.'

She glanced slightly to the left. Turn to the right. There was something horrible between her legs. Oh God, they have inserted a catheter. Elizabeth Webster suffered from a horror of incontinence. A second childhood of nappies and leaking urine yawned before her. She tried to wriggle free, but this was interpreted as distress. The staff nurse materialised, armed with a disposable syringe, determined to suppress the violent thrashing. Elizabeth shuddered as the needle went in.

'The blood tests are back. The scans are clear. She hasn't had a heart attack. She hasn't had a stroke. I don't quite understand it.'

The pilot's boy
Who now doth crazy go.

Smells became clearer. Detergent. Bleach. Urine. Overcooked vegetables. Burnt custard. Spilt orange juice. Washing powder. Furniture polish. Her sight remained compromised. Colours were indistinct. White and cream blurred into a glowing mass as if an apparition had heaved itself into her range of perception. She could not see. She could not speak. But she could still smell the odours of the hospital, some rank, some comforting. And when she was conscious, she could hear everything.

'Poor old thing. Has she had a stroke?'

'Better to let them go when they get like that.'

Elizabeth Webster longed to rise up from her bed of death and hit them. Her anger was transparent, articulate, vivid − like a falling sheet of clear water, but it had no channels in which to flow. She tried to bite her silent tongue and discovered that the nurse had removed her bridge. One half of her mouth gaped empty of teeth. They were taking her apart, like a dilapidated robot, piece by rusting piece.

She slid back into the dream time and saw an angel, all feathered wings, white robes and androgynous Pre-Raphaelite sweetness, lurking above the waters. As she watched, the angel descended and dipped its long silken sleeves into the pool, stirring the surface into choppy froth. Quick, lift me up. Carry my bier to the brink of the flood. Lay me in the foaming whirlpool before the angel goes. Bring me to the waters she has touched and I shall be healed. I need water, not the Word of God. Bring me water.

Burr, burr, burr.

But this was the first clear word that the nurse could discern:

'Water.'

She at once tipped the baby's plastic cup on to the old woman's shrivelled lips. A trail of sweetened dribble ran down her chin. The angel hovered, glimmered, vanished.

And the night staff standing there in the wake of its vanishing were left puzzling over her notes.

'She's been out of intensive care for ages. No change.'

'She hasn't had a stroke.'

'Dr Broadhurst is coming tomorrow.'

'Oh. It's heart then, is it? He's the big white chief in cardiology.'

Dr Broadhurst was a very ugly man. He had oily thinning hair and heavy glasses. His suit didn't fit and his baggy white coat was stained with blue strokes from a leaking biro. He flirted with all the nurses. He remembered every name and details about each colleague's family circumstances. He brought real Swiss chocolates for the entire ward and had a wicked funny leer. Everyone adored him.

'This is Miss Webster. She was brought in on the morning of Tuesday 19 March. She came out of intensive care about a week later and has been here with us ever since. You've seen the blood test results? And the scan? She's anaemic. High blood pressure in the past. Not drastically high now. We don't really have a firm diagnosis. She's semi-conscious most of the time. How are you today, Miss Webster?' The blurred white mass loitering above her clearly did not expect an answer and so she refused to respond. Then the heavy frames and oily clump of hair loomed into view.

His hands were the first things she saw clearly since the dead halt in her sitting room. They were hideous, deformed. The livid skin was peeled back over the knuckles, the scar tissue spattered with puckered spots of brown. The flesh bunched and shrivelled, as if he had fought off a napalm attack with ungloved fists. He placed one hideous scabbed palm upon her wrist. She flinched at once, as if she had been stabbed. The doctor's jowly face broke into a huge gap-toothed smile. He raised both tortured hands in a gesture of acceptance and defeat. And then he spoke directly to her, and only to her.

'I know. Horrible, aren't they? I had skin cancer and this is what severe radiation burns look like close up. I don't ever wear gloves. I never hide them. It seems like cheating.'

He turned his hands over, as if admiring the damage. Elizabeth opened her eyes wide. She wanted to acknowledge this gift of candour. But how? She coiled up all her strength and sent the message to her fading brain. Nod. Smile. She had no idea what happened on her face, which had detached itself from her skeleton weeks ago and now floated at a little distance, like a dancer's mask. She felt nothing, but the doctor squeezed her fingers in his grotesque and puckered hands, leaned close to her and winked. She caught the flash, magnified in the right lens.

'Put her in a room of her own. Let her sleep as much as she likes. Keep her very quiet. I'll come and see her again tomorrow.'

The way back towards movement, sight, speech, the daily task of interpreting the world, had opened up before her.

She knew when he was there because he always showed her his hands. They were his trademark, his password. She relaxed whenever she saw the browned claws and yellow nails smoothing the pillows, cradling her wrists. She was being held in place by a gentle monster who meant her no harm. He gave her a sequence of daily injections. At the end of a week her sight began to clear. She knew

15

morning from evening. She watched the sunset in the basin's glass.

'When will you speak to me, Miss Webster? May I call you Elizabeth?'

She squeezed the burned scabs.

'Thank you. Would you like a chocolate?'

She tried to shake her head. But nothing moved.

'Did something happen to you on the night you fell ill? Can you remember?'

She saw her small green rooms, the vase to the left of the television, her little bookcase with all her treasures, her Larousse and three different French dictionaries on the bottom shelf. The television was murmuring gently, wars and rumours of wars. She heard the climbing rose scratching against the window. A quiet night in a cold spring, the damp settling on the closed daffodils, the security lights at the end of the muddy lane illuminating whenever one of her neighbours came home. No. Nothing had happened. There was no reason now why anything should ever happen.

'Dites-moi, chère Madame, pourquoi vous n'êtes pas heureuse.'

He spoke perfect fluent French. She felt a little shock go through her when she heard the language again. She clutched at her beloved other mother tongue. She watched the late-night films; she tried to ignore the subtitles. She read *Le Figaro* magazine and she had recently discovered *Le Passant Ordinaire* to which she still subscribed because, although she loathed the revolutionary politics, she liked the art photographs and the uncompromising articles, spattered with technical terms from psychoanalysis. But since she had retired from the school and abandoned the embarrassment of grammar, the horror of dictation and the evils of free composition, she had not heard the language spoken. She had not heard the rising chimes, neither murdered by recalcitrant children or perfect in the voice of her student assistant, a young graduate from Caen, who wore very expensive suede shoes with pointed toes. She tried to eliminate the vision of those shoes and concentrated hard on the distorted claw, which settled on her wrist.

'Prenez votre temps, Madame.'

He had noticed the reaction. He was helping her towards the language that she loved; a territory she had once lost for ever now reeled into view. She whispered the words. The burr, burr, burr began, cleared. Her heart filled up like an empty cistern in heavy rain.

'Je ne sais pas,' she gasped. I don't know. I am unhappy. I am angry. I am lonely. I am old. I don't know. Dr Broadhurst sat very still, leering slightly, Patience on a monument, smiling at grief. *Je ne sais pas. Je ne sais pas.* I don't know. I don't know. She said it again and again, for the sheer pleasure of hearing the words of denial and doubt. These were her words. He waited until she fell silent.

'But when you do, you will tell me, won't you?' He continued quietly in French. She squeezed the claw, now clamped firmly in her own freckled, bony grasp. The wooded passage through her shadowed mind opened out into fields, filled with purple flowers and summer light. She heard bees amidst the buddleia.

'How long have I been here?' she whispered.

'Deux mois,' said Dr Broadhurst, 'two months.'

It was summer in a new century. She curled on her side, dreaming time, all ports astern, clear seas before her. Then she realised that the sensation of swaying upon the swell was perfectly legitimate. She was floating on a waterbed, set to a long slow wave. She glared at the doctor's uncanny repulsive face.

'Mais qui êtes-vous?' she demanded.

'I'm the messenger,' he said.

The worst obstacle she had to overcome in the following weeks was the physiotherapy. A muscular young woman with a grisly dragon tattoo and one earring arrived every day for an hour. She pulled and bent and pummelled. Then she threatened Elizabeth Webster with bedsores if she didn't make an effort.

'You always get bedsores in recovering coma cases.'

Elizabeth told her to fuck off in murmured French. The very next day she was whisked away in a wheelchair to the heated pool. Hydrotherapy. At first this seemed like a better bet than the bedroom assaults. She was crammed into a black one-piece bathing costume that was too big for her and hung in baggy folds around her stomach and groin. For the first time she contemplated her bony thighs and slack distended flesh. Her body lay crumpled, hideous, decayed. She had lost over four stone. Young arms lifted her into the steaming water and attached her to a sequence of blue floats. She immediately longed to urinate and grappled with her pelvic muscles. The hated catheter had been removed but she no longer commanded her bowels. It was all too humiliating. She felt the tears rushing down. Get me out. Get me out.

'Is it too hot for you, darling?'

An enormous hairy man hauled her out again. Had he dislocated both her shoulders?

'She's crying. She doesn't like it.'

'Pee! Pee! Pee!' yelled Elizabeth Webster. Burr, burr, burr.

'What's the matter, sweetheart?'

18

The fake sexy tones enraged her. That's it. The screaming bladder would probably have triumphed anyway, but
she let go on purpose. In the spirit of vindictive aggression
she pissed all over the tiles on the side of the tank. To her
surprise the hairy physiotherapist simply roared with laughter.

'Bless you, my love. You didn't want to do it in the pool.
Let's get you over here and hose you down. This always
happens. Didn't they take you to the loo on the way down?
Naughty girls. I'll give them a piece of my mind. Maybe a
spanking if they're feeling lucky and special.'

He roared at his own camp menaces, propped her up in a
white plastic chair above a drain in the tiles, pushed her legs
apart and hosed down her stomach and thighs. The thin
streak of golden urine mellowed and widened, then vanished. She gasped at the fierce jet of colder water. At first
the shock winded her, then oddly enough the force felt
pleasant, even suggestive. She wriggled against the pointed
torrent.

'That's better now! Back in the pool!'

He picked her up as if she were a bunch of weightless
sticks and lowered her gently into the floats. His body smelt
of oil and chlorine. All the hair on his chest, back and arms
floated independently in the water, which gave every limb
a furry aureole. He increased dramatically in size.

'That's it, darling. Stretch those legs out and pop your
head back. You'll float ever so easily. Close your eyes.
That's it. It's not even five-foot deep. Like a great big bath.
Pretend you're Cleopatra. She had a bath of asses' milk,
didn't she? NHS doesn't quite run to that. Stretch your
back. Let your bottom float up. Relax. There we go.'

She lay peaceful and extended on a nap of bright blue in
a room full of hollow echoes. Above her the light exploded

against the girders and the opaque glass roof. The silver bar around the tank nudged her elbow. She was hot, cradled, secure, floating in the amniotic fluid. She began to doze off.

But here he was again, beside her in the water, the hairy creature, full of irritating talk.

'Oh do shut up, you fool,' snapped Elizabeth Webster, all her rusty guns rattling, her voice powerful and abrasive, just as it had once been, billowing out into a nascent rage, addressing the rowdy third form.

'That's it,' shrugged the monster, ruffling all the surfaces, apparently not at all offended. 'Treat me like the blond bimbo that I am!'

But Miss Webster was laughing. The floats were sliding out from underneath her. Wasted grey wisps of hair stuck slicked to her face and throat. She tried to splash water into his face, had no strength to do so and slithered under. He raised her up. She spat out a mouthful of hot, blue, chlorinated liquid. She still had no teeth in the left side of her mouth and wondered where they were. Yet she was laughing.

At last she could sit up in her hospital–issue orange floral gown, which buttoned up the front, all the way to her chin, without her head lolling like a dead sunflower. But she still could not walk unaided, so she was placed back in the wheelchair and whisked away down corridors and into lifts. She emerged in bright sunshine. Here were windows opening on to a lawn. Here was an empty desk with a phone and one open file. Here were family photographs on a teak filing cabinet: children on a mountainside frisking like goats in a panorama of green and blue. A standard lamp with a wooden base. Green carpets, no artworks. A large carton of Swiss chocolates. And here was the doctor with the mutilated hands.

He waited until she had completed her inspection. He watched her assessing the sunshine in the gardens. He took his time. So did she.

'Will you talk to me now?' he asked quietly.

She looked carefully at his hands, which were, as always, placed like a gauntlet on the desk before him.

'Have I had any visitors?'

She was not sure if she had dreamed Dr Brody and the vicar.

'Yes. Your GP has come every week. He's in constant touch with me. Your vicar and his wife have come twice a week ever since you've been here. They bring you fresh flowers from your own garden every time. They have the keys to your house. They have watered your plants and seen to the lawns. They have written to your family in Canada, who are, I believe, your closest living relations.'

Elizabeth Webster looked at Dr Broadhurst's ugly face and thinning, oily hair in horror.

'I didn't tell them to fuck off, did I?'

'And much, much worse. Where did you learn to swear like that? You must have been in the Navy.' The doctor boomed his incredulity and appreciation. They could hear him in the corridor. She sat before the desk, no longer innocent, but open-mouthed, appalled.

'One of your ex-colleagues has been here too. Can't remember his name. He was very impressed. He said that you were excellent at keeping order. Now we all know how you did it.'

So that's what had poured out of her — a torrent of enraged filth. The doctor met her eye, suddenly serious.

'It's quite normal. It often happens. I had a patient with

21

early dementia who told us all that we were rotten, rat-arsed cunts and meant every word of it.'

'I haven't got dementia.' Elizabeth Webster was decisive.

'No,' he agreed, 'you haven't.'

'Then what have I got?'

'You haven't got anything that we can understand. You just came to a dead halt. And you were very ill indeed. And then you became very angry. And now we have to find out why.'

She looked him in the eye. Her lips hardened into a thin white line. Her chin came up.

'But if you do know why, you're under no obligation to say anything whatsoever. You're in hospital, not under arrest.' He was being conciliatory, humouring her.

'Don't patronise me.' She warned him off.

'Wouldn't dare,' said Dr Broadhurst and spread out his ghastly hands before her in a gesture of surrender.

There was a long pause. She saw someone in the gardens, shouting silent orders above the sputter of a mower. She smelt the cut grass of high summer and heard the buzzing from within the great yellow corneas of the daisies. The world glowed magnified, surreal. She sensed something huge, eyeless, breathing, close to her. The doctor sat at ease in the uncanny silence. And now the revolt that was boiling within her began to take shape. She was not under any obligation to apologise for who she was or to justify herself. She had no immediate answers or explanations, but she had that huge, long rage of the warriors who are never defeated, the wounded who die with their swords bared and blood-ied, their eyes fixed on the approaching enemy. Miss Webster's insurrection took the form of refusing to play ball with the eminent consultant. Why should she do all the talking?

'Speak,' she commanded.

'Have a chocolate?' He held out a lavish box decorated with a range of snow-capped peaks, each separate segment of dark, bitter chocolate wrapped in silver paper. She ignored him.

'I speak French,' he began to explain, apropos of nothing at all, 'because my wife is Swiss. She speaks French and German and we have a house at Vevey, above the lake. Your GP told me that you were a French teacher and that you had a passion for the language. That is why I spoke to you in French. You wouldn't listen to English any more. I thought that you might listen to the language you loved, if not to me.'

She nodded. He was telling the truth. Suddenly he leaned across the desk as if he were confiding a secret.

'Miss Webster – or Elizabeth – you haven't yet said that I may call you Elizabeth – I don't think that you are mad. I know that you have not had a stroke. You have had – or are having – a complex form of complete breakdown. Your heart is affected, but the attack was not caused by any form of heart disease. I am a cardiologist, but I am also a psychiatrist. Whatever is wrong needs to be acknowledged, and I really cannot know what is wrong until you tell me. You need to know why this has happened to you, or it will happen again. And you will die, unknowing.'

She did not answer him. Instead she stared past the doctor's shoulder at the huge copper beech swaying in the gardens, the branches stretching low on to the fresh damp grass.

'You may call me Elizabeth,' she said.

He nodded, pleased.

'I want to go home.'

He rubbed his repulsive butchered palms together. 'Good, good,' he said.

She was obstinate and courageous in front of Dr Broadhurst, but it was quite another matter entering the house she had left behind her on a windy night in March, nearly three months earlier. She came back in the ambulance. Dr Brody was waiting on the doorstep. He had read 'deceased' rather than 'discharged' on the fax that arrived in the surgery, and rang the hospital in a panic. Now he stood, wrong-footed, embarrassed, fiddling with the keys, hoping that no one had betrayed his mistake in an excess of black humour. Miss Webster was preoccupied with more basic problems than her own death, which she had always assumed would be beyond her power to organise and control. She had practised walking in the hospital, but was still dangerously unsteady on rough ground. The lane with its dips and puddles presented a frightening terrain. She concentrated on keeping herself vertical with the two canes they had given her and avoided the doctor's eye. He had seen her at her worst in the hospital: toothless, hair unwashed and tortured into thin grey plaits, stinking, abusive, unkempt. She had suddenly become old and mad.

Now she was wearing a shabby pair of trousers, borrowed from the hospital and her once smart cardigan, which swayed about her bony shoulders in horrid folds. Her grey skin dangled in slack sheets around her neck and jaw. The bridge was back in place, but it no longer fitted and a sinister new row of puckered lines furrowed her upper lip. Her watch, carefully returned to her in a labelled envelope, now hung loose upon her wrist. Some of the jewellery she had been wearing had disappeared. Her gold and pearl earrings, which had once belonged to her grand-mother, had clip-on fixtures. The women of her family took the view that only prostitutes had their ears pierced. Jewellery often simply vanished in the hospital. No one had ever seen the little clips of pearl and gold. Or so they said. She had been a trim but solid woman, five foot five, weighing in at eleven stone. Now she staggered towards her own front door like a dilapidated spider, propped up by walking sticks.

'No, I can manage.' She pushed back the doctor and the staff from the ambulance.

Someone had had a go at the garden. The foxgloves and hollyhocks were enormous, but the smoky blue ceanothus had been clipped and contained. The French rose, wrenched away from the windows, sported a fabulous torrent of pale pink blooms. Unscented. The old climbing roses had no scent at all. All their beauty was in opulence. Dr Brody dealt with the ambulance. She looked at his hunched back and balding head. He too was getting old. An old man helping an old patient, a retired spinster who used to fit all the polite clichés: game old bird, sharp as a button, spry and fit for someone her age, iron constitution, never misses a thing, she has a clever way of putting things, never wastes her words. Wasted. She had been laid waste. She had stopped dead in her tracks and the horror hurtling along behind her, like a convoy of articulated lorries, had simply piled into her back. She was flattened in the crash.

'Miss Webster? May I help you in?'

Dr Brody, whom she had told to stick the thermometer up his own arse and go fuck himself, was bowing and bobbing like an eighteenth-century gentleman. How on earth was the old girl going to manage? Surely she had been discharged far too soon? She could see it on his face.

25

Someone had cleaned out and re-stocked the fridge. There was a carton of milk, a packet of processed cheese, eggs, butter, half a dozen tomatoes. The vase to the left of the television was full of fresh-cut garden flowers. She sank into an upright wooden chair that faced the windows and the open meadows beyond, so that she did not have to confront the kindness of unseen hands or the obnoxious bouquet. She could not stomach unsolicited generosity. She felt the bile rising again. Down *hysterica passio*. Let me rot. Leave me be.

Dr Brody was fussing, making suggestions. She heard the gentle stream resolving into words such as 'tomorrow', 'your personal carer' and 'meals on wheels'. She made one last tremendous effort to remove him from her front room without shouting.

'Thank you, Dr Brody. I shall be quite all right.'

She tried smiling reassurance. Smile at them. Then they go away and leave you alone. But the smile had become a fixed rictus before she could persuade him to leave. He backed out through the porch and into the lane, still distributing offers of assistance. She shrank into her trembling heap of oversized and disinfected clothes, then closed her eyes.

She did not retire, she did not resign, she was pushed out, rejected as one of the unrepentant ancien régime facing a new dispensation. The three schools in her neighbourhood had been restructured; St Winifred's, the old Catholic girls only, where she had been French mistress for over thirty years, was absorbed into a much tougher catchment area. Elizabeth Webster had been educating the nation to the best of her abilities. This meant the discipline of grammar, the rigorous pursuit of beauty in poetry, civilising the wild and discouraging drugs and eye make-up. The teachers at the convent had been like the nuns, authoritative, sincere, possessed of a vocation. But now the language of education was transformed around her; here was a new breed of teachers who had not heard the call, did not much care about their subjects, were given to fiddling with their computers rather than reading books, yet were busy moulding their careers in education. They carried clipboards and worried about the school's position in the league tables. She was told that she could not go on teaching the old syllabus. What use was Corneille? Racine? Molière? She was urged to modernise. The language of *l'informatique*, economics, journalism, that's the coming thing. Business French will be of more use to them. They have to understand the finance pages.

> *Ce prince dont mon cœur se faisait autrefois*
> *Avec tant de plaisir redire les exploits*
> *À qui même en secret, je m'étais destinée . . .*

Racine no longer made their hearts beat faster. She used to pack at least half a dozen Catholic girls, desperate for sex, their heads full of *Phèdre*, into assorted colleges at Oxford and Cambridge. Now they wanted to do Media, Film and Communication Studies at universities of which Miss Webster had never heard. What is to be done? Elizabeth Webster fought a quiet but incisive campaign of rational resistance. She was, to use their jargon, 'managed out' over a period of two years. They reduced her timetable, then accused her of not pulling her weight. She was offered a tight-fisted early retirement package. They were liquidating the dinosaur. Time to take care of your roses, dear.

27

Elizabeth Webster did not go quietly. She made a scene in the headmaster's office. She involved the union, who thought she was mad, but did their best to improve the package. She refused to be thanked or given a retirement present. In any case she hardly knew any of her colleagues any more. Only one of the nuns still sat on the board of governors. The old guard had all been eased out and were glad to go. The young new teachers regarded her as an unnecessary antiquity, a dated porcelain piece of little value that would soon fall from the shelf of its own accord. That was the order of things. She was being brushed aside by a giant wave of ignorance and mediocrity, all action taken in the name of a great love for lists and systems. She packed up her classroom and her office in one afternoon and drove off in a rage. She took all the literature textbooks. No one tried to stop her. She sent back her keys by registered post and never set foot in the building again. Her anger remained, undiminished.

But anger proved to be an expensive luxury. Elizabeth Webster had never married. Women of her generation made a choice: marriage and children, or an independent career. Her mother chose marriage, the large country house and the two daughters. The inexorable logic of family life took hold and the mother had then, over decades, been gently but firmly bullied into her green grave. Elizabeth's younger sister made off to Canada as soon as she could save up enough money for the ticket and never came back. She married a rich man, but she still went out to work. The Christmas photographs of houses, dogs and children became ever larger and more affluent over the years. Finally they came by DHL Express, wonderfully wrapped in stiff gilt frames. Miss Webster's younger sister took her husband's name and attended the family funerals. These two things represented her concessions to convention; she tolerated nothing else. She abhorred the death-bed scenes and waited until all was quiet before booking her flight. She too now spoke beautiful French and she dressed with great taste in strong colours and matching accessories. In middle age she paid for a facelift and wore the kind of high heels that Elizabeth had banned, even in the sixth form.

'I was always terrified of becoming like you. You more than Mother, although she was bad enough.' Her sister was all candour and unpleasantness as soon as they had tucked their father neatly into the soft loam. 'I used to wake up dreaming that I had become you. My husband tells me that I screamed and screamed.'

And with that she sauntered back to her land of short, humid summers, emptiness and blizzards. Her responsibilities towards hearth and kin were now complete. The Christmas photographs stopped that year and Miss Elizabeth Webster never heard from her sister again.

What am I like that you were so afraid of degenerating into a resemblance? She got up and looked into the mirror above the telephone. There she saw a stranger's face, old, wizened, shrunken. The eyes glowered misty and huge, the nose protruded like a dæmon's beak, the hair sank crushed and lifeless against the scalp. She had once nourished a very handsome chignon, which she could coil up into an elegant roll and secure with a tortoiseshell comb. Her appearance could not be considered elegant once she turned forty. She was too solid for elegance, but at least she had been smart and suitable, a middle-class English lady of a certain age, fitted out with all the trimmings, like a well-painted dumpy steamer, managing her affairs, brandishing car keys and briefcase, her savings accounts bulging and replete. Now she looked like a plague victim.

Well, my sister, was this what you saw? My future and yours?

She had been forced out of the school five years earlier, lived alone as she had always done, and saw very few other people beyond the inhabitants of Little Blessington. She went to Waitrose once a week. She offered French literature classes to the University of the Third Age, but nobody was interested. They already had a retired professor teaching existentialism. And after all, her fate was not so strange. Many women find themselves alone in their late sixties. Husbands die, children grow up and move to other parts of the country – or turn out to be monsters. There are no insurance policies against loneliness. She had never built any close friendships with anyone; she was self-sufficient and suspicious. Other people either asked you for money or made you listen to their life stories. She had no idea which was worse.

So she joined the bridge club. This was peopled with her kind, a dozen elderly and well-heeled locals: embittered, ironic, eccentric and morose, too savagely disillusioned even to contemplate voting Tory, excellent at cards and intent on winning every game. They played for small sums. No one ever spoke at great length. Her usual partners were men of few words. Only one other woman was a member of the club, the leather-faced wife of a gentleman farmer. The bridge club got on well with Elizabeth Webster, who gave no fatal signs of being feminine and enjoyed a drink. They sent her one Get Well card during her three months in hospital and none of them came to visit her. The bridge club regarded her as one of the Fallen. Someone else took her place.

On the whole, Miss Webster did not like men. She had not liked her father. She did not like the headmaster, who had done his best to have her sacked. She was not fond of the vicar, who was earnest and sincere, yet medieval in his theology. He feared, with some justice, that the entire world was held fast in the grip of the Evil One and endeavoured to work Satan's presence into his sermon on Christmas morning. She did not much like Dr Brody, who fussed and twittered. She did not like men who offered to help and assumed that she couldn't start the car, carry the bags, shovel snow, chop down trees, decapitate the hedge. But there was now an exception. She admired the hideous man with the mutilated hands because he spoke her language and commanded her respect.

Her small store of bottles was dusty and undisturbed. She poured herself a large whisky. The phone rang. She let it ring and ring and ring.

And so it was, during that summer early on in the new century, that year from which a slice was simply lost, remaining alive became an enormous task that was almost too much for her. She knew that she was being difficult, but she found it impossible to admit that she was no longer self-sufficient, and that her odious, garrulous personal carer had become essential. The shopping grew in scale and weight until she felt like Sisyphus, facing the stone. Her sister finally managed to get through on the telephone, late one night when Elizabeth was sitting staring at the blank screen, too discouraged and demoralised even to turn on the news.

'I thought something like this might happen to you. You were always so damned righteous when it happened to other people. Don't expect any help from me.'

'Have you rung up just to tell me that?'

'You've got enough money, haven't you? Make the best of it.'

It was an evil reckoning.

Why should we listen to you, you old cow? One of the children, caught smoking on the school steps had said that to her face. They were little vultures; they knew she was on the way out. They scented the kill. In her day the children had knocked on the staff-room door and begun their sentences with 'Please, Miss, may I . . .' Now they arrived in their own cars, flirted with the younger staff and smoked openly, without let or hindrance, even when they were still wearing school uniform. She bit her lip. Meaning had evaporated from all her maxims and certainties. What mattered? Discipline, order, control. The younger children jeered at her from a safe distance. They skulked behind the privet on the way to the car park and made loud farting noises when she lowered her arse on to the driver's seat.

Elizabeth Webster had been autocratic and sharp-tongued. Now she was an old woman. She was therefore fair game.

You need to know why this has happened to you. Or it will happen again. But nothing ever comes round again. I shall never stand before my class or have the small moments of power and satisfaction every teacher has. I shall never see my pupils succeed nor receive those happy cards when their exams are over. I shall never teach Racine or Flaubert or Gide or Camus or Colette again. Nor will anyone else. The textbooks with the helpful introductions and glossaries are all upstairs in unmarked cardboard boxes, left over from the convent. The soft words of judgement rang in her head. I shall never again be happy, I shall never again be young.

Elizabeth Webster conjured her own death out of shadows. He whirled before her, skeletal, black-winged. He failed to impress. His visual manifestation seemed stagy and predictable. She possessed no material goods about which she still cared, she loved no other human being; she could therefore afford to dismiss him. One irritable flick of her head and the strange rush of darkness receded. If the world really was clasped in the grip of the Evil One, as the vicar said it was, then the Almighty had failed to assert Himself. He too had been slack in matters of order, discipline, control. She realised, with gathering indifference and contempt, that she believed in nothing. She faced a world that was empty and unsafe. She was on her own.

She became everything she most despised: querulous, forgetful, indecisive. She tottered down the lane to the shop, propped her sticks in the umbrella stand, then found that she had forgotten what she was doing there. Everyone addressed her in hushed tones. When she tried to be waspish, she uttered platitudes. Her personal carer, a middle-aged mum who talked about her children and cleaned the kitchen, bathroom and downstairs shower with indecent vigour and energy, ticked her off for leaving any hot food on her plate or rotting half-eaten meals in the fridge. Elizabeth came to dread the sound of her key in the outer lock and her cheerful greetings. She insisted that she could manage for at least part of the week on her own and reduced the visits to Tuesdays and Fridays. Then she found herself seized with a sort of joyful paranoia and took to bellowing, 'And how are we today then, dear?' to the empty sitting room on the days when she was spared the carer's presence.

Her brain was dissolving into a vegetal state. She read French aloud in the evenings to counteract the trend, but heard her own sentences trailing off. The language faded and became unintelligible. She could no longer understand anything that happened on the television. The *Radio Times* metamorphosed into a jumbled map of instructions written in cramped, meaningless numbers and codes. She slipped in and out of present time when images that she could not interpret lurched across the screen. She once actually confused *The Midsomer Murders* with the news, and sat there, transfixed, upon the green striped sofa, horrified that the BBC dared to show real bodies of rich people butchered in their desirable residences. She turned off the television and stared into space.

She forgot to wash, then found herself tugged back into the world by disgust at her own stench. She began to avoid her visitors. Someone on the parish council sent round his gardener to re-establish order in the undergrowth. The woods invaded her garden. She saw badgers and foxes cruising across the remains of her lawn. Their eyes glowed, phosphorescent in the light from the kitchen. She had long ceased to care, but the village was upset. Everyone remembered the luxurious perfection of Miss Webster's cottage garden. The gardener must be sent in, for the look of the thing. As he hacked and pruned, Miss Webster realised that she loathed honeysuckle, mock orange, clematis and sweet peas. She wished her plucky row of gladioli at the bottom of the sea. She planned a world of asphalt and stone, clamped over the rampant upward thrust of green. I want a world where nothing grows. Once more, she had come to a halt. Everything else that progressed, evolved and flourished was an offence to her tired eyes. On the days when she was safe from the carer she no longer bothered getting up or getting dressed. She lived in the last house at the end of the lane. Few people ever passed. She settled down to face the wall.

Eventually she was roused by the itching on her scalp. Her unwashed long hair, descending over her shoulders like a witch's crown, smelt dank and fishy in the August heat. She sensed her own uncomfortable descent into the lower depths. I'm falling to pieces, she grimaced at the mirror. Her sister's mask-like face, all the lines stretched away, tucked behind the ears and underneath the chin, sneered back at her.

'Look at you, you disgusting old crone.'

Elizabeth Webster flung all her hatred at the mirror, then staggered away to the bathroom to get dressed.

She took the bus into town, as she had not driven the car for months. It lay under green canvas in the garage, the battery irreparably flat. Elizabeth Webster never travelled by bus. Behold the lower depths of rural public transport. The huge blue vehicle grunted to a standstill, filled with exhausted, deranged and decrepit people. She had never seen any of them before. She didn't have an appointment so she slunk into her usual hairdresser's and sank into a seat by the door, waiting to be noticed. The girl who had always washed her hair in the old days was a sweet plump blonde called Sophie. She had been promoted to junior stylist in Elizabeth's absence and now wore a smart white shirt, nail polish and a little badge. She didn't recognise Elizabeth. But Elizabeth didn't recognise her either.

'Good afternoon, madam. Do you have an appointment?'

Elizabeth rose up unsteadily, clutching her sticks. She swayed over the small table, shabby and hesitant, still clutching a gossip magazine filled with celebrity weddings and conspiracy theories. Sophie rummaged through her list. The dryers roared behind her.

'No, I don't.'

'Miss Webster?' Something in the voice made the girl look up.

Sophie forgot both her manners and how to be diplomatic in the face of catastrophe.

'Oh Miss Webster! What's happened to you? Your beautiful hair! It's awful, it's ruined.'

She rushed round the desk to take Elizabeth's hand and to touch the tangled, filthy mess that was tied back with orange plastic strips torn off the bottom of a bin bag. No part of the ensemble that had been Elizabeth Webster had been heralded by anyone as beautiful, no, not for decades. Those on the receiving end of her tongue had called her a hatchet-faced bitch; beauty didn't come into it. Those who admired her courage and asperity never dared to open their mouths. Not even to utter compliments. It took someone as simple and ordinary as the girl from the hairdresser's, utterly unaware of the dragon's teeth, to speak the truth and to recognise the extent of the calamity that had befallen the old woman. Her hair had indeed been beautiful – thick, gleaming, heavy, a clear lucid grey shot through with shafts of pure white. It had never been coloured, it had never been thin.

Sophie gathered her up and ushered her to a safe and private corner.

'You've been very ill. I can see that you've been very ill. Come and sit down over here. I'll fetch your sticks.'

Sophie plucked at the remains of the bin bag in horror.

The shop barely noticed the intrusion. Elizabeth Webster looked dingy, ragged and frail. She had therefore become invisible. But Sophie could still see her, and it was this that moved Elizabeth to tears. Her face was wiped with warm scented towels; she allowed the kind young hands to scrub her mouldering scalp and spread out the disaster on the draining board.

'Thank you, Sophie,' she murmured again and again, 'thank you.'

She had all her hair cut off. It was the only acceptable solution. A new face emerged beneath the scissors, with a spiky butch bob. She looked like Gertrude Stein, square, unsmiling, resolute. As she stared back at the unadorned and shrunken head, which now looked curiously fresh and naked, she managed to hint at a smile.

'Thank you, Sophie, thank you very much. That will be fine.'

She missed one appointment with Dr Broadhurst and the hospital began a campaign of harassment. His assistant pestered her with troublesome phone calls at odd times, catching her off guard. They offered her a row of emergency appointments, pinned her down to dates and times and arranged for the day ambulance to pick her up. She retaliated, arrived early in a taxi, and sat down, savage in the waiting room. For the first time she sallied forth without her sticks. She felt insecure without them, but refused to yield.

I come and go as I choose. The consultant's assistant eyed her up, irritated. And so she alighted once more in the quiet room looking across the gardens towards the beech trees with the doctor sitting, calm and expectant, before her. She touched his damaged hands without looking down at them, as if she were verifying his identity. The uneven purple skin felt dry and scratched, like the bark of an old tree. He turned them over. The rough surface of the doctor's palms marked the distance she had travelled.

'Your haircut is very smart.'

'None of my clothes fit.'

'Good excuse to buy new ones. Are you eating three meals every day? I bet you're not.'

Silence.

'Who are you?'

'I've told you who I am. You know who I am.'

'All right then. You tell me where I should go. What I must do.'

'You are to go far, far away from here. You will find a country that is francophone. Then you will be at home in the language. But you must not go to France itself as that is a country you know too well. Everything must be different – the culture, the people, the food. You must go somewhere that is very strange to you, somewhere that is utterly unknown, and then you will be told what to do.'

There was a long, long silence. And it struck her as odd that inside this silence she could hear nothing, neither the sounds of the mowers in the gardens, nor the traffic on the bypass, which usually hummed and hissed in a tense, swift rush at midday, nor the soft tap of the computers in the neighbouring office. Then she heard the doctor's voice again, coming towards her like an approaching procession that she had last seen at a great distance.

'I'm going to change your prescription. I want you to take these tiny pills four times a day. One at each meal and one before you go to bed. I'll write to your GP and let him know.'

Elizabeth Webster had the distinct impression that a brief rift in time had gaped open and swallowed her grasp of the remembered present. Had she hallucinated the doctor's command to depart into the wilderness? What was still real? She left the room clutching a National Health prescription with instructions to go straight to the hospital pharmacy and then to seek out a desert on the rim of the world.

My pills.

Where are my pills?

She scrabbled at the bottom of her handbag. My papers? My passport? Oh God, I've given them all to that Arab in pink. I must have been mad. She looked up at the black man, anguished and frantic.

'My pills. I haven't taken my pills.'

'May I hold your other bag? Then you can look for them.'

He relieved her of the tartan hold-all. She retrieved the pills. Everything she had packed was still there. Elizabeth Webster twitched and shook, paranoid and insecure, fearful of strangers. But she was no longer on home ground. Anger and despair are emotions that need a secure base and known surroundings to flourish in tranquillity. She had begun to loathe her garden, her house, her furniture and her television because they were all still there, battered but intact, while she fretted and struggled against the process of dissolution. But here she was, in the transitional flux of a foreign airport, where the air felt thrice-breathed, and all known markers vanished, swallowed down by the strangeness of the languages around her. Despair thrives on stagnation. Elizabeth Webster had packed her bags and moved on. She was no longer angry either, for the place was too strange. She had been shaken out of her hole, like the vixen that had missed the sound of the hunt breaking cover and found herself exposed in open fields. She blinked, bewildered and unsettled, at the black man whose steady, abstract gaze met her own.

He had stretched out a small pile of documents before her as if awaiting her judgement and inspection. Here was the sullen black girl with dreadlocks coiled round her head like the Medusa. CRIME OF PASSION KILLER GOES FREE. And here was another image of a glamorous woman in a lavish blue dress, her breasts shiny with light, making love to a microphone. TRAGIC FATE OF JAZZ SINGER. She peered more closely at the huge eyes mired in dreadlocks. The coils were decorated with tiny shells and eyeless faces. Crimes of passion. Was it a crime to be passionate? Were these dead girls the images of the women the old black man was pledged to avenge? She leaned over the photographs.

'Lost, lost,' she murmured.

'She is lost to me,' agreed the black man and the disconcerted Miss Webster realised that the photographs had deceived her. The glamorous woman and the mutinous street girl were one and the same.

And now before her fluttered the sudden apparition of the pink satin Arab, whose moustache vibrated with polite formulas.

'Voilà, Madame! I have checked the flight and confirmed that your luggage will be transferred. Everything is written down here for you. We will escort you to internal departures.'

She was marched across the atrium to yet another security gate. The guards stood at ease, watching the shifting lines of passengers, their hands on their machine guns.

40

'There are lots of soldiers.' Elizabeth scuttled anxiously between her two guardians, only just keeping up.

'Ah, yes,' said the Arab, 'there have been other threats since the last attacks.'

'Attacks?'

The black man shrugged, irritated.

'Don't alarm Miss Webster, Hassan. The level of alert here is no worse than London.'

But the Arab was bent on terrifying explanations.

'It was all most unfortunate – two terrorist attacks, on a hotel and on a restaurant, within minutes of each other. Everyone is saying that it is Al-Qaida, but nothing has been proved. This kind of thing puts off the tourists. People feel unsafe.'

She contemplated death by unseen and unsolicited explosion. This seemed far less terrible than being lost in the street. They reached the departure gate for internal flights. The two men began making noises of reassurance and farewell. She returned their kindness with whispers of gratitude. She could never repay their generosity. The black man raised his hand as if he was silencing a congregation; then he began a speech.

'Miss Webster, here is my card. This is my mobile number, which will work in this country. But put 00 44 in front of the number and drop the first 0. It will then work like an international call. I am here in Casablanca at the Grand Hôtel Royal. If you are in any further trouble please do not hesitate to call me.'

She peered at his name. Percival Leroy Jones in silver italics. There was a lunatic pomposity in the embossed pretentiousness, but a posh address in St John's Wood backed up his self-importance. She clutched the card. He bowed.

'And now we will escort you to your flight.'

As she watched them walk away down the concourse she noticed that the black man rested his hand on his companion's shoulder. The younger man looked up, trusting, comfortable. She saw their unlikely colours, pink, white, touching, merging, as they gathered one another closer to pass through the crowd. They looked – and sounded – like men from two radically severed worlds, but their obvious intimacy suggested years of shared experiences. Their connection was palpable, unequivocal. They were friends.

2

TAXI DRIVER

S omeone had blundered. She ended up in an expensive hotel far outside the great walls of the kasbahs, rising one above each other with their dark medieval streets, and far from the balconied buildings of the old colonial town. This was a smart new hotel with a view of seven palm trees and the endless desert beyond. The taxi stopped in twilight. Opposite the hotel entrance she perceived a dim expanse without colour, lights or buildings. Far away, a truck, its canvas roof torn and flapping, lurched down a long straight road, raising a giant cloud of dust which never settled but simply lengthened, like a jet's trail. The air tasted of cooling dust. Half a dozen children doubled up like empty gunny sacks were loitering beside the hotel's entrance, under the red walls and towering oleanders just beyond the security gates. They sprang into action as she reeled out of the car, and tried to snatch her bags. 'Un cadeau, un cadeau,' they shrieked in chorus. The taxi driver shouted back in a language she had never heard before. Elizabeth Webster beat them off with one of her sticks.

'They just want to help.' The taxi driver glared at her and rang the bell.

The receptionist and the porter looked like costumed

extras on the set of Indiana Jones and the Desert of Doom. The woman was wearing chains of gold: gold falling from her ears, gold encircling her neck, gold draped in her hair, and a long black gown with a tight bodice, stitched sequins sparkling. The porter was stuffed into a tomato-red uniform with gold buttons and a fez. The glittering tassel swung madly round his head as he drove the children back under the wall. Suddenly the feeble twilight was engulfed by the black pool behind them. All the light sank into the ground. They retreated into the illuminated courts. Who had paid the taxi? Elizabeth Webster now felt very uncertain on her feet. She looked up, steadying herself on the gravel with her sticks. A large blue and yellow neon script announced the hotel bar as the Desert Rendezvous and promised a Foretaste of Paradise at Happy Hour. She heard voices and shrieking giggles. A long facade of identical pointed doorways faced a courtyard of rustling bougain-villea and tiled fountains. She could smell jasmine and sense textures, but could not distinguish any colours. Elizabeth Webster decided that she had at last arrived in hell. She was hot, she was dirty, she was tired, she was limping, she was old, she was late.

'Welcome, welcome. Please let me carry that. Come in, come in . . .'

The costumed woman plumped her down amidst embroidered cushions and offered her a tall clean glass filled with sparkling mineral water.

Don't drink anything if it isn't bottled.

'C'est de la Badoit.'

The receptionist spoke fluent French and had eyes ringed with kohl like an Egyptian deity. Her skin was pale olive and her forehead high and domed. All the wealth of the desert smothered her in gold. She smelt of cinnamon and rose water.

44

'My name is Saïda, Madame Webster. You must come to me whenever there is anything you need.'

It was like having a personal djinn. Miss Webster's luggage vanished and soft hands ushered her upstairs. Rose petals floated across the bed and her bathroom, paved in blue and white tiles, equipped with large bath, power shower, bidet and hair dryer, glowed with comforting, luxurious modernity. The sheets were ironed white and the light cream covers had been turned back. A tiny jewelled lamp lit up the carved wooden screen and a bowl of exotic fruit – figs, dates, apricots – stood on a small table of inlaid cedar and mother-of-pearl. Somewhere at a little distance she could hear water falling in the fountains. Her anxiety ebbed away. Someone else was looking after her. Someone else was in charge. Someone else was pointing out the way.

In the days that followed the hotel staff approached her mouthing concerned clichés.

'Ah Madame Webster, you look so much less tired. You looked very strained and exhausted when you first arrived.'

'Madame Webster, voulez-vous prendre votre café au lait ici ou dans le jardin?'

'Mees Webster? Is the music disturbing you? I will ask the young people to turn it down.'

'May I bring you a glass of mint tea, Miss Webster? If you sit outside in the gardens then you must drink a lot because of the heat.'

The garden was a miracle of colours, sustained entirely by a network of irrigation channels and humming electric pumps. The hotel was built on a deep well, barely fifteen feet beneath her feet. The water rose up from the dark earth, ancient, cold and sweet. It smelt of riches and prosperity. Palm trees, neatly pruned into symmetrical rows, lined the walkways and the old walls; roses with magnificent peeling faces loomed white and red in well-turned beds of imported soil. A huge hibiscus, now well past its best, some flowers still hanging limp and bleak upon their stems, stood up to the bougainvillea. But the place she preferred was a hidden stone bench in front of a mountainous wall of jasmine that oozed a strange dismal perfume into the afternoon heat. A sequence of exotic tiled fountains in ochre, red, blue and the subtle green of Islam punctuated the gardens, imposing as medieval fonts. One of these stood in the midst of a pond whose cool waters were protected by a surface of pale, scented water lilies. The flowers appeared to darken to a deep rose in the evenings. At night the temperature fell by over twenty degrees; every surface, patterned, paved and tiled, cooled at a different pace. Every opening or entrance seemed curtained, veiled, shuttered or screened. It was as if she were under constant surveillance. Someone watched her, constantly, from behind the silenced windows.

During the days Saïda appeared and disappeared in hushed slippers. The woman stalked the arcades and staircases like a beautiful giant cat, padding between guests. At night she burst forth in high heels and phoney Oriental chiffon. She chatted, merry and brisk, with the young people and lavished cocktails upon them; her manner was formal with the staff. She inspected their work – each detail was checked, from the measures of alcohol in the Desert Rendezvous to the arrangements for collecting guests from the airport. She clearly suspected all her employees of being skivers, profiteers and thieves. Everything was locked up. She carried the keys. She checked the mini-bars herself. Her tone with Elizabeth Webster was always careful, respectful and apprehensive. A cardiac crisis would be bad publicity for the hotel. The old woman must be humoured and cherished. The hotel was full: many French people, mostly older couples on autumn breaks, and a young Dutch crowd who stuck together and roared out on quad bike adventure trips across the desert. Yet the sounds of laughter from the swimming pool and the bar always seemed to be in the distance. Miss Webster noticed that she was being protected from intrusive disturbance. Everyone seemed to know that she had been very, very ill.

On the third day Saïda greeted her in the gardens beneath the wall drenched in jasmine. The old woman was reading Laclos. Saïda looked at the book.

'Ah, *Les Liaisons Dangereuses*. Mais c'est choquant, n'est-ce pas?'

'It was at the time. Do you read the classics?' The receptionist suddenly struck her as interesting.

'A great deal. I was never sent to college. My father did not think that girls were worth educating. If I had daughters I would send them to school, to university. I would not let them marry until they were educated. I would insist on that. An education is as good as a rich dowry.'

'Then you have no children?' Elizabeth Webster enquired politely. She was under the impression that Muslim women were summarily executed or cast into outer darkness if they failed to produce infants. But no, the other woman lit up from within with pride at her biological achievements.

'J'ai un fils,' she said, as if her entire existence was justified by this revelation.

'How nice.'

Elizabeth Webster delivered this arrow with careful contempt. But both women were speaking in their second language. Saïda failed to notice the shift in register.

'He is young, he is handsome, he is very clever. He will study at the university. And it is my dream that he will study abroad – in France or America or in your country. He will rise in the world and be someone to reckon with. You see, Madame Webster, we are poor people. We come from the desert tribes. We have only just begun to live in houses and to eat from tables. We are a long way behind you. It is my dream that my son should have a better and an easier life than his father or his grandfather before him. I want him to do more than drive camels and goats.'

She checked herself. The speech had been delivered with inappropriate vehemence. She pulled herself up short. Elizabeth Webster came to the erroneous conclusion that Saïda had remembered that she was staff and that the English woman was a wealthy guest. Private lives should not be discussed. No such thought had entered the other woman's head. Saïda gazed at the old English lady, stricken and contrite. She had said too much. She had boasted of her child to a woman who had no husband and no sons.

'Pardonnez-moi, Madame. I spoke without thinking.'

'Don't mention it.' Elizabeth could afford to be gracious. She was here on a very temporary basis. 'I would like to hear about your family. You must tell me more about your people and your son.'

Saïda misunderstood this too. She did not hear a polite confirmation of permission granted with minimal interest expressed, but an intimate request, a gesture of connection and friendship. She was delighted and confused.

'I will bring you some photographs of our village and my son,' she promised. She wanted to give something in return. The English lady was too solitary, too isolated. She had never ventured outside the hotel. She was un-accompanied. She ought to visit the film studios and see where the grand producers had made *The Jewel of the Nile*, *Gladiator* and *The Mummy Returns*.

'You must see the town and the desert. It is, comment dire?, un endroit sauvage, but very, very beautiful. I will arrange a tour and a guide.'

'Not too expensive.'

Elizabeth Webster was being cautious with her money.

'The price will be arranged and agreed in advance.'

And so, much against her better judgement, Miss Webster procured a yellow hat and a muslin veil, a fine shawl and a pair of dark glasses. She dressed for battle with the local sights and presented herself, armed with sticks, basket and parasol, in the foyer shortly after dawn.

The taxi lurked by the gates, a battered, unmarked black Citroën with slanting headlights like a monster's eyes. The roof rack was roped up with unspecified sporting tackle, four long planks that looked like skateboards or wind-surfing equipment. She peered at them while the driver held the door. Each plank glimmered in the blue light, closely decorated with perforated bottle caps, nailed in patterned lines. Hers was not to reason why. She climbed in among the worn leather and tacky orange cushions. The rear-view mirror had grown a tail, swinging with prayer beads and a golem, its lids barely open. The radio played belly-dancing music and the whole thing smelt of carpet cleaner and cigarettes. The driver dipped and bowed, his head encased in an impeccable white turban. The turban added a little height and majesty, for his entire form was swathed in white – the djellaba was clearly a costume and a little too big for him; he shrank, diminished in its ironed white folds. Even the embroidered hem gleamed clean and uncreased. She noticed a very old pair of trainers poking out beneath the theatrical draperies. But I know you –

surely this was the same taxi driver that had driven her from the airport?

'Bonjour. Je m'appelle Abdou,' grinned the creature, revealing a sinister row of blackened teeth with many gaps. 'I am your guide. I speak French, English, Arabic and German. What is your language of choice?'

'French,' snapped Elizabeth. 'And we've already met. You ticked me off for being sharp with the children. Remember? So you also speak German?'

'I achieve a lot of Germans,' smirked Abdou, as if he had eaten them all. He didn't acknowledge the fact that he had seen her before.

'Please turn off the radio.' She decided to assert herself at once.

'No can do,' Abdou produced an authentic Gallic shrug. 'It gives me the weather forecast and my instructions.'

'From whom do you take your instructions? I'm paying you.'

Abdou ignored her, turned up the volume and cruised away down the atrocious, dissolving stony road, nodding to the palm trees and the crouching children who all seemed to be old friends.

'Town with rare library, ancient kasbah and pots, or desert with magnificent oasis and date palms? Desert first, before it is too hot. Town tomorrow with souk and exhibition with carpets.' He decided for her, and swung the old car on to the path that led beyond the seven palms and into nothingness.

There was a road of sorts, uneven but stable. Far in the distance, now clearly visible, now merely a black outline, roamed another moving truck. It could have been the same one she had seen on her first night. They neither lost sight of the truck, nor gained upon it. The faint black square and the dusty cloud in its wake were still there as the light gained ground across the alien landscape. Elizabeth Webster looked out into the void. There was no sand to be seen. She had imagined giant dunes and strange patterns, rippled like the sea, changing with the wind across endless slopes of radiant gold. Instead, as the light strengthened, she saw an endless flat gravel plain interrupted by boulders. The deep purple shadows unfolding across the emptiness before her began to lift, leaving her jolting across a frozen ocean of bare rock, settling into grey, a visionary dreariness bereft of all life, all green, all human habitations. The only human point before them remained the truck, receding into endlessness.

'Why is there no sand?' yelled Miss Webster above the wriggling thump of Abdou's music.

'We see sand later,' Abdou shouted back. 'The desert is mostly not sand. It is mountains and it is like this. This is hamada.'

Hamada. She found it in the glossary. *These great plains of gravel and rock are the desert pavements across which the caravans have always preferred to pick their way. Travellers who understand the risks will avoid the uncertain banks of unstable sand. Sometimes the dunes will bear the weight of a jeep, but you must be familiar with the prevailing winds. There will be soft sand on the windward slope, which is being constantly exposed . . .*

'No, no. I don't trust the sand,' roared Abdou from the front seat of the Citroën. 'I show it to you. But we stay on this good road.'

The good road shuddered and bumped beneath them. The taxi reached a steady speed of fifty kilometres per hour and sputtered onwards into the waste. She grew accustomed to the light and to the fact that there was no end to the horizon and nothing to see. The colours before her

51

never varied: black and grey, lit by a dusty white glaze as the sun climbed. The landscape gleamed, featureless, endless, blank. The hamada extended on into infinite distance, utterly barren; there were no palm trees, no bushes, no animals, no people. There was no water.

'I will show you water,' Abdou announced, as if predicting a miracle. 'In two hours' time you will see water.'

Two hours. She contemplated the grim, unchanging endlessness before her. Elizabeth Webster had been an adventurous woman, used to travelling. She loved to see new places, new countries. She enjoyed remarking the subtle differences between all the rich worlds of Europe: the tilt of a roof, the fashion in shutters, decorated facades, gardens with gnomes, chateaux whose gracious lawns and gravel paths sported peacocks, the shift from slate to tile as she drove south, the grazing cows gradually yielding the fields to sunflowers and olive trees. She liked to observe the public buildings, each nation's pompous little gestures, the town halls, the arts centres, the grotesque civic sculptures installed on roundabouts. And she adored movement, change. But what confronted her in this abandoned place of frozen violence was unchangingness. The car moved ever onwards, into nothing. Even the appalling music reproduced itself with a steady monotonous sequence of pounding wails and howls. Infinity unfolded before her.

The cumulative effect of this unaltered endlessness proved most peculiar. At first she was angry and bored. An hour passed. She fidgeted uncomfortably amidst the orange satin cushions, watching the reds and blacks of the boulders and rocks becoming grey. The palette of colour by mid-morning had evened out into a desperate, unyielding grey waste. Nothing moved. Nothing changed. Nothing appeared over the edge of the landscape before her. She closed her eyes in rage and horror. Why had she come to this desolate place of futile heat and eerie nothingness? Who had sent her here? It was inconceivable that she would ever choose to make this journey of her own free will. Rage and frustration gave way to a terrible sensation of misery. She sank, wretched, into herself.

Abdou, who had been silent for a long time, followed her disturbed and baffled gaze. Suddenly he said, 'There is an old desert saying that Allah removed all surplus human and animal life from the desert so that there might be one place where He could walk in peace, and so the great desert is called the Garden of Allah.'

Elizabeth Webster listened to this declaration, incredulous. Islam was clearly a religion invented by madmen. Before her stretched the level plains of emptiness, hostile and austere. But Abdou had hit upon a rich vein of sententiousness and would not give it up.

'We have another saying, Madame. We say that Allah, the Almighty, Lord of the Creation, the Compassionate, the Merciful, King of Judgement Day, is as far as the stars, and as close as the pulse in your jugular vein.'

At this point he caught her eye in the mirror, grinned, displaying all his decrepit teeth, and then sliced his throat cheerfully with his hand. Elizabeth Webster caressed her own carotid artery with a sensation of real alarm. Allah, the All-Knowing, the All-Powerful, the mysterious sharer of all secrets, was suddenly present in the taxi. The light became a cauldron of flame, and the desert had produced an ominous line of grey spikes, as if the army of dragon's teeth was beginning to rise. There was nothing near at hand or far away. Distance did not exist. Abdou had begun to speak.

'Hamada is not always good desert surface. Sometimes it is evil, very evil. It rises in sharp pointed stones that tear up the tyres and the camels' feet. A whole Roman army had their sandals ruptured by hamada. They perished, every one – soldiers, servants, baggage train. The whole caravan. Their polished skeletons are still out there in the sand.'

Abdou abandoned the wheel, looked out upon the desert and rubbed his hands as if greeting a cherished collaborator who supported all his endeavours.

'Are you from somewhere in the desert?' asked Elizabeth, now deeply wary of the taxi driver.

'Oh no. I am from a tiny village in the Valley of a Thousand Kasbahs. The desert people are very different. We watch them coming into town. If they come with camels, the camels are exhausted. If they come in jeeps and trucks they will be about to break down. They cannot see us clearly and the sand is in their bones.'

'Will I see where Saïda comes from?'

'Yes and no. Saïda is born of the desert people. They were once nomad. But she is Berber and she comes from a settled family. Her husband is from the desert. He is Imohagh. The French say Tuareg. It was a bad marriage which brought ill luck to her. Avec les hommes comme son mari, tu joues avec la vie et la mort. They are a ferocious people. They are all over the desert now. They are the camel masters. The wilderness is in them. The men wear the tagelmoust, the dark veil of indigo. The French call them 'les hommes bleus'. The women do not wear this. So Saïda does not. But her husband did not stay with her. He went away, back into the desert. No one knows where he is; some say he is in Mali. So she is neither widow nor wife. And she works in a hotel.'

Abdou made the hotel sound like a third sexual option. He chewed on the end of his turban for a moment, his eyes glassy, staring at the depths of endlessness before him. Then he said, 'She should take another husband.' This did and did not explain Saïda's interesting situation.

'She mentioned a son –'

'Ah, Chérif. Ha! He has his father inside him and she will not believe it.' Abdou glared at the desert's fixed face and then increased his speed. Elizabeth sank back, puzzled. Then she lowered her veil, and pushed her dark glasses higher up her nose.

'We've been driving for well over two hours,' she declared.

'Water is very close,' sang Abdou.

But all around her she saw nothing, nothing but long stretches of grey rock. When she opened her eyes again they were grinding up a little incline. A small jeep trundled towards them. She stared at this apparition emerging from nowhere. Both vehicles stopped and negotiated one set of tyres off the edge of the road in the potentially murderous hamada. Abdou turned down the radio and leaned out. A black man with shining polished skin lowered his window. His hairless arm was a deep blue-black and his face a mass of lines and folds. The conversation was conducted in broken French, so she could follow what was said, but the content seemed utterly surreal.

'Peace be with you.'

'Peace be with you also.'

'Are you well?'

'Praise be to God, I am very well. Are you well?'

'I am well.'

'Your family is well?'

'Yes, thanks be to God, they are very well.'

'And your family?'

'They are well.'

'May God protect everyone dear to you.'

'May he bless you and all of yours.'

'Have you seen the pool hidden in the hills of Tinnazit?'

'I have seen it. The water is plentiful and sweet.'

'Were you alone there?'

'No one else came.'

'May God preserve you and your people.'

'May He bless you and all your sons.'

'May God go with you upon all your journeys.'

'May He be present in all your travels.'

The taxi lurched back on to the road and the jeep continued, draped in sheets of dust. Abdou turned up the radio. Elizabeth began to wonder if she had hallucinated the entire thing.

The light boiled, hard and angry, glinting on every surface, near and far. She removed her dark glasses briefly only to replace them at once. The rocks shimmered, as if alive, grinning brilliant and purposeful, directly into the taxi's windows. She closed her eyes again. She was being carried forth into eternity by the unknown charioteer, to an accompaniment of raucous dance music, interspersed by passionate outbursts of Arabic.

'Madame Webster! Awake! Look! We have arrived.'

She jolted back into the fiery, scorching world in a state of shock. A rushing breath of hot wind stirred her veils, her lips felt cracked and dry. She was still propped up, a little lopsided, in the back of the taxi. The music vanished. A giant silence, tangible and vast, embraced and held her, tense and startled in its grasp. There was Abdou, wonderfully pleased with himself, holding the door.

'I will install you by the pool. Then I will arrange the picnic.'

Another sound came to her. It was the sound of water falling gently into water. She clambered out of the taxi and staggered forth into the rocks. The landscape itself breathed heat, but remained apparently bereft of every living thing. They had abandoned the road and were parked beside an enclave of leaning boulders, all taller than a man, which appeared to be plotting or praying, bound together in a sinister huddle. And from somewhere down amid the rocks came the sound of water. She peered into the precarious gulf before her, and saw, some twenty feet below, a tiny green place, a secret hidden crevice that smelt of water. She grabbed her sticks and tottered down the path, supported by Abdou who had gathered up a handful of sweaty cushions and a folded rug. All she could smell now was fresh, clear water.

The tiny ravine represented an oasis in miniature. She beheld a miraculous patterning of small trees, acacias, thorny mimosa, shady tamarisk; bright moss and tiny ferns actually clung to the side of the pool. The small pond of uncertain depth was replenished by a steady, assiduous runnel of clear water pouring out of the rocks. Elizabeth Webster stood over the pool, marvelling at the clear waters beneath her feet. She imagined that she saw something move, flicker and vanish among the curving stones below the surface. Abdou inspected her shoes and then carried out a sedulous, investigative form of housework on the flat stone resting in the shade. He brushed it down and peered round all the sides.

'Scorpions!' he announced. 'I like to be careful.'

She looked at him, horrified.

'They crawl into beds at night,' he waved his hands, 'or fall from ceilings. But don't worry. I will clear them all out. Nothing can come near you.' He handed her a bottle of Fanta and a straw.

'Don't drink it, if it isn't bottled.' Abdou delivered this maxim as if it was another piece of desert wisdom about the goodness of Allah. When he returned, staggering down the path with a plastic cool box and a giant umbrella, she was perched on the cushions sucking at her straw like a child, peering delightedly into the pool, relishing the emerald moss and the deep shade of the tamarisk.

'Abdou!' she burst out, for she believed herself the witness to a miracle, 'there are fish in this pool.'

He nodded, very pleased.

'Picnic first, then siesta!' he commanded, his dreadful teeth making him look like a murderer. Miss Webster could think of no way to convince him of the urgent need to replace them with a gleaming set of fakes.

There was always water in this great desert. We can still see the ancient watercourses cutting through the giant massifs. If you dig down in the dried-up wadis you can find water, sometimes fifteen, maybe twenty feet beneath you. It is harder to find the wells in the desert. They can be marked by a simple pattern of sticks in the sand. You could walk past them without knowing. But far beneath you, buried in the deep rocks, left there from the days, many millions of years ago, when the great lakes covered the desert, huge caverns of water lie hidden, the reservoirs known as the fossil aquifers. The plains here were once savannah grasslands, peppered with lakes. Antelope roamed here, grazing on the long grass, moving from lake to lake, following the rivers. Here zebras browsed by the pools, and drifting herds of buffalo, and even elephants, patrolled the plains. We have found their bones buried deep in the salt depressions that were once the great lakes. And the water still lies beneath us. It has ebbed away and descended, down, down, down through the porous rocks to the great buried spaces in the sleeping earth, but it is still there, still waiting, secret, hidden.

Elizabeth Webster dreamed this crepuscular buried mass of water. It saturated her brain. She heard the rumbling crackling mass of the flash floods bursting the sandbanks, desecrating the mud houses of the lost desert peoples. She saw the giant black rainstorms sweeping the masses of the Ahaggar and the swelling rivers beginning again in the gravel valleys of the Anti-Atlas, rushing away down the wadis only to vanish without trace in the rolling wilderness of sand. She looked back into the crevasses and ravines that had been barren only days before, and beheld the gleaming green moss of fresh plants, which the floods had seeded, nourished and then abandoned. The rising flood had proved that its promises were fickle. For this is a place where nothing lives for very long.

'It is an old desert saying that the date palm must keep its feet in the water and its head in the fire.'

Had she dreamed that too? Abdou specialised in garrulous trivia. For indeed her feet were in water and her head was on fire. The siesta had transformed her forehead into a furnace. She swallowed two aspirins with a gulp of Fanta and subsided once more into the copious cushions. Gradually, she sank into a comatose lethargy, like *La Grande Odalisque*, whose public had deserted her now that she had grown old. When she awoke her temperature had dropped and the desert, whose rocks showed their fangs above the green ravine, was peopled with long bounding shadows. Abdou finished reciting his prayers and wrapped up a little carpet upon which he had carried out a brief transaction with Allah. Elizabeth Webster gazed up at the giant sky, which had gulped back down the white haze of fire. It was still very hot, but the desert no longer held a vicious swab of scorching air against her mouth, daring her to breathe. She stood up, wavering, and jabbed one of her sticks into the pebbles, like Aaron's rod.

And then they were bobbing along the gravel once more. It was a complete mystery to Elizabeth Webster how Abdou knew where he was going. There were no landmarks of any kind that she could discern. The music was re-instated, but it was softer, more melancholy than the thumping dance music, and more appropriate to the later hour, a strange braying song, backed by a zither, that accompanied the shudders and jolts of the Citroën. She stared out of the dusty windows, hypnotised. And then she saw the dunes.

Directly in front of them, with no warning given, several long banks of caramel sand, shivering with threads of gold, suddenly materialised out of empty space. As the car thudded towards them they grew in scale and loomed high above the roof of the vehicle. The great dunes shivered and rustled in the light; there was an illusion of movement, yet they remained still. Here they were at last, the sandscapes of legend, sculpted into ripples, ruffles and flutes, kissed by the hot wind. She looked up at the sharp crest; running down the flanks of the dunes was a constant trickle of blown sand.

Harmattan.

'The wind has another name in every place where it blows,' said Abdou, 'and the grains are dirty like smoke in the big storms. It gets into everything. Everything! But you miss the worst. The big blow comes later.' He hunched himself up in a despairing shrug, keeping one claw on the wheel. And then they were driving on sand. The road was washed by sand. The road vanished beneath the sand. The dunes pushed towards them, horribly close, now nearly twenty feet high, looming up beside the black taxi which crawled like an escaping beetle along the windward edge.

'You wanted sand. Voilà les sables!'

She lowered the window and stared at the great hump-backed dunes, unable to gauge their extent and size.

'It's the wind that embraces the dunes and gives them their identities,' said Abdou. 'They have all different shapes. And sometimes they build up, huge, like a holy dome, but then I come back a week later and they are gone.'

The shivering dunes were streaked with red and gold, luminous with subtle, leaping shadows. She stared at their slopes and crests. The desert now spoke to her disoriented soul. I am neither merciful nor malignant. I am neither cruel nor compassionate. I am neither intelligible nor opaque. I neither spare nor kill. I do not make peace or create evil. I am simply here, before you. I am I am I am.

Abdou heard the old woman whispering to herself and immediately feared the worst. Sunstroke.

'Have another Fanta. You are not used to heat. You must drink.'

He passed her another bottle. It hadn't been that hot as far as he was concerned. Thirty-five degrees at midday was quite normal for this time of year. And it was already much cooler. They were having a good day.

'I am,' murmured Elizabeth in English, her cracked lips quivering at the austere, rustling dunes.

'Mais bien sûr,' agreed Abdou cheerfully, looking out for the first crowns of the date palms amidst the mountains of sand.

★

61

The oasis town solidified like a wondrous apparition sprouting from the desert: suddenly, there it was, like a theatrical magic turn, fabulous as the overwhelming dunes. At first she saw a huge *couronne*, a bizarre crown of green palms encircled with thorny scrub, then, as they descended into a little depression, they were surrounded by gardens and squat, unpainted buildings. Some houses had no glass in their windows, just blankets pulled across blank square gaps, as if the eyes of the buildings had been put out. The red and umber walls crumbled gently at the corners, clearly made from packed mud. Some roofs boasted real ridge tiles, others, covered with the same thick, dried dirt, slapped on with trowels, looked less reliable. Several two-storeyed buildings guarded the main street; one of these had a striped orange awning set up on the roof. Many others had rough stick and tarpaulin shelters projecting out over the doors. A tin-shack garage disgorged the innards of a dozen dismembered cars into the sand. Two men grappling among the remains waved to Abdou as the taxi crawled into the street, the only street. The road beneath their tyres was solid and flat, but thickly coated with drifting sand. Further away she could see a huge battered sign advertising the HÔTEL DES VOYAGEURS. Between the houses she caught glimpses of irrigated vegetable patches, fenced off and defended against the nibbling goats. Chickens darted across their path, and then suddenly the taxi was surrounded by a mass of running children. Abdou coasted to a halt in front of a general store. An insane collection of goods, laid out side by side, dusted with sand, confronted them on a makeshift porch: teapots, carpets, pumps for tyres, pumps for bicycles, pumps for siphoning liquids, pumps for unblocking drains, packets of screwdrivers and pliers in different sizes, storm lanterns, fertiliser, seed packets, plastic buckets, two green

Hammerlin wheelbarrows, rolls of wire, rope, all colours, all sizes, tins of putty, nails and wrenches, tarpaulin *querbas* made of goatskin for carrying water, two leather saddles for giant camels, highly decorated, a box of pumice stones, a dozen jerricans and a mass of tacky-looking carrier sacks with zips on the top. Just inside the doorway she could see a stand with every known form of battery, a pile of blankets, grey, dark blue and maroon, and a row of plastic models representing Arnold Schwarzenegger as The Terminator.

Abdou stepped out in front of the store, pretended to rush the children, who began screaming delightedly, and then commenced yelling in a language that might have been Arabic. The children mobbed the taxi. A big man in a tatty brown djellaba surged out of the shop and bundled them out of the way. He loomed in at the back window.

'Madame Webster! Welcome. I am Saïda's brother-in-law. She told me that you were coming.'

He proudly produced a cellphone from his pocket and made it play the theme tune from *The Lord of the Rings*. Elizabeth Webster, now completely drenched in the great I AM, had decided that nothing would surprise her. He kissed her hand and she descended from the taxi like a queen. All the children backed off, tantalised and impressed.

'Enchanté, Madame. My name is Massoud.'

'Ravie de vous connaître.'

The children gawped at the veiled old lady, open-mouthed. A small crowd of boys gathered to watch her sweep past the outlandish bazaar, through the dark shrouded shop and into a cloistered, irrigated courtyard. Flecked blue paint peeled from the concrete arches, but beneath them lurked a cool swept space, equipped with low seats ripped from defunct vehicles and decorated with carpets and cushions. The garden blossomed scents and colours. After the vast monochrome austerity of the desert she gazed into a living kaleidoscope. She realised that everything rising from the tended earth was edible: aubergines, peppers, carrots, chillies, pumpkins and two magnificent lemon trees. Irrigation channels built of packed earth glistened between the rows. There was a stone well at the centre and a fine modern diesel pump set up beside it.

'We acquired this from the World Food Programme,' said Massoud proudly, indicating the pump and making the process of acquisition sound like an excessively clever theft. He settled Miss Webster on one of the car seats and presented her with a range of soft drinks, from Coke to Orangina, in real glass bottles. Don't drink it if it isn't bottled. Miss Webster knew that these particular Orangina bottles had been discontinued in France years before. Massoud also proposed a draught of water from the well in an authentic pot-bellied pottery carafe. Abdou assured her that it was safe to drink, as it had been drawn directly from the rocky entrails of the earth.

'It is very sweet and clean. The water here is famous.'

'Thank you, Abdou. Thank you, Monsieur. I will have a mug of this water.'

The two men bent double under the burden of their own copious hospitality. She wondered where they hid the women. So far, woman appeared to be a species either rare or extinct. Yet, these children must have surged out of a human womb. They cannot have reared up from the sand like earthworms. She looked at the suggestive swelling purple of a well-watered aubergine and saw, just beyond the plants, an olive face surrounded by jewellery, a woman's face which resembled Saïda's – rounder, fuller, older, but just as beautiful. The other woman squatted before her and clasped both her hands in her own.

'Welcome, Madame Webster. My sister has told me so much about you.'

Yes, this was the other sister who had remained in the desert. The French was not as confident, the eyes less fiery and more speculative, and the voice had the soft insistent trickle of the sands. Elizabeth read the face shrewdly and she was not wrong. That servile cunning, never far from the surface of Saïda's glance, could not be detected in the face of this desert woman. Saïda had been contaminated by the habits of service, her polite smile purchased so many times that it stared back fixed, like a mask stitched to her face. This woman retained the freedom to meet anyone's gaze. Yet she was watching, waiting for her husband's gesture of permission to remain beside her guest. She presented a tray with an ornate silver teapot, several glasses painted in different colours and a plate of dates. When she set it down Elizabeth noticed a tiny pool of fine white sand collected beneath the stubby little feet of the pot.

'I am called Fatima.'

The men melted away. The tea tasted very sweet. The conversation came straight out of *Alice in Wonderland*.

'You are alone, Madame.'

'What do you mean, alone?'

'You travel alone.'

'Yes. Is that odd?'

'Here it is odd for a woman to travel without her husband and her children.'

'I have no husband and no children.'

Fatima bowed, but expressed no indication of pity or surprise. She had expected that answer. The entire exchange evolved as an elaborate charade. Elizabeth Webster drank some more very sweet *thé à la menthe* and waited to see what would happen next. She became fascinated by the devious shiftiness of the people amongst whom she had been sent. She sensed the existence of a hidden agenda, and waited for Fatima to declare her hand.

'My sister wishes for you to meet her son. She wants him to study abroad. He is a very brilliant young man, but he loves the desert. He will miss the heat and the light if he travels to Europe. I have seen pictures of England and it is a green place of perpetual rain.'

'This is perfectly true.'

Elizabeth wondered how to ask for the lavatory without appearing to lose interest in the family descriptions.

'I too have a son. I have four daughters and one son. My son is called Mohammed. My sister's son is called Chérif. They have grown up here together. I shout for them and still expect to see two dirty children come running out of the dust. But no, they are young men now. They are both more than twenty. Mohammed is just as brilliant as his cousin. But we cannot offer him the things that Saïda can offer to her son. Saïda has a good job and no other children. She can save money. Our lives here are more precarious. We depend on desert people, who are often poor, and passing trade. We would like our son to study. Mais nous, nous n'avons pas les moyens.'

Elizabeth listened to this speech carefully. She understood at once that she had been chosen, picked out as the recipient of a careful, subtle sales pitch, an obscure discourse of demand and expectation. A market in clever young Arab men was being proposed to her, but she was not interested. It would have been easier to sell her shares in the Hôtel des Voyageurs or a Bedouin carpet which she didn't like and didn't need. She went on to the offensive.

'What do you want from me, Madame?'

Fatima looked startled and not a little shocked. The question could not be answered because the manner in which it had been posed was too ungraciously direct.

'My sister would like you to meet her son.'

'Then I should be delighted to meet him. Send for him at once.'

She had been settling the hash of other people's sons for many years, ever since the convent ceased to be Girls Only. She settled deeper and more comfortably into the recycled seat of a defunct Renault and attacked the dates. Elizabeth Webster had decided, unbeknown to herself, for this process had taken place deep in her unconscious mind, to live at risk. Safety does not come first. All her life she had been wary, suspicious and cold. She had spent sixty years frozen into a posture of refusal and denial. Now she decided to open the doors and allow herself the entertainment of unsolicited adventures. Why not? I've saved up so much money that I actually count as rich. I may be retired, but I still pay tax. There are no tricky situations which money can't solve. Let me see your sons. And then I shall be able to work out what it is that you have brought me here to witness and to do. And then, only then, can I decide.

'Massoud!'

Fatima clapped her hands and her husband answered from the dark shop behind them. Elizabeth shifted her feet and discovered an outline of sand had appeared around each stout white walking shoe, into which her soles had melted. A rapid exchange between husband and wife in the local dialect concluded the business: someone was despatched to find Mohammed and Chérif.

But this proved to be no simple task. In an oasis village containing thirty dwellings they were nowhere to be

67

found. They had been seen cleaning buckets in a neighbour's house. No, they had been looking at a camel one of them wanted to purchase. They had been sent out into the desert by the *garagiste* with his mechanic to help with a lorry that was leaking brake fluid. They were asleep in a nearby grove of date palms. They were digging a new irrigation channel in their cousin's herb garden. They were watching CNN in the saloon bar of the Hôtel des Voyageurs with two German tourists. They were teasing their sisters behind a grain store. They were working in the Frenchman's *lotissement* for a disgracefully low wage. They were far away from the oasis tending goats that were all perched in trees. They were sought in every house along the street. Their names rebounded in the sand. Mohammed! Chérif! But they could not be traced. Search parties were sent out, the children were enlisted. Then others were sent to find the ambassadors that had already gone and also vanished. Every doubtful trail and false lead was followed up. They had been seen playing dice, or updating the website's weather map at the hotel. They were sweeping sand from the window sills at their uncle's residence. Wherever they had been seen they were not there now. They were certainly together, but nowhere to be found.

Abdou grew impatient.

'If we don't leave now it will be by moonlight that I drive that road.'

Elizabeth Webster began to think about dinner at the hotel and a long foaming bath. Fatima erupted, distraught at the failure to locate these errant sons, and proceeded to suspect a conspiracy. Her paranoid anxiety overflowed in an unintelligible dialect and ended in a desperate prayer. Elizabeth paid no attention to the chaos. She did not belong here and refused to feel responsible. The lost boys remained irretrievable. They were gone. Abdou finally hustled her back into the taxi just as the light changed to evening. Rested and refreshed, she promised to view both missing sons should they reappear within a fortnight and could make it into town. The taxi and its occupants were waved off like royalty by the massed search parties in the excited street. Abdou's dusty Citroën banged away into the desert with the crackling radio switched to maximum.

The desert appeared to change shape and volume in the sharpening shadows. The dunes rose up, humpbacked, like gigantic dolphins negotiating an unearthly element, their backs flexed and supple, rippling with shadows. The hamada opened out like a nomad's veil, huge, spreading, indigo. She saw the half moon unfold, yellow and vast, lightening their road. The void increased dramatically in size as the darkness above and below stretched out into infinity, like an immense black hand. The temperature plunged. She retrieved her shawl from her basket and peered out into the fabulous, luminous dark. The shadows darkened. Each rock nurtured an eerie double, which lurked beneath, mirroring its shape. The world before her, now completely alien, to which she had neither maps nor compass, proclaimed itself a savage place, without paths, landmarks or hope of rescue. She was in the hands of her guide, who was himself unknown, a figure from fairy tale. But the risks now represented no terrors for her. She sat back in the chariot seat of her dark taxi and gazed out, content, at this miraculous and inexplicable world. Abdou drove the dark horses faster, faster. She asked no more questions. She had learned how to trust him.

They saw the lights up ahead from a great distance. Abdou immediately slowed down.

'Something's happening. There's nothing to be seen on this side of town.'

She leaned forward and they both peered out at the unintelligible leaping shapes far ahead. As they approached they saw several trucks lined up along the road like wrecked hulks washed ashore. Several men standing on the roadside were gesticulating at one another. They heard shouting.

'What is it?'

'I don't know.'

The taxi crawled forwards and was suddenly in the midst of a mass of uniformed police and armed soldiers swarming over the vehicles. A battered car was being emptied out under torchlights, the driver protesting with excessive gestures. Two soldiers, one with his machine gun trained directly upon them, stopped the taxi. Abdou put his hands in the air and surrendered at once. Elizabeth was unable to follow the exchange, but she did not like the warm smell of oil that exuded from the sleek black barrel.

'Do they want us to get out, Abdou?'

'Yes. Quick. Leave the basket.'

A slight wind, now cooling fast, tugged at her shawl. Her knees felt stiff and she was unable to stand up easily, but neither of the two armed men bent to help her. Abdou and Elizabeth Webster stood together, silent and bewildered, beside the black Citroën. Elizabeth realised that Abdou was trembling. She stood up straight at last, unafraid but very puzzled.

'Vos papiers, Madame.'

'What is going on? Please explain.'

'Vos papiers.'

'I don't have them in the taxi. My passport is at my hotel. The Hôtel du Désert.'

This caused some confusion and irritation. They concentrated upon Abdou instead and began to ransack his boxes of papers and tapes. The taxi's documents were spread out all over the bonnet and examined with a large square beam, powerful as a searchlight. The soldier shone the beam directly into Abdou's face whenever he came across a document with an official photograph. Elizabeth Webster tried to wander up the line of trucks with the intention of finding out why a roadblock was there in the first place. There were no ambulances or recovery vehicles, no carts overturned or groaning squashed camels, no signs of an accident and no cars or trucks coming from the direction of the town. All the traffic had been stopped. She was unable to see very far into the dark, as the headlights were confusing; then she was briskly dragged back to the taxi by one of the soldiers.

'Is this how you treat tourists?' She raised her voice in indignation. A uniformed policeman approached. He rose to the challenge.

'It is for your own protection, Madame.' He spoke English.

'Would you be so kind as to tell me what is going on?' She drew herself up in the dark and wrapped her shawl around her with a contemptuous flick. The policeman looked a little dusty, but had been well ironed that morning. He sported an excessively neat, clipped beard, a natty piece of facial architecture which appeared scrupulous and vain. She could not see his eyes, so she lowered her veil and made sure that he was unable to see hers.

He hesitated for a second, then he said in English, 'There has been a terrorist attack on the main marketplace. A car bomb. Four people have been killed and many more injured. The death toll will certainly rise. And there has been a warning, or at least a rumour, that another bomb is timed to explode somewhere else. We have no idea where. So the town is sealed off.'

'When did this happen?'

'About three hours ago.'

'We have been visiting the desert all day, officer. We therefore cannot possibly have been involved in this bomb. And as you well know, the Hôtel du Désert is outside the town walls. I beg you to allow my driver to return me to my hotel.'

Elizabeth Webster presented this as a formal request, but her manner was both fearsome and severe. The delivery suggested a command. The officer hesitated. She pounced.

'We have no need to cross the town. We can go round by the desert tracks. Please call off these soldiers and allow us to depart. I will vouch for Monsieur Abdou. I am his employer.'

For a terrible moment the outcome was in doubt. Abdou watched her without appearing to do so. He had not understood her words, but he had grasped the method. Make them think that you are more important than you are, and that if they don't look sharp there'll be consequences. Then the officer stood aside and roared at the soldiers.

'Quick, Abdou!' said Miss Webster. 'We're off!'

She climbed into the back seat unaided and then realised that she had been walking without her sticks. Abdou pulled the taxi out of line. There was now a queue of drivers behind them being bullied and menaced, their vehicles threatened with immediate dismemberment if any irregularities were discovered in their papers.

'I assume that you can find a back route that is passable.'

'With my eyes shut. Thank you, Miss Webster. Accrochez-vous! We will escape!'

And off they went, shuddering across undulating gravel at crawler speeds. A row of sitting camels loomed up in the headlights. Abdou passed so close that Elizabeth could smell them and heard one belch. A small brick shack with a paraffin lantern hung outside the doorway materialised from hulks of darkness. They saw three sepulchral faces, gaunt and fixed like images on tombstones, peering fearfully at the approaching lights. Abdou turned on the radio, but the dance music didn't come on line. Instead he picked up explosions of static and thin muttered voices.

'I can get the police channels.'

Everything was in Arabic, or as Abdou explained, approximately Arabic. Elizabeth clutched the front seat and bent over, straining to decipher a language she would never understand. Abdou translated the essentials.

'They are still searching all the public buildings. The death toll has risen. My cousins were in the market today. No one has claimed responsibility. There is a news blackout. But the news has got out anyway.'

The torpor of the day vanished; they both sizzled with adrenaline and muffled terror.

'Abdou! Are you sure we're going the right way?'

It occurred to Elizabeth that they might be heading straight for another roadblock, or that they would be taken for escaping terrorists and liquidated by mistake. She imagined bullets, fine as sand, peppering the taxi. The unruly desert juddered beneath her as the taxi bucked and swung.

'Mais non. Je suis bien sûr. I know where we have to go. Sit back, Madame Webster. It is very rough underfoot.'

The headlights rose and dipped, like a ship at sea. Suddenly the car wallowed and slumped. They were stuck in a patch of soft sand. Abdou cursed and leaped out. He scrabbled around the back wheels, which had the effect of burying the taxi ever deeper. Miss Webster became aware of a decided list to port. Abdou abandoned the futile attempt to dig the taxi out with his bare hands and grappled with the ropes on the roof rack. Elizabeth Webster finally glimpsed what the surfboards were actually for. She climbed out and helped Abdou lay the boards under the tyres. As she grovelled in the dirt she noticed that the deeper sand was still warm. They could hear someone crying and a chorus of yells and howls, far, far away. As their eyes became used to the moonlight they managed to wedge the ends of the surfboards on a solid gravel surface.

'Get in. Drive. I'll push.'

'Madame Webster! You are a lady. You cannot push.' Abdou looked desperately around at the all-encompassing dark and the distant fiery lights above the town. If she didn't push no one else was going to.

'In my country, ladies push. Get behind that wheel and drive. Go on, get in,' she snapped, and he did.

And so Elizabeth Webster, who a month before had barely been able to walk one hundred yards to the village shop, sank up to her ankles in warm sand, heaving an old black Citroën on to the surface of the *tôles*, whose purpose she had at last understood. Our situation is not desperate and we will soon be home. The radio hissed and crackled as the taxi crept along the barely visible trails in the dark. It was midnight before they saw the seven palms outlined by the security lights. The gate was guarded by two uniformed men who raised their guns as Abdou drew up in front of the hotel. The children had vanished. There were very few lights on in the main buildings and no music floated out on to the terrace of the Desert Rendezvous. Everyone was inside, clustered into the salon, watching alarmingly local horror on CNN.

'Abdou! Miss Webster! Thank God!'

Saïda rushed down the steps, her high-heeled sandals, an evening speciality, clattering beneath her. In the security lights her jewels winked and glittered, sinister as the eye of a toad.

'How did you get through the town? There are road-blocks everywhere. Oh Miss Webster, thank God you have returned safely. Four of my Dutch guests are missing. They were out in the town. We have no idea where they are or what has happened to them. The bomb went off in the main square – where there are all the restaurants and clubs . . .'

'Really? They said it was in the market.' Miss Webster liked to get things right. Abdou was unpacking all her equipment. She ignored the soldiers and the guns and accepted her basket from his hands. 'Thank you, Abdou. Please don't worry about me, Saïda. The English are quite used to bombs. The IRA has been blowing us up for decades. I have been in good hands, quite safe and very comfortable. We had the pleasure of meeting your family.'

Everyone clustered around them, anxious to hear the whole story, as if they were shipwreck survivors. But she spoke only to her guide. They kissed each other on both cheeks in the French style and then shook hands warmly as if they had served in the same company and survived the assault together. The little taxi man no longer looked cheeky and confident; his white djellaba was crumpled and soiled, his turban had been destabilised by the episode in the sandbank and his teeth now looked like an un-fortunate dental disaster, rather than a special effect. The old English lady stood up straight in the glossy night. She carefully balanced her sticks, basket, shawl, veils and hat, and reached into her jacket pocket. No one could see how much money she gave him as it was carefully folded into a roll. The transaction remained private.

'Thank you, Abdou, for a wonderful day. Here is a little extra recompense for all your trouble, and thank you for bringing me safely home.'

3

THE VISITOR

Why had anyone bothered to bomb a public square in a small desert town on the remote edge of the Atlas Mountains? The square contained a mosque with an elegant minaret, a daily market, a donkey park, two cafés, a small hotel, three restaurants, one of which was in every known guide to the country and much photographed on account of the green, ceramic tiles around the dining room and its old French colonial décor. What was there to bomb? Terrorists went for capitals, for spectacular atrocities, which would kill thousands at a stroke. The masterclass had been given by the 9/11 bombers. But even the Al-Qaida experts were forced to make two assaults on the World Trade Center before they got it down. Practising, that's what my local terrorists were doing. That was a practice run. And a great success it turned out to be – I don't think. Two dozen dead and scores of wounded, some of them maimed and crippled for the rest of their lives. Four Dutch tourists and all the rest their own people. Inefficient, that's my view. Far better to pick off the white Western tourists with crack snipers. After all, they're easy enough to spot, wandering round the market nearly naked in skintight shorts and off-the-shoulder T-shirts. But maybe they are after their own government. Maybe it'll be the king's palace in Rabat next time. Or the police headquarters. A bomb left inside the lift. Or maybe a guided missile attack on the British fleet nestled in the lee of Gibraltar? Theatre is the language of terrorism. They need an audience to witness the event; otherwise the performance is worthless. If they could hire Jean Michel Jarre to do the fireworks, or that fat madman who filmed all the Tolkein, and get them to design the special effects on the tie-in computer game, they would. Maybe even terrorism has to be commercially viable. Late September, and time to get on with clearing up my garden before the winter. Oh my God, just look at my rhubarb, wolfed by slugs.

Elizabeth Webster, two weeks back from her eventful sortie to the land far away, to which she had travelled, obedient and puzzled, without knowing why, now stamped round her receding flowers and shrubs, pruning back dead shoots and clearing out the first fallen leaves. She bagged up the rubbish. Not enough yet for a bonfire. I'll have one at the end of October. She rubbed mud off her gloves and stood leaning on her rake. And what have I gained from going far, far away to a land that I shall never see again? She looked up at the apple tree, demanding an answer. The huge mass of ripening apples leered down at her. She collected all the decent windfalls that were not pierced by the invisible worm that flies in the night in the howling storm. I have come home, she thought. I was not myself. I had become old, frail and twittering. And I was lost, even in familiar surroundings. But now I have come home. She smiled at the Michaelmas daisies and last year's Christmas tree, which had rooted nicely.

She purchased a discreet haul of new skirts and cardigans and stashed the walking sticks in the coat cupboard. Miss

Elizabeth Webster lifted her chin and tightened her lips. Business as usual. She rummaged deep within the shoebox and retrieved her cherished galoshes. Miss Webster set great store by her log stove and her elderly galoshes. Everyone in the village, who saw her at church or in the shop, told her how well she was looking.

'Amazing what good a little holiday can do.'

'Well, you look quite transformed.'

'That haircut really suits you. Chic!'

'Oh Miss Webster, your nose is all sunburnt. But you do look well.'

(This contribution supplied by Sophie at Snippets.)

'I say, you weren't anywhere near those frightful bombings, were you?'

She no longer ripped their heads off when they made personal comments; instead she heard genuine concern rather than impertinence. She began reading again and renewed her subscription to her foreign language book club: New Books in French and German. She signed up for a course of t'ai chi, ten lessons, at the university sports centre and felt full of energy after the first session, swaying and rising in rhythm with the teacher, a woman sculpted in muscles, who wore a kung fu headband, struck fierce poses, and then held them, her face expressionless. She bought a DVD player that was on special offer at Dixons to watch French films, also available from the predatory book club. This was an ambitious move and the SCART leads unfortunately defeated her. But she put it aside and summoned up the local TV men to make all the necessary adjustments. She was no longer catapulted into rages when inanimate objects put up a malevolent resistance. *Tant pis*, I'll do it tomorrow.

★

Miss Elizabeth Webster was sitting on the green striped sofa beneath her Anglepoise reading light, at 10.45 p.m., watching *Newsnight*, in precisely the same position she had occupied at the very moment she came to a dead halt, six months previously, when the doorbell wheezed and sprang into life. She took a long time drawing back the heavy velvet draught excluder from the porch door. The t'ai chi had had an unexpected effect on her knees and she wobbled into her porch, stumbling over her shopping bag and umbrella, which both fell away from the wall and landed on her toes. The shape outside in the gusty night, illuminated by her automatic floodlight, was curly-headed, young and male. She flung open the front door and glared at him.

'Yes? What is it?'

The young man had the kind of beauty which silences crowds and persuades elderly pederasts to reach for their flies and their cameras, for their time of joy has come again. His smooth olive features and merry dark eyes met hers with confidence and amusement. He knew exactly who she was.

'Bonsoir, Madame Webster.'

He spoke perfect French, with the kind of intonation that no one normal ever acquires from their mothers. More alarmingly, he was carrying a large suitcase, a rucksack and a bulging paper carrier bag. Elizabeth instantly smelt a rat.

'Who are you? And what do you want?'

'Je m'appelle Chérif. Je suis le fils de Saïda. And these are for you.'

He pressed the poisoned gifts upon her. Inside the paper carrier bag was a mass of bulky packages, wrapped up in glittering paper. There was no room in the tiny porch for the smiling Chérif, the suitcase, the rucksack, the bag of presents and Elizabeth Webster. Someone had to go out or come in.

'Well, you'd better step inside for a moment. Entrez, entrez,' she gestured impatiently. What kind of visitor turns up just at the moment when all decent people are thinking about locking the back door, finding themselves glasses of water and putting the cat out? The unsuitable hour worried her more than anything else. Was he staying at Everglades, the B&B? Should she call a taxi? They stood in the middle of her orderly green room, staring at one another. Chérif looked around him, curious, at ease. He had wide, dark eyes and long lashes. He studied the books, the television, the abstract paintings, the watercolour of a slate mine in North Wales. Each china ornament – including the maiden with goats, hand-painted, made in 1845, very valuable indeed – was examined in turn. This scrupulous silent inspection, which was too innocent to be rude, came to rest above the wood stove, not yet lit, and steadied before another face, which scowled back.

'Who is the man becoming a tree?' he asked at last.

'It's a green man. Un homme vert. He's a roof boss in the cathedral cloisters. They were once found all over Europe, mostly in churches. Some scholars think they are a fertility symbol, but no one really knows what they mean.'

'He is a soldier in camouflage,' said Chérif, peering at the evil gilded face, who suddenly transformed himself into a harmless comic squaddie.

'Would you like some tea?' Elizabeth Webster remembered her manners and Abdou's strange conversation with the anonymous driver of the desert jeep, whom she would also never see again. 'Is your mother well? Are all your family safe and well? I hope there have been no more bombs.'

'She is well, thank you. Yes, they are all well. Et Dieu soit béni, God be praised, we have had no more bombs. But many tourists have cancelled their winter bookings because they are afraid.'

'What stuff and nonsense. They are just as likely to be blown up here.' Elizabeth marched out to the kitchen. 'Put down your suitcase and rucksack and I'll make you some tea.'

'Why not open your presents?'

She grappled with the mass of bright parcels laid out on the kitchen table, and as she tugged at the shining paper she saw why he had asked her to do so. There was a beautiful silver kettle, engraved with tiny abstract swirls, a decorated silver teapot, squat but noble with four stocky feet, and six perfect hand-blown gilded glasses with golden rims and exotic patterns etched in the glass. Everything felt heavy, precious and expensive. The glasses were carefully wrapped in an Arabic newspaper. Her heart clenched when she saw the strange dots and swirls of the unknown tongue. It had been real. She had been there. But the presentation was not over. Chérif began to unravel a large bundle wrapped in blue plastic, extracted from the bulbous rucksack. This, the most alarming gift of all, overflowed from his hands as he pulled it from its wrappings; an endless carpet, which, like Draupadi's sari, bloomed into voluminous folds. Each section of the carpet was intricate, meticulous, hand-woven; the deft touch of beauty stretched casually across her kitchen in a torrent of crimson and gold.

'She shouldn't send me such lovely things. I was only a guest in her hotel.'

The complexity of the gesture and its origins in bribery only gradually dawned on Elizabeth, who was not used to receiving anything, let alone unsolicited gifts. But the unknown young man, gorgeous as a god, stood smiling before her, amused, insistent.

'These are for you,' he said.

She stood back and looked at him carefully. He was wearing ordinary Western clothes: a dark blue T-shirt with a red star, no slogan; a loose furry fleece, the zip undone; black jeans and trainers. He stood there in her kitchen, meeting her gaze, patient as the Angel Gabriel on the left side of the triptych in a Renaissance painting, waiting to be noticed and addressed. He had not removed the padded anorak. It smelt new, unworn.

'Let me take your coat.'

Saïda's only son felt solid and safe. The only extraordinary thing about this young man was his eerie beauty and grace.

'Shall we use the new teapot? I will give it a good scrub, just in case.' Chérif effortlessly assessed her kitchen and sorted out the prodigal gifts. Elizabeth found herself settling his coat into her cupboard. She had a sudden urge to check the pockets and actually did so. But apart from an English train timetable and a taxi receipt, there was nothing there. She went on to the offensive.

'It's actually quite late. Where are you staying tonight, Chérif?'

He looked at her, unabashed, brandishing the teapot.

'I don't know. I was hoping you could recommend a hostel. Somewhere not too expensive. I have an interview at the university tomorrow. And if it goes well I have a place to study mathematics and chemistry. I'm very good at maths.' The smile beamed huge, inclusive, the teeth straight and gleaming and apparently all his own. 'I won a prize. That's helped with expenses like the flight.'

Elizabeth suddenly heard herself being inhospitable,

83

suspicious and unkind. This was the moment when she could have turned back, refused to initiate the long chain of events that followed and remained shut up in her dark past. She could have ended everything by saying no. But safety does not come first, and yes, she was disarmed by the boy's loveliness. And for this young man the flat green fields and oak clumps of provincial England constituted the northern desert, the unknown barren space, a wilderness dangerous to the unwary and the ignorant. Traditions of hospitality exist in every desert, traditions that must be honoured.

'You are very welcome to stay here tonight and we can find somewhere more suitable through the university accommodation office tomorrow.'

The surprise appeared unfeigned. He had not expected to stay in her house. She smiled, reassured. So did he.

'Merci, Madame Webster. Vous êtes très gentille.'

He actually bowed, teapot in hand. Chérif had breached the gates and could therefore be blessed by an innate generosity, of which Miss Webster was completely unaware, for hitherto it had never been tapped.

'Would you like to ring your mother and tell her that you have arrived safely? Or is it too late at home?'

'I did that at the airport. I thought I'd send her an e-mail tomorrow. She picks up her e-mails at the hotel.'

For the first time the boy looked anxious. Elizabeth saw the furtive shudder of exhaustion in his eyes and shoulders. She dug out an opened packet of ginger biscuits.

'Tea. Then bed,' she declared.

Everything salvaged from her mother's house had been dumped in the spare bedroom. When she ventured into what appeared to be a vista of old-lady-land early next morning, clutching a mug of very sweet tea with no milk, Chérif's dark curls were practically submerged beneath chintz armchairs, lace dripping from the pelmet and a vanity dresser, its surfaces coated in protective glass, replete with coloured crystal perfume bottles and boxes of scented powder puffs sporting views of Swiss lakes. Elderly beauty equipment crowded round the bed, drenched in lavender and dense with embroidered flowering roses. The towels flirted with each other on a varnished wooden rack, presenting a dashing camp mixture of violet and pink. Even the silver-backed clothes brushes, laid out on the sheer glass surfaces according to size and depth of bristle, were covered in dancing maidens. The only thing that still bore witness to Elizabeth's more neutral taste was the pale yellow wallpaper.

'Good morning, Chérif. Here's some tea.'

He considered her for a moment, baffled. Then his eyes settled on the luxurious floral glut of artificial colours and widened in alarm. Elizabeth hastily opened the curtains to reveal the apple tree. She remembered what he must have seen every morning: date palms, white sand, grey rock. Before them unfolded a sunny autumn morning, ripening into a cool windy day. The whole world brimmed with late heavy green, bruised yellow at the edges.

'Bonjour,' he murmured, staring in wonder at the size of the apple tree. The marvel rattled back against the panes.

'Chérif, do you speak English?'

He switched languages effortlessly to reassure her, but reproduced the faintest tingle of Internet America.

'It's better to speak English. Maman told me that you loved French. We had some French teachers at school. But I should practise for my interview.'

'What time do you have to be there?'

'Eleven-thirty.'

'I'll take you in. You can have a hot shower downstairs.' Some unsettling instinct warned her to keep him out of her bathroom.

What on earth does he eat for breakfast? Muslims don't eat bacon, so the fry-up is out. Toast and fruit and yoghurt. That's safe ground. Honey. I have real honey in a honey-comb. She decided to be daring with the homemade marmalade. Chérif reappeared in the kitchen, damp and scrubbed.

'I've saved all the basin water for recycling,' he declared.

They spent half an hour apologising to each other for her acceptance that water was something to be wasted and his inadvertent exposure of this domestic scandal. She reassured him that she always tipped the washing-up bowl over the roses to slaughter the greenfly and the ubiquitous black spot; he begged her to let him do it. She watched him from the kitchen window dowsing each late rose in turn. Not a drop was spilt on the brick path. As he emptied the plastic bowl he swung the thing triumphantly in the air. She saw him smiling at the bedraggled, dripping roses.

He sauntered into the back porch and said, 'My mother says it rains and rains in England. The earth is damp, so it must be true. Everything is so green.'

'Well, it rains more than it does in the Sahara. Did you know that we sometimes get the red dust from the desert here? Carried on the winds?'

'The harmattan,' said Chérif dreamily, 'the name means the evil thing.'

He wandered back into the garden and lifted his eyes to the great tree with its hanging globes of red and green. He stood at the edge of her soft lawns, stroking the fuchsia, looking up. She pondered this curious mixture

86

of sophistication and childishness. Sometimes he appeared to possess the knowledge and assurance of an experienced traveller; sometimes he seemed bewitched by wonders. Surely these people knew everything about the West? They watched the films, the news, they scudded about the Net, climbed aboard planes, cadged books off tourists, talked endlessly on their mobile phones. But here stood this young Arab man, gazing at the apples and the extravagant torrents of red, green, purple and gold in her autumn garden, transfixed, as if confronted with a miracle. The light plunged dappled through the apple tree and swirled across his face and chest, now light, now dark; each shadowed plane glimmered, shone, faded. No one had ever stood in her garden before, worshipping her apple tree.

She switched off the central heating and called him from the back door.

'It's time to go,' she said.

The university was founded forty years before in a frenzy of ideological conviction. It was now much the worse for wear, for it is almost impossible to renovate bald, cracked concrete. The elderly brutalism had been softened in odd corners by Virginia creeper. Chérif stared at each new scene with desert eyes. She realised that the whole thing unrolled before him like a foreign film without subtitles, finally as insubstantial as a mirage. It was all too close, too coloured, too green. She pointed out the building to which he should report. Term had begun and the walkways were swarming with young people. It was warm in the sun. They all tied their jackets and sweaters around their waists and necks. Chérif stared intently at the girls. These massed members of the young fair sex wore metal, jewels or bones skewered through their noses and eyebrows; their ample bosoms, stomachs and bottoms, much of which was on display, oozed over zips and belts, untidily packed into tatty black clothes far too small for them.

'Shall I wait?' They were sitting in the car.

'No. It may take a while. I have to do a language test and see the dean of studies at two-thirty. Can I ring you and tell you what has happened?'

'Of course. Let me give you my number.'

'No need. I have it here.'

She was already neatly recorded in his little red book.

Elizabeth Webster hoovered and polished like a fifties housewife stricken with cleaning frenzy, one eye upon the phone. He might have to stay the week. If they do find a room for him the rental would start on 1 October. That's a week away. Or maybe they have entire halls of residence for foreigners. What on earth can I cook? I can't offer him frozen packets of chips from Waitrose. I should get some fresh vegetables and roast something. They aren't supposed to drink. But the Desert Rendezvous was always mixed, half locals, half tourists, knocking it back in a smoky haze of rock and jazz. That's why I never stepped over the threshold. She spied on the luggage in the chintz boudoir. He had packed up all his belongings and remade the bed. So he isn't intending to stay.

The phone rang.

She flung down the hoover and heaved the whole phone off the window sill.

'Chérif? How did it go?'

'Miss Webster? It's the TV Repairs from Great Blessington. Sky installation systems. You left a message on the answerphone. Was it the aerial needing repairs or a Sky dish and box that you wanted?'

'Oh no, no. I can't deal with that now. I'm expecting a call. May I ring you back?'

She sat down firmly on the green sofa looking out at the meadows and the windy autumn light. This time she was ready. Purse. Glasses. Keys. Just as soon as he rings. She rubbed her knees, like an athlete ready for the gun. But when he did ring he was not crowing or triumphant, he was worried.

'Yes, yes. It was fine. I did OK on the English. But it's not over yet. I have to do a maths test on Friday and they won't accept me officially until the bank draft clears and I have written proof that I can pay the fees.' He paused. 'I'm at the accommodation office. They don't have much. Term's started.'

'Hang on. I'll be there in forty minutes.'

The accommodation office was run by two prophets of doom. They addressed themselves entirely to Miss Webster, as if Chérif were either dumb, illiterate or autistic.

'He's going to have real problems finding anything anywhere, Miss Webster. Everything's taken. We haven't anything on campus and his budget isn't very big. It's expensive in town. He doesn't have enough for a flat. He can't pay the agency fees or the caution. You really need three months' rent to begin with. So that's out. And we've got no flat share offers left. We have this room in Wickham, but he'd need a car . . .'

'Well, is there anything at all?' Miss Webster began to tap the desk. Her bony fingers rose and fell like the hammers in a piano. The prophets wriggled uneasily before her.

'These people in Highwater, out beyond Stanford St Mary, are renting a room. It's not expensive and it's a twenty-minute bus ride round the ring road. There aren't any extras for water or electricity. No cooking facilities. Shared bathroom. It's just that – well, I was trying to explain –'

'Ring them. We'll go and look.'

Chérif's face had set fast, his mouth tightened into a grim line. Had something happened? The young woman clearly found it difficult to hand over the address. Miss Webster snatched up the card and stalked out; she hated embarrassment and indecision.

Highwater was on the rough boundary of town, beyond Great Mills DIY, Dobbie's Garden World, Dixons and Asda. They turned into the estate beside a burned-out telephone box and a shattered bus shelter. The dustbins toppled into the street and a featureless patch of straggling grass, criss-crossed by muddy tracks, served as a playground. The houses were neglected and too close to each other. A pile of wooden pallets loomed like a barricade in front of a battered corrugated iron shed.

'Oh dear, this doesn't look hopeful.'

Highwater. The address began to take shape in her mind. One of her indigent pupils had moved here, a sensitive timid little thing, the youngest in a large Catholic family, and the boys on this estate, or some of them at any rate, had used her guinea pig as a football. Elizabeth Webster worried that her Clio would end up with the windows smashed in, her umbrella stolen and the tyres slashed. There were no black faces anywhere to be seen. It was a white man's estate. But Chérif had recovered his optimism. He peered at the houses. She realised that he was not reading the overflowing skips, the yellowed net curtains or the cars propped up on bricks as she did. She was calculating poverty, he was counting the door numbers.

'I think it's this one.'

Two small children were destroying cardboard boxes in the front garden, then sitting in them and pointing plastic guns at each other. One of them had a patch over her left eye. It was unclear whether the patch concealed an ailment or served as a prop in the game of pirates and castles. They both rushed to the doorway when the alien car pulled up and screeched for their mother with harrowing intensity. A skinny bottle-blonde slithered sideways past the pram and bicycle wedged in the hall.

'Are you from the college?'

She looked at Elizabeth's smart cream mac and clean shoes. Then she saw Chérif. She stopped dead and stared. The arresting beauty of the strange young man was like a trump card, laid down on the broken concrete path between them. A man with a self-inflicted blue tattoo on his forearm lurched out behind her.

'Mr Leering?' Miss Webster looked down at the card and then up at the man. He smelt of oil and hadn't shaved. 'We've come about the room,' she said, her heart clenched. Then she stood aside. She was taking over. This was Chérif's call. She would never set foot in a house as ugly as this one. The man pushed past his wife, ignored Chérif and looked suspiciously at Elizabeth.

'This one's not your grandson, is he? Can't be. He's too dark. Well, I'm sorry, but we can't accept Arabs. The college said that he was Arab and that he doesn't have any references. We can't take them if they don't have references. And we can't have any Arabs. I've got kids and I'm not taking risks.'

Elizabeth stood before them, dumbfounded. The

children abandoned their boxes and came to stare at the old lady with short spiky hair and the beautiful silent man. Nobody said anything.

'Sorry. We can't take him,' the man repeated. He never looked directly at Chérif.

Miss Webster exploded. 'How dare you be so rude!' Her skin tingled and her mouth went white. Chérif intervened in French.

'Madame Webster, it's all right. They've said no. And why. Ils ont dit non. Et pourquoi.'

Now the entire family gaped at Chérif. He addressed the old lady with deference and respect, but the strange language suggested a shared, exclusive code. The monster Caliban had begun reciting poetry. He pulled gently at her sleeve.

'It's all right. Let's go.'

Elizabeth glared at the children, who shrivelled against their father's trousers, then she stormed back to the car. No one had ever dared to be rude to Elizabeth Webster when she was in her prime. There were consequences whenever she was crossed or contradicted.

'You aren't even an Arab, are you?' she thundered at Chérif, 'you're a Berber!'

'What's the difference to them?'

Elizabeth felt the rejection in her stomach and behind her eyes. They drove back to the cottage in silence. The sky was gigantic, pink and gold. She was still in a pale rage when they arrived. Nothing would pacify her. She threw her car keys down on the coffee table and rang the university accommodation office.

'Yes, Miss Webster, the Leerings did ring,' squeaked one of the hapless administrators, flattened by Elizabeth's torrent of menaces and her electric delivery. 'They say they're very sorry. It's not your – um – young man they object to. It's just that they've made a decision –'

'To be intolerant and racist. I grasped their motives perfectly, thank you very much. I shall be making an official complaint against them and against you for harbouring such people on your books. I shall be in touch via my lawyers. Goodbye.'

She hammered the phone back into place. Angry letter. Copy to the press office and the vice-chancellor. And threaten them with the newspapers. She must have snarled the last word aloud. Chérif stood helpless in the middle of her sitting room, clearly more devastated by her outburst than by being turned away from the inn.

'The newspapers would probably support the Leerings.' He sounded wretched.

'Did you suspect that this would happen?' Elizabeth launched a fresh round of accusations, more sharply than she had intended. Chérif winced. She eyeballed him aggresively. Impasse. He stood accused of being in on the whole thing, and staging his own exclusion.

'It will be easier to find somewhere when I know other students.'

Once more he had failed to understand her anger and assumed that he was its cause. She wanted him out of her house. That must be the reason for this rage that welled up from a secret place, fathoms deep. But her wrath arose from a very simple source: Elizabeth Webster loathed being thwarted or denied. She was used to being heard and obeyed. Anything else was intolerable.

'Don't waste money and time on these people. You don't need to find anywhere else. You've got to start your course. Buy books. Settle in. You're staying here. There's no point besieging the estate agents until you know for sure that your cheque has cleared and that you've passed your maths test. And you'd be better off saving your cash. Even a B&B costs a fortune.'

'B&B?'

'Never mind. You're staying here.'

'Are you sure, Madame Webster? Je ne veux pas m'imposer.'

His hesitation gave her the licence to insist.

'Nonsense. I'm inviting you. An invitation. Do you understand?'

There was a long pause, and then he said, very simply and quietly, 'Merci, Madame Webster.'

'Oh, forget it all. I hated that place and those people. They murdered one of my pupils' guinea pigs. Un petit cochon d'Inde. I'd love to have you here. And we should be celebrating. If you aren't wanted for murder and haven't stolen the money, you've got a place to study for your degree.' Elizabeth Webster's face crumpled into laughter wrinkles. She looked older and younger at the same time. 'How shall we celebrate?'

'Tea!' said Chérif.

The bank account required her word that he was a fit and proper person, but the fact that he lived in her house helped enormously. Miss Webster's reputation and the scale of her investments whisked them past all obstacles. She counter-signed all his documents, upon which he was variously referred to as her ward, protégé and godson, all in one day, by confused officials who needed to put a name to the connection. Chérif flung himself into the programme of induction seminars, laboratory tours and library visits. He came home with files full of unnecessary information.

Elizabeth spread them out on the kitchen table and read every word. Sexual harassment. Hardship fund. Chaplain's visits. Sports insurance. Health and safety regulations.

'Are you on the seminar lists and have you been given a personal adviser?'

They hunted through the lists and yes, there he was.

'I think Friday's a rubber stamp affair, Chérif. Especially if you're such a hot shot in maths. After all, you're paying foreign student fees. Has the bank draft come through? Unless you turn out to be penniless or go for the dean in a mad knife attack, you're in.'

'Why should I want to knife the dean?'

'It's an English figure of speech.' He stared at her for a moment, then burst out laughing. He was slowly learning how to be teased.

'I will pay you rent,' declared Chérif, shoulders back, decided.

'You can pay me a peppercorn rent so that there are no obligations either side. And you can contribute to the food. For the rest you can help me cook and dig the garden. That's it.'

'Peppercorn?' He frowned. Was she to be paid in grain and vegetables? But she was laughing again.

He rang her on Friday. By then they had known one another for precisely five days.

'My money has come through at the bank and I've paid the first set of fees. And I got 91% in the maths.'

'Well done. Are you coming home? Or shall I come and pick you up?'

'I'm at the supermarket by the bus stop. Shall I get anything? There's a bus in ten minutes. I'll come home by bus.'

'Get some more milk. Full cream. Pas demi-écrémé. See you soon.'

Half an hour later she found herself looking out down the track through the porch window, anxious at the wind and drizzle. Did his anorak have a hood? He should have taken the folding umbrella that would have fitted inside his rucksack. For the first time in her life she was waiting for someone to come home. Then she saw him running down the track, a plastic shopping bag banging against his rucksack. The rain shone on his thick black curls, darkened the shoulders of his anorak, glistened on the face of his watch. She bundled him inside.

'You should have taken the umbrella. I told you to take the umbrella.'

'But I love rain,' he smiled.

It was just over a year after the 9/11 attacks, the declaration of the War on Terror and the assault on the Taliban in Afghanistan. In the gruesome wake of accumulated atrocity, the television was filled with synopses of events, historical assessments and never-before-shown footage of catastrophe. It was also the first truly chilly evening of the autumn. When she put the rubbish out she could smell the bonfires in the early dark. Dr Brody's wife was also out there, two gardens away, gathering in the chickens. Elizabeth heard her making mad clucks and chuckles at the dissenting hens. Chérif lit a fire in the stove. The first fire of the year. They watched it bristle and crack as the sticks went up. He didn't bother with the firelighters and used only the minimum of newspapers. Even his movements were frugal and careful. He saved everything. Elizabeth understood this. Someone who lived so close to abjection and nothingness would know in his guts what it costs to live in this world.

The two towers of New York stood smoking on the television. Some of the hijackers were not much older than Chérif. She looked at his cautious pile of tiny sticks and then back at the extravagant courage of absolute sacrifice. Two jets, two vast buildings, thousands and thousands of lives flung into dust. Who knows 3,000 people? It was unimaginable.

'Do you often light fires?' She acknowledged to herself that this must be a redundant question, for behold the practised hand, cupping the flame.

'Every night. To cook. We cook outside.'

Elizabeth nodded. What was the effect of repetition? What did it mean to see this huge descending tower folded in upon itself and rushing downwards in an explosion of dust, again and again? When something is repeated its meaning changes. *Tyger, Tyger, burning bright, In the forests of the night, What immortal hand or eye, Dare frame thy fearful symmetry?* She looked round at Chérif. He was sitting in front of the stove, collapsed like a deckchair, with his arms around his knees.

'And where were you when it happened?'

'In the Hôtel des Voyageurs. Watching CNN.'

Elizabeth Webster had never been to America and had no intention of doing so. In her considered opinion the United States was the source of disgusting food and consequent obesity, appalling films which took place at grotesque speeds, but hooked you all the same, unintelligible accents and bad taste in clothes. America was a nation of petty bosses with no trade unions to kick their shins and politicians who didn't even bother to cover up their own corruption. There was therefore nothing more behind her next question other than simple curiosity.

'Did your people think the Americans deserved what

they got?' Elizabeth Webster thought the Americans had had it coming for some time.

'Of course. Some people did. The people of my village were horrified. It is forbidden to take innocent life. That is what we are taught. But we have supporters of the Palestinians. Mostly young people in the cities. They get very worked up.'

Elizabeth did not follow Middle East politics in any great detail. It had become an insoluble barrage of accusations and reprisals, quarrels between old men, who sent the young to their deaths leaving behind unburied bodies, shattered buildings and blood on pavements. She disliked disorder, riots and injustice. Her temper was easily disturbed by self-serving righteousness and gratuitous declarations that changed nothing; she therefore often watched the news in a rage. Before them on *Newsnight* the second tower crumpled with the precision of a computer-generated special effect in a disaster movie.

'What on earth did that have to do with the Palestinians?'

'They are a dispossessed people. They are our people. The Americans support Israel. But it's not only that. It's hard for me to explain.'

'You don't think all that wanton destruction is justified, do you?'

'No. Mais bien sûr que non. Mais moi, je comprends la rage derrière de telles horreurs.'

'Don't mix your languages,' commanded Miss Webster.

There was a long pause. They listened to the instant punditry and an alarming clip of the mad mullah installed by popular acclaim at the Finsbury Park mosque, declaring jihad in a leafy North London street. A Black West Indian Muslim, who was in charge of the Brixton mosque, suggested point-blank that the sooner the hero of

Finsbury Park was arrested and deported the better. The mullah had only one hand; the other hand had been replaced by a hook, which he was waving in the air to excellent effect.

'Look, Madame Webster! It's the captain from *Peter Pan*. And here comes the crocodile. Tic, tic, tic!'

The home secretary appeared, looking fierce, and declared that the mullah's days of freedom to preach terrorism were numbered. A police car revved across the scene.

'Good Heavens. Did you read J.M. Barrie when you were a child? Whatever next!'

'It's a film,' grinned Chérif, 'Disney!'

Chérif had some difficulty accounting for Miss Webster's solitude. She never mentioned a family; no photographs of grown-up children decorated the shelves and no visible evidence of a husband, alive or dead, disturbed her arrangements. Then he found a set of working power tools stored in the cupboard with the vacuum cleaner and was reassured. She must be a widow who could not bear to look at photographs of her late beloved spouse. She had cleared out all his clothes and shoes, even his spectacles, and handed them over to refugees of the Turkish earthquake. Then Chérif made the mistake of referring to her departed husband.

'My late husband? What are you talking about? I never married.'

A shiver of alarm crossed Chérif's face. He had clearly been misinformed, for by now he was persuaded that someone had mentioned the deceased husband. Elizabeth read the flicker incorrectly; she anticipated a mixture of scorn and pity for the spinster, the woman not chosen.

'I didn't want to marry. I would never have married. I wanted my independence.'

This was quite beyond Chérif's comprehension. In his world women had to marry. It was a disaster if they did not. And they all wanted children. Children were their raison d'être.

'I didn't want children,' thundered Elizabeth Webster, her irritation uncanny and appropriate, 'so why should I marry?'

Chérif began to panic; his skin prickled. She could read his mind. Elizabeth was becoming dogmatic and irrefutable. She attacked the boy's bewildered alarm, all guns blazing.

'Do you understand why I didn't want children and why I never married? Well, young man, do you?'

'Pas vraiment.'

Chérif slunk back into French, where he felt more secure and knew that he could avoid being rude. Elizabeth checked herself. He was her guest, after all.

'Listen. Have you seen any of those Agatha Christie movies? Not Poirot. The ones with the little old lady in the English village?'

Chérif remembered *Murder at the Vicarage*, which, when he first saw it, aged twelve, in black and white, might as well have been describing life on Mars.

'Do you remember Miss Marple? The old lady in the hat on the bicycle with the wicker basket? Well, I'm like Miss Marple.'

'Ah,' cried Chérif, radiant with illumination, 'you worked as a detective!' So, all was revealed – English and Belgian detectives never married. It was a condition of service.

'Oh my God.' Elizabeth gave up on the explanations. 'Put the kettle on, will you?'

But neither of them was disappointed or annoyed by this conversation. Chérif felt that he had learned something significant about Miss Webster's past and Elizabeth felt that she had told this young man a thing or two about English women. At least he had assumed that Miss Marple exercised a worthy profession. Even if he now imagined that it had been her own. A detective. A pleasant amateur sleuth gentility descended over Elizabeth Webster as she hunted down the coconut biscuits she had noticed that he liked more than the ginger ones. Yes, maybe she was something of a detective.

'I taught French for thirty-eight years,' she announced, sitting down before her new teapot. 'Go on. Pour the tea as you do in your country.'

Chérif sniffed the mint.

'You have a flower bed full of mint in your garden. Do you always have tea like this?'

'No. I use it for mint sauce. With leg of lamb.'

Chérif tried to imagine the consistency of Miss Webster's mint sauce and failed.

Sometimes misunderstanding is no bad thing. Were we to grasp every unintended insult, every irritated gesture, every accidental slight, and to take it badly, we would spend our days and nights at one another's throats. Miss Webster and Chérif did not comprehend each other's meanings. Their methods of communication were always approximate, for they had no first language in common. They were from different generations, cultures, nations. But even these things did not divide them so much as their separate conceptions of what it meant to be a woman. She was one of the warrior sex; the women with whirling blades attached to their chariots, the one-breasted Amazons galloping fearless towards the enemy host, with their bows drawn. He had never conceived of the existence of this particular species of woman, let alone encountered one, but she did remind him of various women he had seen in Hollywood films, who were usually far younger, more beautiful, and always came to bad ends. For her, he represented a generation that she was inclined to dismiss as arrogant little bastards sporting feathery beards, thoroughly brainwashed by some mad imam, and so up themselves that they could hardly see their own feet. None of this was auspicious. But he had wandered into her world and looked to her to explain his surroundings.

The need for explanations called forth the best in both of them. Elizabeth Webster had always defended her pupils, whoever they were and whatever their views. Someone in her class was one of her own; even when they did not like her or she them, she stepped calmly before them as guardian and shield, inspired by fabulous and patronising delusions of what it meant to be a great leader. Chérif fell, by accident, into the category of vulnerable beginner, someone who was learning slowly, but showed promise. She decided to invest time and energy in his sentimental education. He was clever, and therefore worth the trouble; she intended to introduce her desert dweller to the modern world.

In the mornings during those first weeks he was already up when she came down at seven-thirty, to greet the gleaming chill of dew on the lawns and the faint trace of white frost in the shadow of her potting shed. He had prepared her tea tray, with the mug she always used for her first cup, early in the day, and the kettle had boiled. But he was never in the kitchen. He was always sitting motionless on the back doorstep, wrapped up in a football jersey, staring at the birds. A squadron of tits jostled for landing positions on the feeder. There was a block of stale cake sitting upright in the toy house, but a strictly limited range of access. Frequent fights broke out. A starling arrived on the fence, then another. The bigger bird fluffed himself up a little. He clearly planned to intimidate the fray before launching an attack. Chérif stared at the sudden dips and jabs as the birds assaulted the cake. He smiled up at Elizabeth when she peered out of the kitchen window, but continued watching the birds. The disorganised aggression unrolled in twitters and shrieks. The cake crumbled and the raids intensified. A chunk plunged over the edge, only to be hotly disputed in the wet grass. When he came in, Elizabeth checked out the thickness of his jersey by running her fingers over the sleeve.

'At least you have some warm clothes.'

'It snows in the Anti-Atlas. I have a huge woollen djellaba that doubles up as a blanket,' he grinned, 'and it freezes in the desert. The rocks sometimes explode at night when the temperature falls. We sleep around the coals. I'm used to winter cold.' He nodded to the birds. 'I love them. They never give up.'

She drove in to pick him up from college at five o'clock on Thursdays. He waited outside the lodge, tired and quiet. But he looked exactly like all the other students wandering past, heading for the union, the sports centre or the halls of residence. She found this reassuring, but did not examine why she did. He walked round to the driver's side, un-thinking. He was used to left-hand drive. She leaned across and opened the door.

'Other side, Chérif. Would you like to see your camou-flaged soldier? The real one on the cloisters' roof?'

She drove back to the centre of town against the traffic and parked just outside the cathedral close. Chérif was fascinated, not by the Gothic spires above, but by the cobblestones beneath them.

'These are sea stones,' he said, 'we must be nearer the sea than I thought.'

'Maybe an hour's drive? We can go to the sea later on in the term if you like. Before it gets too cold.'

She was already planning outings, trips. But she pulled herself up short. I can't monopolise him. And he mustn't disappoint his mother. He has to work hard and do well. He needs to meet other young people, have friends his own age. He can't stay with me, embalmed in chintz. She shook herself back into her usual chill sensibility and marched before him into the damp stone mass of medieval glory.

'All right?'

He had hesitated at the first step.

'You don't take off your shoes. I know that you don't take off your shoes here.'

'There aren't any carpets. It's all stone. Have you been in a church before?'

'Yes. There's a chapel in the desert. It's part of a monastery. Just seven holy men live there now. But it's very simple. White lime walls. No tiles or paintings.'

They were inside the cathedral. The forbidding hollow void loomed huge and dark above them. High in the organ loft someone was flicking through the pages of music, illuminated by one virulent spotlight. The cathedral's echo carried the rustle and slap of each turned page. She saw and heard the building breathe in and exhale as if it were an alien thing. The great, undecorated columns of the nave sank into the aisles, pushing the long rows of empty chairs together. There were lights in the choir stalls, but the ambulatory behind the high altar shaded away into grey dark, deepening in the chapels. Chérif peered at the dead knights and bishops on their marble tombs. He looked down at the memento mori of the rotting skeleton, sculpted in the base, and the ruthless stone faces of the clerics in their rigid shrouds. Maybe they don't have graves in mosques. No, I'm sure they don't. He must be wondering why we sit here in twilight and cold, surrounded by the dead. They wandered deeper into the increasing dark. The cathedral shop closed as they passed by and the long shafts of light, displaying postcards, pencils, paperweights, fluffy toys, life-size brass rubbings and pressed flowers under glass, suddenly clicked off, generating a stranger and more terrible darkness in the great cold space above them. She could just see the windows, but the stained glass remained lifeless and obscure. The dark sucked the shop back into the shadows creeping up the Gothic side-chapels. Elizabeth felt for the wooden latch, which led into the cloisters, and nosed out the steps with the toes of her boots. The padded door thudded shut.

A rush of chilly damp air flung itself into their faces, but the light re-kindled into early evening, with a sky the colour of grey silk.

'I hope we'll be able to see him.'

They set off round the stone square, elegant and austere, encircled with blossoming marble columns and patterned porphyry, staring upwards. The roof bosses, recently restored in authentic medieval colours, smirked back down at them in vulgar blues, green, reds.

'Look at this,' cried Chérif, delighted, 'Noah's ark!'

And there was the emblem of the world's survival, all the

named animals marching up the ramp into the ark of the covenant, two by two by two by two, ducks and swans and cockatoos, the elephants and the kangaroos, everything that you find in zoos . . .

'Two by two by two by two by two,' sang Elizabeth. She remembered the chant from her Sunday school childhood. She glared at the tiny giraffes pinned to the roof above her and suddenly voiced one of her deepest festering resentments.

'The world is organised for twos. Or more than two. Two plus two. I've always been one of one. And made to pay for it.'

This complaint was intended to be understood literally. Elizabeth Webster paid single-room supplements on package holidays or was charged extra for single occupation of double rooms, missed out on special family deals, could not afford villas and gîtes with views and swimming pools, because they were all tarted up for couples, groups or families. It was more expensive to be one of one. She paid through the nose and grudged every Euro.

But Chérif heard a lament, a candid declaration of loneliness. He found himself more alone now in this strange place than he had ever been. He had always been one of two, Moha and Chérif, the two boys raised in the sand beneath the date palms. At dinner he had been one of twelve, the men of his family, the uncles, cousins, grand-sons, sitting on his heels before a tagine of lemon chicken, rice and roasted vegetables. At school he had been one of thirty-eight in a ramshackle classroom, trying to learn all he could to qualify for the senior class where he could be one of twenty-three and get more of the professor's attention. In all his short life he had never, ever experienced that state which could be described as alone. Elizabeth stumbled as she snarled upwards at Noah's ark. The flagstones were uneven; pools of damp formed in the hollows. Chérif took her arm, chivalric and serious.

'Now you are one of two,' he said. And he escorted her all the way round the cloister. This was Chérif's first conscious act of friendship towards her, and Elizabeth did not understand his deeper meaning. What she did know was that she was not as stable on her pins as she had once been and that this young man had clearly been properly brought up; he offered an old lady his arm in a gesture of supportive respect. He was well on the way to being a gentleman.

They had missed the green man. He clutched at the roof like a succubus on the far side of the cloister. Elizabeth consulted the plan on the wall and they set off again in twilight, certain that they would no longer be able to pick him out in the shadowy vaults. But suddenly there he was above them, his fixed mad eyes staring down through the golden mask of leaves, which spread like tentacles across his face. They stood beneath him, heads thrown back, meeting his returning gaze.

'Who is he?' asked Chérif.

'Lots of theories. Nobody really knows,' said Elizabeth.

Chérif was way ahead of his year in mathematics and way behind in chemistry. His tutor arranged extra lab sessions with one of the research students to cover the lost ground, but this involved getting up in the dark and being there, ready to perform and take notes by eight o'clock in the morning. Elizabeth set the central heating for five-thirty so that he would come downstairs to a warm house. She offered to reduce the excessive floral arrangements in his room, but he refused to have anything changed. She cleared a bookshelf for him. His small stock of textbooks began to reproduce itself along the shelves. Together they transformed her mother's tripod of vanity mirrors and glass surfaces into a working desk. She never used the downstairs shower and he cleaned it himself. He never entered her bathroom. Not a word was ever said. They silently divided the house between them. She made a rule to herself that she would never go into his room if he wasn't there. But sometimes she crept in to close the window or turn up the radiator. During these fleeting raids into alien masculine terrain she absorbed odd details, which became strange treasures, endearing mysteries about the boy who had come out of the night to live with her.

He had a tiny cache of books in Arabic. Their subjects remained indecipherable. She lacked the code. She wondered if any one of these was the Qur'an, and if so, was he a fervent believer? He had not mentioned his religion once, not even in passing. She rang the university chaplaincy in a spirit of supportive enquiry. Was there a mosque in town? No, but the small Muslim community met for prayers every Friday at the old Quaker meeting house. She took down all the details to give to him, intending to do it at once, but then could never find a convenient opportunity.

She never made his bed, but laid out the clean pile of sheets and towels upon the now hugely unsuitable embroidered flounce that had once been her mother's living-room curtains. At the end of the third week she noticed a small ring-bound notebook stuck under the pillow. A pencil, marking the page, rolled out. She picked it up from the carpet and then bent down to put it back. Tucked inside the page next to a closely written block of Arabic, was a photograph.

She did hesitate. She remembered hesitating before taking up the photograph and studying the image for many minutes. But had she been interrogated on her motives, her replies would have been jumbled and confused. Who does he care about? Whose image does he keep close in the night? To whom has he given his heart? She had expected the image of Saïda or of a young woman. But it looked like a blurred family shot; a favourite memory of a happy day when someone loved came home. Two smiling young men with their arms around each other were standing beneath a date palm in an otherwise empty desert. The sun was just behind the person with the camera, so that her outline was inscribed upon the sand before her. This was a woman's dress; that was her *foulard*, the long scarf covering her hair which all the desert women wore, a little un-tucked, blowing sideways. Her hair escaped in a dark stringy cloud, as if it had been worked into tight plaits or rats' tails. She was young. Here was the sharper waist and the wide, long skirts of a young woman. Elizabeth drew the photograph closer to her glasses and examined the boys. One was a smiling, sunny Chérif, happier than the one who had left for college that morning in the lifting dark. The other was shorter, slightly heavier in build, with a much darker skin. Chérif, dressed in Western clothes, could almost pass for white; only an intense and perceptive inspection revealed his origins. This other boy was a black man, a desert dweller, someone from the south wearing shepherd's robes. He had a different beauty, the beauty that always accompanies someone who is fearless and walks lightly across the earth. Both of them flung vivid joyous smiles back to the camera and the strange young woman whose bare elbow and fine strong arm cut a stinging silhouette across the sand.

There were three young people in the photograph. Elizabeth studied the shadow figure traced upon the earth. Who was she? The blown outline, troubled by the wind, did not suggest Saïda, who never wore the *foulard*. Was this the girl left waiting in the desert for Chérif's return? He had never once asked to use the telephone. He had an e-mail account in college, but he never mentioned news from home. No letters came for him, and no one ever rang her number. He did not have a mobile phone, or at least she had never seen one. She pondered the background of the photograph. There was the endlessness she remembered reduced to four by four. An odd right-angled shadow loomed behind the woman's left shoulder and disappeared across the edge of the picture. That might be a car, or a building. She could gather no further information. And so she hastily replaced the photograph and scuttled out of the room, feeling guilty and ashamed. If she had caught him in her bedroom she would have turned him out of the house. She had no business being there. She had no right to look.

The TV men came down the lane at eight-thirty on Saturday morning and blocked the track with their van. Chérif was still asleep. They walked round to the back of the house and proposed to climb out of his window on to the flat roof and then up the back brick wall to the aerial.

'Are you sure you didn't want Sky? It says so here on the order form and we've got the box and the dish.'

'No. I just wanted the DVD to work and not to interfere with my reception. But my lodger has fixed the DVD, that works perfectly now, but we still have some interference on Channel 4 and sometimes the picture shudders on BBC 2. He says it must be the aerial.'

'OK. We'll check the system. But we still need to get out of that window.'

'Chérif!'

He stumbled forth in hasty jeans, jersey and bare feet. The TV men gaped at him, astonished. Sleep made his face more open and more vulnerable. His curls had got longer. He looked like one of Byron's boys, a Greek beauty, simple and as fragile as a girl, yet remote and withdrawn, like a difficult and much-importuned god, who always withheld his blessings. The TV men apologised for the disturbance with more fervour than was necessary, not to Elizabeth, but to Chérif. He clearly had no idea who they were, but accepted their oblique homage as a matter of course. They handed him the list of Sky deals on offer. He turned it over on the kitchen table while Elizabeth filled up the kettle.

'Sky TV!' His excitement warmed the room. The summary of news packages lay beneath his fingertips.

'Which package have you ordered? Oh, Madame Webster, if you got this one we could see the news on Al-Jazeera and Al-Arabia and Sky and CNN!'

And in that instant, her hand on the taps, the filling kettle slippery in her grasp, facing her October garden washed in pale sunshine and drifting leaves, Elizabeth Webster decided on the £47.00 package, which gave her world news from every known station and thirty-eight channels of digital nonsense, reality TV and interactive shopping. She marched out the back door and yelled at the ascending engineers who had not yet reached the aerial.

'Get the dish! We're going for Sky!'

Several distant neighbours who were sweeping leaves, or preparing for the shops, heard the shout. Miss Elizabeth Webster, whose acid opinions and savage tongue had plagued village committees for years, and whose near-demise had unleashed creeping evil thoughts, some as nakedly unkind as, 'the old cow deserves all she gets', was heard shouting down the back gardens – saying yes to afternoon game shows and UK Gold, yes to *Paradise Island*, *Antique Auction Bargain Slot* and *Most Haunted*. That voice that had always been raised in contempt and dissent was at last proclaiming herself one of us. That spell in hospital changed her for the better. She's much more human now.

This was certainly one section of opinion expressed at the bus stop and in the shop. But another school of thought, those involved in the church and the campaign to have the telephone mast sited elsewhere, had absorbed the fact of Chérif's presence and did not like what they saw. That young Arab boy from the college who is living with Miss Webster – have you seen him? Oh yes, he takes the early bus every morning. The Sky dish looked ordinary. But there was the uneasy combination of young Arab man – an unknown foreigner who spoke several languages – and a recently installed, highly sophisticated communications network, which troubled the torpid consciousness of an English village. Little Blessington was too far away from the city to be a safe harbour for strange faces. The self-contained huddle of old houses, with only one new row behind the pub, remained a village that was untroubled by students, overflowing dustbins, abandoned cars, burglary or petty crime. The pond gleamed with water lilies, not floating plastic bags, everyone recycled their bottles and knew the names of each other's children and pets. Whatever announced itself as new and different was noticed and picked over. The new Sky dish was carefully observed and discussed in detail. Someone had heard that Miss Webster's lodger arrived on her doorstep in the middle of the night and that she took him in, never having seen him before and having no real idea who he was. What can she have been thinking of? She never used to be so imprudent. It will all end in tears, you mark my words.

No good can come of this.

4

UNSUITABLE MUSIC

The vicar came to see them on a Thursday night just before Guy Fawkes. By this time Chérif had been resident in Miss Webster's house for well over a month. The vicar was not exactly spying, but on something of a fishing trip. Everybody wanted to know what was really going on in the cottage at the bottom of the lane. Miss Webster's attendance at communion seemed no more irregular than usual, but her stony-faced concentration had mutated into something reflective and peaceable – entirely uncharacteristic of the old girl. She gazed thoughtfully at her surroundings more often than she used to do. She forgot her collection envelopes, then slapped a ten-pound note and some loose coppers on to the dish when it approached her pew. No one ever put cash in the collection bowl, and so the congregation present pretended not to notice. The spare change rattled with a vulgar clink. *Let your light so shine before men that they may see your good works.* 'Stuff and nonsense,' muttered Miss Webster, audibly objecting to the collection of church funds being represented as a charitable act that demonstrated Christian virtue and benefited others. Her neighbours heard her, but they were used to muffled, enraged muttering and occasional sudden departures. She sat there oblivious, scratching her spiky white hair, as if she had developed lice. Dear me, she looks like an escaped lunatic. After this minor incident the vicar's wife gave him a prod.

'High time you plucked up courage and visited Miss Webster. I hear she's stopped being abusive and that she's got one of the students as a lodger. Good thing too, considering how ill she's been.'

And so the vicar was disposed to think well of Chérif. If the old lady keeled over again she wouldn't lie dead, undiscovered and decomposing, for days on end. Someone would raise the alarm. We are, after all, each other's keepers. Chérif opened the door, but Miss Webster was right behind him, peering beadily at the visitor.

'Oh, hello Vicar, it's you. Well that's all right. Come in and have some *thé à la menthe*. We're perfecting the mix.'

Two things upset the vicar: Chérif's arresting beauty and the fact that Miss Webster said 'we'. Beauty always appears sinister to the paranoid, because it blinds you to other things. And as for the cosy plural – the gorgeous lodger was clearly more deeply embedded in the household than he should have been. Keep it short, friendly, professional. He crouched a little as he entered her small sitting room. Miss Webster had elderly bits of farming equipment hanging from her ancient oak beams which gave the room a rustic look and were designed to put paid to anyone over five foot ten. The vicar glared at the green man who stared grimly back from the fireplace. There was a new hand-woven carpet of intricate and cunning workmanship covering the original dull green. The tapestry glowed red, ochre and white. Filled with alarm, the vicar backed off. The thing glowed with heat and deserts, but appeared too beautiful to be trodden on, like the victorious treasures over which Agamemnon himself had hesitated.

'It's Ramadan,' announced Miss Webster, 'so Chérif can't eat anything until sundown. Thank God it gets dark after four. Otherwise I'm not sure I'd last. We're having our *petit déjeuner* now. Dates, milk, fruit, tea, croissant, cakes and sugar with everything. And we eat dinner much later on. You're very welcome to join us.'

'Ah, Ramadan. I take it you're a Muslim.' The vicar addressed Chérif and managed a fake grin of idiotic broad-mindedness. 'Well, Miss Webster, you must have got into all this while you were in Africa.'

'Oh yes. I've quite given up pork. Chérif doesn't eat it.'

The spiky haircut was far more alarming than the sudden conversion to Mohammedism.

'Do sit down, Vicar,' said the old lady pleasantly, 'and you can walk on the carpet. It won't attack you. Chérif! Tea!'

The vicar eyed the young man with well-disguised caution. The boy wolfed down a glass of milk and set into the cakes, every one of which came from Maison Blanc, creamy, delicate and expensive.

'And I gather that you're here to study?'

Foreign students. Like all the 9/11 bombers. That's where they learned about radical Islam. Not in their own bloody countries, but while they were pretending to be engineers in Hamburg. The vicar caught himself thinking the worst. Chérif explained his degree course. Maths. Chemistry. Well, at least he wasn't doing the MA in Weapons of Mass Destruction. The vicar mistrusted the university's biology programmes after discovering that Saddam Hussein's top scientist, informally known as Dr Death, had done her research work at that very institution down the road. He looked at the boy over the top of his bifocals. Handsome devil, English excellent, accent slight.

'You must miss your family.'

They all had huge families. So there were always spare candidates for martyrdom.

'I keep in touch by e-mail. We write regularly. Phoning is expensive.'

'You're welcome to ring Saïda from here, my dear. You know that. His mother has my number, just in case. I stayed in her hotel back in September. Well, you know that if you were ill, I'd ring the hotel straight away.'

'I know, thank you.' The boy seemed anxious to please. He anticipated Miss Webster's empty glass, observed her gestures, nodded, deferential, whenever she delivered her judgements. This, at least, was one of their good points, respect for their elders. But that hadn't stopped the Taliban, most of whom were hardly more than children, insisting that everyone grow beards and that women, even their mothers and grandmothers, should be banished from the schools and streets. The vicar looked at Chérif's dark curls with increasing mistrust. He had never suspected Islam of being an attractive religion and found it inconceivable that anyone would choose to be a Muslim without having a scimitar pressed against their throat. The boy's beauty glowed like a talisman, a warning. The vicar sank steadily downwards into the green sofa. He felt less and less secure. The strange, decorated glass of sweet tea was burning his fingertips. The liquid tasted like a honeyed drug. Miss Webster was now telling him about the cannon they fired off from the barracks every evening during Ramadan to announce the ending of the fast.

'. . . so everyone stops together. Very practical. It's harder for Chérif here in England. The other students keep offering him chocolate biscuits. It's better if he comes home earlier. I have the whole thing ready so that we can pounce like vultures on the cakes.'

'And are you following Ramadan too this year, Miss Webster?' Green leaves of mint floated in the bottom of his exotic tea.

'I am indeed. It makes the cooking so much easier.'

'I see.'

The vicar put down his glass.

A week later an incident occurred at the village shop. Miss Webster's cottage was right at the end of the lane, the last little brick and flint house, facing the meadows, before the woods closed in and the village gave way to tangled deciduous green. The trail continued onwards, narrowed and smothered by bushes, until it finally ended in a derelict muddy farmyard, which, contrary to all appearances, was still inhabited. A few antique, scratching chickens clustered in the mud. But the farm people used the road leading to Bolt, the next village beyond the ruined abbey, which was actually nearer, thus no one except Sunday walkers ever passed the cottage. The way back to Little Blessington led through slush and puddles. There had been a co-ordinated move on the part of the inhabitants of the other three cottages to asphalt the lane, which was under shared ownership. All four properties had to agree, under the terms of the leasehold, and share the costs. But Miss Webster refused. Her objection, which she never explained, was incomprehensible to her immediate neighbours. She lived nearest the woodland. She had more of the uneven track to negotiate than any of the other residents. The expenses would be shared between the four cottages;

therefore she stood to benefit from the improvements more than anyone else, and at no extra cost. Still, she refused to countenance the scheme, without ever giving her reasons, and nothing could be undertaken without her consent. Chérif had to run the gauntlet of her antagonists' front windows on the way to the shop.

No one actually wished Miss Webster dead, but there were a certain number of rueful shrugs from the pro-asphalt lobby, which accompanied their congratulations at her escape from the hospital. They were not as well disposed towards Chérif as the vicar had been. Opinions varied. Who was this pretty Arab who made his theatrical late-night appearance so rapidly upon her return? Was he taking advantage of her hospitality and her solitary, vulnerable situation? Miss Webster had been very ill, indeed out of her mind, and was almost certainly not quite recovered. Nothing else explained the Arab. He appeared to have installed himself on a permanent basis. The less tolerant among the neighbours wanted to know: where did he stand on the question of asphalt and did he have any influence with the old hag?

Now, Miss Webster could never be described as generous, not even by the most fervent well-wishers, and she was usually as vulnerable as a reinforced iron cauldron. People who make it clear that they have chosen to live alone and are not the victims of tragedy – unforeseen accidents, fiancés killed in wars, inheritance disputes and duplicitous offspring – are always suspect. They might be perverts or spies. They are certain to manifest signs of being eccentric, odd or mad. Miss Webster chose solitude and other people were afraid of her. The pro-asphalt neighbours interpreted her cropped hair and diminished figure through a mist of malevolent clichés. But they did not dare to prey upon the old woman directly. And so there was no conspiracy.

Nothing was actually said. Any comments they exchanged aloud were pitched in terms of incomprehension and regret. But the cottages arrived at a tacit consensus. They would take it out on the boy. None of them spoke to him. He was ignored at the bus stop, and gently avoided whenever he passed. Then came the incident at the shop.

Chérif had been sent out by Miss Webster to purchase kidney beans, butter, self-raising flour and an uncut loaf of brown bread. The village shop stood four-square, facing the bus stop and the school gates, a substantial affair with two aisles that did steady business all year round, because they were so far from the city. Mrs Harris, a fervent member of the pro-asphalt lobby, could see right to the end of both passages from her lookout post behind the till, where she defended the alcohol, newspapers and cigarettes. A system of traps and hidden alarms were placed in key locations, and the shop had stopped selling fireworks after an incendiary incident with a firecracker.

Chérif wandered round the shelves gathering up his prospective purchases. He knew he was being watched, but proceeded, unhurried, apparently relaxed, towards the cash desk. Shopkeepers were always wary, suspicious, vigilant. He got out the purse. Mrs Harris stared at him and then at the purse, a black-and-white tweed square with a dog-tooth pattern and a tarnished snap clasp.

'Wait there.'

She retreated into the cubbyhole where she kept her mugs and kettle and seized the telephone. Chérif stood nonplussed amidst the newspapers, then began reading the football results. He could hear the woman talking but not what she said.

'Miss Webster? Your lodger's in the shop. And he's paying for his shopping with money from your purse.'

'What?'

'He's using your money. He's got your purse.'

Miss Webster pulverised her telephone in a sudden onset of enlightenment and roared out of her front door. She rampaged down the muddy lane, hatless, in her cardigan and slippers, slicing through the puddles like an armed destroyer, her stockings muddied, all her guns trained on the shop door. She took the corner by the gas canisters at speed and burst forth between the aisles, sending the postcard rack spinning.

'Out of my way, Chérif!'

The boy recoiled, amazed, into the Coke cans and wine bottles.

'Now listen to me, you racist cow, if that child has my purse it's because I gave it to him. I sent him out to do the shopping. Are you refusing to serve my lodger? Do I have to call the police? What's gone through your head, eh? Do you think I don't know what goes on in my own home?'

'Miss Webster, don't take on so,' Mrs Harris decided to overlook the verbal insults, as she had heard from Dr Brody's wife that Miss Webster was capable of far worse. 'I only thought −'

'You didn't think. None of you knows how to do it. Now take this boy's money and let me get out of your infernal dustbin of a shop.'

She snatched the purse, hammered a ten-pound note on to the counter, grabbed the self-raising flour from Chérif, thrust the purse back into his confused grasp, executed a rapid pirouette, resuming her former flight path, and pounded out of the door, leaving Chérif staring bewildered at the white-faced Mrs Harris. The shopkeeper was, however, used to crises.

'I was only trying to help. Here's your change. You

know, with that temper Miss Webster'll have a stroke one of these days. You can't tell her anything.'

'A stroke?' Chérif queried the one word that didn't match his interpretation of the sentence; to him a stroke was a caress.

The language problem for Chérif was more complex and ambiguous than ever became apparent in ordinary conversation. By disposition he was quiet, and concentrated hard on understanding the mysteries of dailiness. He tried to work out the world according to Miss Webster first, through observation and deduction, before pestering her with questions. It is untrue to say that traffic instructions are universal. Chérif puzzled his brains before the motorway garniture that he saw every day and which resisted obvious interpretation. Sometimes he emerged utterly stumped, despite his heroic effort at comprehension.

'Madame, qu'est-ce que c'est le Hard Shoulder'? "Hard", c'est dur et "shoulder" c'est épaule, non?'

Elizabeth Webster was trapped in the fast lane and not in the mood for lucid explanations.

'It means "accotements stabilisés". You can stop on the edge.'

'But it says No Stopping on the 'ard shoulder –'

'Chérif, just shut it, will you? I'll explain later.'

And so he learned not to interrogate her when she was driving, but because he held back he made some hilarious assumptions. The funniest of these, which kept her chuckling for days, was the meaning of the sign at GROVE FRUIT. They drove past the fruit farm whenever they went into the university. GROVE FRUIT was a large market garden, which, despite its name, actually concentrated on vegetables. They had decided to launch into strawberries earlier that year and put up a huge sign with a badly drawn spiky red blob perched at the end, which read PICK YOUR OWN STRAWBERRIES.

'Do they have great trouble with thieves?' asked Chérif.

'Eh?'

'Thieves stealing fruit.'

'I don't think so. Why?'

'Well, it says pick your own strawberries.'

'And leave mine alone? Chérif, you're a treasure. No, it means what's yours is mine. Come and pick my strawberries and when you've paid for your punnets they'll be yours.'

'Punnets?'

Chérif stared at the prickly red blob, which remained swathed in mystery.

After the debacle in the village shop they initiated a weekly joint sortie to Waitrose. Chérif loved doing the shopping. He wandered round the bright store, now already overflowing with Christmas goodies, giant boxes of crackers and crystallised fruit, and a large cardboard sledge trailing glittering, useless things. Elizabeth learned how to linger and gloat, instead of slamming fourteen bald necessities into her trolley and making for the checkout. He hovered, translating the labels. If her feet gave out she plonked herself behind the *Guardian* in the coffee bar. She never bawled at him for dawdling, for she was tasting the pleasures of the slow lane. He brought his discoveries to her, delighted.

'Look! I know where these dates come from. I know this town. I might even know the people who cut them down from the top of the *palmiers*.'

'Date palms. Don't mix languages. Do you want to buy those?'

He wrinkled his nose in horror.

'At that price? It's a robbery.'

Elizabeth Webster laughed. She often laughed now at Chérif's puzzles and observations. The lines on her face had begun to change; they were deeper and more beautiful.

'My mother grew up in South America. She felt like that about avocado pears. But why quarrel with the import costs? If we don't pay, we can't eat them. That's the way it goes.'

They clattered out to the car park and the chilly fog, beneath the feeble orange lights. Elizabeth sat for a long time behind the wheel, cleaning her glasses. The country lanes before her were pitch-black, as were the streets of Little Blessington, for the parish council had unanimously voted against streetlights.

'Can you drive?'

'Mais bien sûr.'

'I'm going to put you on my insurance. Do you have your licence?'

But it turned out that Chérif's licence, a battered pink piece of cardboard in French and Arabic, had been purchased. As was the custom. He had never actually passed a test. Not as such. This emerged when they filled in the AA forms.

'Date of test? You're only twenty-one. You must remember.'

He clearly remembered handing over the money. It had taken months to amass that much. But he had been driving large lorries since he was fifteen; he had driven his uncle's delivery truck. He had borrowed Saïda's Citroën to take his grandmother to hospital. He even owned a battered motorbike. And once he had tried out Abdou's taxi, but just the once.

'I think you'd better take a few lessons. I'll ring BSM.'

The driving lessons went off swimmingly and Joan, the frosty local instructor, sauntered round the village declaring that she was completely in love with Miss Webster's young man, and if she wasn't forty-six and old enough to be his mother, well, she would be pursuing him down that muddy lane herself. This counted against Chérif with the asphalters who now described him as 'the snake charmer'. The big shock came with the AA insurance quotation. There were too many alarming discrepancies. Number of years' experience. Seven. Number of years with valid licence. One. Age of driver. Disturbingly young. Place of birth. Foreign. Sex. Male. Miss Webster's insurance increased a thousand-fold to the spectacular and unbelievable total of seventeen hundred pounds. She rang the AA in a fury. A rush of placatory excuses were offered in exchange.

'It would make a big difference if he was a near relative.'

'What do you expect me to do? Adopt him?'

They sat in the kitchen and listened to the news. The weapons inspectors were playing at cat and mouse with the Iraqi authorities. Chérif reflected carefully on the consequences. He expected her to have an answer for everything.

'Do you think they really do have weapons of mass destruction?'

'Of course. Everybody does. So what does that signify? We've got weapons of mass destruction. Every known form of weapon. Biological, chemical and nuclear. They're stacked up in Berkshire.'

Chérif stared at her, amazed. How on earth had she accessed all the secret files and located the laboratories?

Could this be common knowledge in England? Why weren't the authorities terrified of terrorists looking up the address in Berkshire, strolling past, and leaving with phials and fluids that could kill millions once they touched the air?

'What will happen?' he asked. The radio news was terrifying; the world steadied itself for war.

'I'll pay the seventeen hundred pounds of course,' snapped Miss Webster. 'I want you to be able to drive the car.'

It took him a moment to understand that she was no longer concentrating upon the political situation in Iraq. 'But it's a lot of money.' No one in his village ever bothered with any kind of insurance.

'I've got pots of money. I've saved all my life. And for bloody what?'

'The rainy day,' smiled Chérif, who had recently absorbed this phrase in college and came from a country where it so rarely rained your money would always be safe from wastrels. Miss Webster was adamant.

'Well, now it's raining.'

Nobody thought he had actually stolen the car, but they watched the curly-headed Arab heading off for college in the Clio with suspicion and mistrust. And within the secure precincts of the shop, the recycling point and the gardening club polytunnel, they prophesied an appalling and inevitable doom, certainly for the Clio – such a pity, low mileage, almost new – and possibly for Miss Webster whose imprudence knew no bounds.

Miss Webster and Chérif decided to build a bonfire for Saturday night. The derelict farmer hacked down two trees, which had been hanging over Miss Webster's garage and polluting the gutters with a soggy black mass of dead foliage. The trunk was chopped up and carted off for firewood, but there remained a spiky pile of dead branches blocking the lane. Miss Webster therefore decreed that Guy Fawkes would be celebrated for the first and only time at her house. This necessitated a long historical explanation of gunpowder, treason and plot. Chérif listened, fascinated. Miss Webster clearly thought all forms of government should be blown sky-high. She attributed this to being independent-minded and living in the country where governments only ever interfered with you by raising petrol taxes, planning a new bypass through the local nature reserve and banning hunting with dogs.

'There was an assassination attempt on the King's life in the 1970s,' said Chérif, 'but I wasn't born then and I don't think there's been one since. People in my village love our king.' He didn't sound convinced.

'And you don't?'

'I don't know.' Chérif looked blank. 'My cousin says our government is corrupt. But all governments are corrupt, aren't they?'

'Absolutely. It's a necessary evil.' Miss Webster was contemplating fireworks, had lost interest in politics and was looking up the weather forecast. 'Fine and clear. Light frost towards dawn. New moon. Can you handle explosives?'

'Bombs?' Chérif flushed. He had endured enough silly jokes in college about the use to which he intended putting his knowledge of chemistry and had acquired the not entirely kind nickname of Chemical Ali. He now reacted to all suspect insinuations, however innocent. Miss Webster noticed nothing.

'Fireworks. We have to have fireworks.' She suddenly looked up, saw his embarrassment and made the connection: gunpowder, Arabs. 'On second thoughts I'd better buy them. I don't think there's a shop in town that would sell you anything you could use as a fuse.'

And so after lunch on Saturday Chérif was discovered building a towering inferno of dead branches, rotting cardboard boxes and a broken old cupboard found abandoned in the shed. Browned grass and pale grey ash marked the regular spot for a bonfire, well clear of the fence and trees at the bottom of the garden. Miss Webster decided to go for bust and made a substantial Guy out of discarded nylons and the remains of her sister's old clothes, which had been abandoned in her mother's house and never claimed. It gave her no small satisfaction to send that pert bitch up in smoke. She sat the lumpy horror of indeterminate sex down at the kitchen table. The bald nylon head lolled forwards and the thing gave a sinister shudder. Miss Webster topped it off with a woollen bobble hat she no longer wore on winter sorties in the garden. As she contemplated the elongated blank head something came over her. The creature must have a face. She dug an old thick felt-tip out from the kitchen drawer, which dated from the epoch of grammatical points on flip charts, and ran it under the hot tap. Then she attacked the orange nylon lump. A moment's brisk scratching and a face, grinning and evil, leered back at her. The felt-tip leaked black ink over her fingers, as if the malice in her intentions overflowed. She flung it into the dustbin and gazed with satisfaction at the wicked angel seated at her table. It did look uncannily like her sister, wearing the old tomato cardigan and sagging, fingerless green gloves. She wanted to gloat over her monstrous creation.

'Chérif! Come and see what I've made. Chérif!'

He was absorbed in piling the remains of the rotted gate, now replaced, around the base of the bonfire as if the interior needed extra defences to build it up. He must have heard her, but for an instant he did not react. Then he turned; a baffled frown flickered across his remote, peculiar beauty. There were many ways of reading this hesitation, but Miss Webster was too astute not to be aware of its significance. She knew what it meant; in her heart she had always known.

'Chérif!'

The reaction was too late, too strange, too staged. *He did not know his own name.* Miss Webster drew herself up and prepared for battle.

But she had no time to say anything barbed or ambiguous because the doorbell, artificially amplified so that she could hear it in the garden, howled through the house. Who comes past on a Saturday afternoon without ringing beforehand? She flung open the door. And there before her on the porch step stood a young woman wearing a brown leather flying jacket and white scarf, Biggles in a miniskirt, with thigh-high beige suede boots. She had a cheerful mouse-brown bob of hair, no handbag, and was swinging her car keys.

'Hi! Is Chérif in?'

'And who are you?' snapped Miss Webster.

'I'm Karen. I've come to cut Chérif's hair.'

Elizabeth Webster was mystified rather than annoyed by this fresh apparition. Of course he was chased by pretty girls. Probably by pretty boys too. Just as well the girl has got here first. This smiling figure on her doorstep embodied yet another sign that Chérif had a life separate from her own, a life of which she knew nothing.

'Do you have another name?'

'Sorry?'

'A last name?'

'Oh! Yes. Wallis. But we always use first names at work.'

'And you're a student too, I suppose?'

'Oh God no. I'm an estate agent.'

'You'd better come in.'

Karen gave a little scream of shock and joy when she saw the Guy lolling at the table. 'Oh, he's brilliant! Huge. And really scary. Did Chérif make him up for you?'

'No,' said Miss Webster, irrationally gratified by her success at creating a Frankenstein, 'I made him myself. Chérif's building the bonfire.'

'Are you having a party? Can I come?'

The demand was so innocent and excited that it never occurred to Elizabeth Webster to say no. She had guarded the gates of her home for years, with a ferocity that would have been a credit to Cerberus; now her house had become a refuge for strangers. She flung open her back door and welcomed the damp rush of cold.

'Chérif! Your hairdresser's arrived.'

Karen established her beauty salon in Miss Webster's kitchen, borrowed the meat scissors, and snipped away at Chérif's wet curls, while he sat at the other end of the table from the hideous Guy, making faces at the monster. He had a large clean towel folded over his shoulders with his curls hanging wet and limp about his ears. He looked shrunken and vulnerable. Karen clearly wasn't very good with curls. She sipped her coffee and, reflecting on the damp heap of clean hair, appealed to Miss Webster.

'What do you think? How short should I cut them at the top?'

'Why not dry them out a bit, pull a chunk out straight,

and cut off the same amount all round. Maybe an inch. Or two? They've got very long. Then let them go. They'll bounce back like mattress springs.'

'That's how Ma does it at home,' said Chérif helpfully. Miss Webster was touched by his childishness.

'You've never called Saïda "Ma" before. Or at least not in my hearing,' she observed.

'She doesn't like it.' Chérif blushed a little and fell silent. Karen duffed up his curls with a vigorous rub. Miss Webster set a cup of coffee down in front of the Guy.

'Go on. Drink up, you old cow. Any last requests? By eight o'clock tonight you'll be toast.'

'Oh, it's a woman, not a man,' exclaimed Karen.

'It's my sister. She's being incinerated in absentia,' declared Miss Webster, cool as a contract assassin. 'And she's going to the stake wearing all her own clothes.'

Chérif and Karen were mightily impressed by the subtlety of this revenge. Neither dared to ask what crime the sister had committed. If Miss Webster condemned her to death then she deserved it. Later, outside in the garden, Karen expressed her candid admiration for the eccentric old woman with the interesting vicious streak not usually associated with sober cardigans and clean kitchens.

'She's wicked, your landlady.'

'She used to work as a private detective. Like Miss Marple in Agatha Christie movies,' explained Chérif, 'and she may still be armed.' Karen stared at him and then at Miss Webster's frail, smoky figure washing up the lunch dishes behind the murky glass of the kitchen windows. They saw her carved into vertical lines by streams of condensation. She appeared illusive, hallucinatory, provisional.

'No kidding? You sure?'

Chérif nodded. Miss Webster dissolved in steam.

And so a new phase in the evolution of events began that night as they stood upon the damp lawns with the dead leaves sodden underfoot, clutching mugs of mulled wine and dodging the shower of rushing sparks. Miss Webster's sister caught nicely and was gone in seconds to their united roar of comic approval.

'You don't have to worry about her again,' shouted Karen with delighted sadism, as if they had just executed a heretic. Chérif too was impressed by Miss Webster's ruthlessness and decided that in the course of her undercover work she had probably killed many men. For Miss Webster had begun to encroach upon his imagination. It was as if she had become more than one person. The instability in her identity troubled him, like a subtle shimmer on the edge of his vision, because he was not used to observing women closely. The veil should be drawn across the eyes of men. He looked down, away, as he had been taught to do. He never stared directly at the women in his family or in the streets. But he belonged to the sex that was celebrated and cherished, not the servant sex. His self-confidence was somewhat shaken by these women who did not wait for him to speak first and had their own opinions, wore better and more expensive clothes than he did, drove their own cars and earned more money in one month than he had in a lifetime. Suddenly the world seemed less simple than it had done. And naturally enough, Karen had made the first move.

'Nice girl. How did you meet her?' The old lady began her interrogation as soon as they had waved Karen off down the dark lane and Chérif was forced to acknowledge that he had been wooed and courted and won. He had never so much as lifted a finger in the process.

'When I wasn't sure I could stay here I went to the estate agent that had "rooms to let" in the window. Karen works there. Then she fixed up her mobile phone for me. It works on a card. I paid for the card. So that she could let me know if anything suitable came up.'

'And so that she had a number she could ring.' Miss Webster grinned. Chérif was unable to follow the sexual plot.

'Yes. To tell me if she had heard of rooms.'

'No, you goose. So that she could speak to you.'

Chérif had not even seen the trap.

'And I bet that she somehow always forgot to take back the phone?' Miss Webster's recent liberation from her sister's malevolence had improved her mood. She crowed with victory. 'Voilà! You don't even need to tell me the rest. She told you she had a room for you to see and when you decided you'd stay here she asked you out.'

Chérif gazed at his unpredictable landlady, helpless before her investigative acumen.

'Well, she's a very sweet girl. And exceedingly pretty. You can invite her round any time.'

The next invitation came from Karen herself, and was addressed to both of them. Miss Webster had her doubts. She had never been to a rock concert before and wasn't sure that she could support the necessary level of decibels. Surely the young people would rather go on their own? Karen was obviously put out on the other end of the line.

'But it's a sit-down, not a rave. And they're a really good band.'

Miss Webster had never heard of The Usual Suspects, and said so. Karen was incredulous.

'Not heard of them! You're not serious. They're always on telly and on MTV. Anyway it's a benefit for the Carmen Campbell Defence Fund. So it's a really good cause.'

Miss Webster had never heard of Carmen Campbell.

'But you must have done! She's really famous. And it was all over the papers. Less than a year ago.'

Miss Webster had been in hospital, semi-conscious and sinking without trace into a pond of terrible despair when Carmen Campbell's desperate fate had hit the headlines.

'She's a great singer. Really amazing. I have all her CDs. She's as good as Joan Armatrading, Diana Ross, Billie Holiday, Bessie Smith . . .' Karen tried digging up every black jazz and blues singer she had ever heard or read about in an attempt to reach into the empty crevasse of Miss Webster's knowledge concerning popular music. Miss Webster had heard of Bessie Smith. '. . . And anyway, she disappeared early last year. She had this lover who tried to kill her. He was working for the Special Services. You know, like MI6. So it may all have been a plot. He followed her to Spain where she was singing at a concert in Barcelona. Did you really never read about it? It was all over the front pages for weeks. And he tried to stab her in a bar. There were witnesses who saw it happen. He did stab her. A crime of passion! But she knew he meant it when he said he was going to kill her, so she was prepared. She pulled out a gun and shot him. It was self-defence!'

Karen chuckled, triumphant. Point proved. Carmen Campbell is innocent.

'Calm down, my dear. You're beginning to sound like a *News of the World* exclusive.'

A somewhat sulky silence uncoiled at the other end of the phone. Chérif came into the red and green sitting room and stoked up her stove. They were still burning the wood that he had cut for the bonfire. He mouthed questions at her in French. *Est-ce que c'est Karen au bout du fil?*

'Chérif's just come in. I'll pass him over.'

'Oh Miss Webster, please come.'

But Miss Webster remained non-committal.

And so it was with some surprise that Karen saw her, squired by Chérif, approaching the theatre on the following night. It was Saturday 30 November and Miss Webster had known Chérif for precisely two months. It was indeed the anniversary of his arrival upon her windy doorstep. Karen bounded towards them, brandishing the tickets.

'We've got great seats. I knew you'd come.'

Miss Webster seated herself like a chaperone on the edge of the row, so that she could stretch out her knees. She looked round at the gathering public and noticed that she wasn't the only person present who had advanced to the stage of white hair and a large home-knitted cardigan. She had not, however, set foot in the theatre for years. It still glowed crimson, an Edwardian gem which had acquired a new layer of red velour, fresh gilt and cheeky little lamp-shades topping out the house lights. Balconies and boxes perched like pigeon lofts all round the edges and the seating in the circle and the upper balcony stacked up straight, like a supermarket shelf, so that everyone was near the stage. There was a famous acoustic. The slightest whisper uttered near the backdrop could be heard in every stall of the ladies' lavatory. This made the middlebrow murder mysteries, popular all year round, in which the butler had always done it with the help of the lady of the house, exceedingly thrilling. Any form of amplification was entirely unneces-sary. Yet the stage was littered with huge black boxes, destined to magnify electric sound, and a fearsome array of speakers, one set five feet tall, trailing wires, and men in grimy white T-shirts sporting headphones. This conventional theatre presented itself as an utterly incongruous and unsuitable venue for loud bangs and unexpected explosions.

'Would you both like a drink in the interval?'

Miss Webster insisted on providing the drinks so that she could stroll up to the bar and inspect the premises. She didn't ask either of the young people what they wanted. The bar, usually a hushed mutter of middle-class conversation and the odd plume from an isolated cigarette, vibrated with pounding hard rock. Behind the elegant ebony counter, once decorated with free peanuts and olives, men with death's heads plastered across their chests sauntered to and fro, issuing Bacardi breezers to teenagers who were clearly too young to be drinking anything other than fizzy orange pop with straws. Miss Webster ordered a gin and tonic and two Cokes for the interval. This entailed a good deal of shouting on both sides. Turning down the volume was clearly out of the question. Part of the point of her withdrawal was to give the young people time alone to talk. Miss Webster did not misunderstand this situation, which was well within her experience. The canny observation of youthful courtship at a distance emerged as one of her fields of expertise. Chérif was being reeled gently in; the hook wasn't yet locked in his gullet, nor had he swallowed the worm. Karen had not yet officially declared herself on the hunt; this evening established the continuation of her investigative prowl. Miss Webster liked girls who took their time.

Either party could draw back at any point. Therefore Miss Webster's role as safety device on the erotic pressure cooker proved essential – manifestly so – or she would not have been invited with such lunatic insistence. The old woman perched on a window ledge halfway down the staircase and added up what she knew about Chérif.

Not much, in fact.

He comes from a tiny sandy village on the brink of the Sahara. He has no father now and may never have known his father. His mother has a good job managing a hotel in a town four hours' drive away from that village. She has a job no other woman has. He is clever and silent. He eats enough for six. His cousin is called Moha and he treasures a photograph, which he keeps under his pillow, of said desert, another young man, who may or may not be Moha, and a woman's shadow. He is extremely gifted with electronics. He has set up my DVD and is responsible for my purchasing a sinister black parabolic dish and, on a monthly basis, thirty-eight channels of hot and cold flowing burble from the TV. He is obsessed by news. We watch at least two bloody hours of news every night. He is not particularly interested in films, but will watch one with me if it doesn't interfere with the news. He has mended the car's rear door, which was sticking fast, and changed the oil. He loves doing the shopping and has dug the garden. Twice. He watches the birds. His English is better. He asks intelligent questions. He makes me laugh. He works very hard at his studies. He receives no letters or phone calls – or at least not at my house. He loves rain. He is good company because he never intrudes. He has the trick of vanishing.

But what did one ever know about young people anyway? They lead their own dark lives. And it would be a mistake to imagine that whatever thoughts roared through their brains were of more than passing significance. Except that, without much reflection, they are inclined to make that dreadful leap across the abyss from thought to act. The lurking act, which flicked incessantly into her mind, happened to be murder – mass murder, privatised murder, sexual murder, self-murder.

The French courts were still trying to make up their minds concerning a shocking case of a young boy who had murdered his playmate, a girl of thirteen. He had taken her into the garden to play, then proceeded to dress up as *The Scream*, complete with white horror mask and butcher's knife. He stabbed her fifty-two times, but could give no reason why. He must have had a reason, even if it could never be spoken. Another adolescent murdered his parents wearing the same costume, which you can buy in novelty shops in every high street, Europe-wide. They were becoming known as 'the Scream Killings'. Elizabeth Webster pondered the past. Had she wanted to kill her parents? Most certainly so. Of course she had. Everybody wants to do that. And had she not burnt her loathed sister in effigy, not a fortnight since? We are all perfectly capable of becoming *The Scream*.

The vicar thinks Chérif is a terrorist. She had seen it in his eyes. Here was a young Arab, aflame with the love of Allah, but keeping it well hidden, hell-bent on sending the Houses of Parliament and all that therein is, straight to eternity. Or perhaps a suicide plane, bristling with armed explosives, cutting through the lawns at Balmoral. Maybe it's the end for the university, which had once harboured Saddam Hussein's ravishing Lady of Death, the only wo-man in his government. Is Chérif following in her footsteps and genning up on poison gases? Are his tutors teaching him to tinker with weapons of mass destruction? We must take responsibility for this, she thought. We've trained them all. Even the Americans taught their own 9/11 bombers how to fly jet planes into buildings. You can do anything in America, pay up front and no questions asked.

What puzzled her most was the fact that terrorism was impersonal. You need not hate those that you kill. You need not even know who they are. I know that I shall meet my fate, somewhere among the clouds above. Those that I fight I do not hate, those that I guard I do not love. Terrorism is therefore exactly like an act of war, and just as self-indulgent, dissolute, corrupt. Elizabeth Webster did not believe in just wars. Murder should be personal and passionate, whether planned or spontaneous. An act so momentous and decisive as the ending of a life should be executed with verve, panache and a deliberate, responsible devotion to the consequences. You murder the one you know well, the one who is close enough to do you harm. You murder the one you love.

But what tipped normal people over the edge?

And why was she thinking about slaughter, personal or otherwise?

Ah! She was looking at a murderer. There before her, sinuous in a dress of blue scales, Carmen Campbell, the singer of whom she had never heard, greeted her from the poster on the stair. Miss Webster looked straight into the eyes of the haughty gorgeous face, beautiful as the Black Goddess. The singer clasped a microphone and countered her stare. The old woman, unimpressed by glamour, addressed the image. They say you killed your lover in self-defence, but can it ever be so simple when the one you kill is the one you loved? Surely there were many times you wished him dead? What made you do it then? The woman in the poster shrugged and turned away. But as she turned Miss Webster suddenly heard a strange jingling clink, the sound of coins or seashells rebounding off each other. Had the poster really moved? She fixed the image. Crimes of passion. Was it a crime to be passionate? CRIME OF PASSION KILLER GOES FREE. But I have heard of you. I know who you are, snapped Miss Webster and found herself, teetering on a bare concrete fire stair in a provincial theatre, talking out loud to a poster on the wall.

I must be going mad.

A bell rang somewhere in the building. Two minutes. As she scampered down the staircase to the stalls she caught sight of Chérif in the doorway, looking about anxiously, clutching his ticket. He suddenly smiled when he saw her.

'Oh, we got scared that you'd gone home.'

'Thought I'd done a runner, did you?'

'A runner?'

'Never mind, Chérif. Come on. Where's Karen? I've organised the drinks.'

The concert was horrendous. A support band, which appeared to consist entirely of girls who had been beaten up in the green room and staggered forth with black eyes, performed under the name of Big Bang. The lead singer read out an overlong ideological statement in support of Carmen Campbell which never actually mentioned what she was supposed to have done. Elizabeth shifted about in her seat, irritated by the fact that she kept encountering stories everybody else already knew. She was not used to feeling ignorant and out of date. The band thumped and droned their way through twenty-five minutes of bad taste cover versions and, worse still, their own compositions.

'They're local,' shouted Karen, in the lulls above the eponymous big bangs. 'I heard them in the Black Lion. Not very good.'

The audience rustled and clapped without conviction. Elizabeth Webster marvelled at the fact that a rock concert could be a sit-down affair. All the televised occasions she had glanced at in passing showed hordes gathered in parks enjoying a bout of hysteria, flinging themselves at the stage, their eyes crazed, their mouths twisted like *The Scream*. Chérif sat between them. She noticed that Karen was holding his right hand. Good, good. Progress. The girl wore a tacky gold identity bracelet with 'Karen' inscribed in italics. He'll soon be wearing that thing for the duration, however long it lasts.

The Big Bangs subsided and the technicians again invaded the stage.

'Should we go upstairs?'

'No, it's only a pause. There's a proper interval between the two sets.'

The women talked across Chérif.

'Do you like this sort of thing?' Elizabeth asked him directly. It turned out that Chérif had never been to a rock concert either, but that the entire evening had been his idea. Miss Webster looked at him, amazed; he too had clearly gone quite mad.

'I saw Carmen Campbell on the posters,' he said.

'But have you seen or heard this band before?'

'The Usual Suspects? Oh yes,' he said cheerfully, 'on MTV.'

'My dear child, you appear to have spent your entire life peering at a screen.'

'Sorry?'

'Never mind.'

Karen giggled.

And then all around them, the audience erupted. Five mangy men of uncertain age stormed the stage like gladiators, several wielding their guitars. They grabbed the microphones and blazed forth in a torrid blast of surging rhythm. Some members of the audience could remain in their seats no more and had to be contained by a row of bouncers, who appeared from nowhere. The Edwardian theatre changed colour and shape as air-raid lights of blue, red and white began to pick out pale, screaming faces in the crowd. A peculiar stream of mist trailed across the musicians' feet like the seventh plague of Egypt and tipped over into the orchestra. The atmosphere of the arena gripped them all. Elizabeth Webster looked on, curious and disconcerted; would these insalubrious entertainers be gobbled up by the hordes? Would she be able to sit through these terrible pounding howls? The words to the songs could not be heard at all. To her horror she realised that Karen was singing along to the peculiar enraged shriek. Once again she confronted a culture everyone else had effortlessly occupied and claimed as their own while she had passed by on the other side of the road.

'That's their big hit,' yelled Karen above the roar of eulogy. 'They'll have to play it again at the end as an encore.'

Miss Webster sat through four more numbers and then took an unscheduled break in the corridor, her hands sunk deep into her cardigan pockets. Even the carpet vibrated with the noise. It was disturbing, but not unpleasant. The band flung everything they had into their act. The drummer tore off his T-shirt and hammered his cymbals in a torrent of sweat, indeed the entire tribe shone and glistened, pouring forth an excessive flood of energy. The lead guitarist pranced and bellowed like a charismatic preacher whipping up a revivalist gathering to the proper level of communal passion, so that if anyone present had not already given their lives to Jesus, they would feel compelled to do so. Elizabeth Webster approved of people who worked hard at their jobs. The band were clearly working very hard indeed; she was therefore on their side.

The last song at the end of the first set was dedicated to Carmen Campbell. This was the song that had made her famous, written for her by The Great Richard Thompson – Miss Webster had never heard of Richard Thompson – written for her smoky voice, her sinister, suggestive presence, her sexual allure. This is 'The Way that it Shows'. A deep clamour of recognition surged out from the mass in the theatre and greeted Miss Webster as she regained her seat. The green searchlights picked her out, grappling with the handrails, and she felt inadvertently exposed.

'You must listen to this one! They do a great version.' Karen leaned across Chérif and urged her on – welcome to your secret initiation into the world of rock. Miss Webster made a serious effort to concentrate. The song began softly and for the first time she could hear the words.

> *You're going to give yourself away*
> *One of these nights . . .*
> *It's the little things betray . . .*
> *Must be the enemy within*
> *That's the way that it shows . . .*
> *A slip of the tongue . . .*
> *Your artful stammer, a little too rushed*
> *All passion to the eye, all cold to the touch . . .*
> *A crack in your defences . . .*
> *And that's enough . . .*
> *That's the way that it shows*
> *The way that it shows . . .*

Miss Elizabeth Webster suddenly looked at Chérif in horror. He had appeared on her doorstep in the middle of the night, become the super-serviceable young lodger, charming, vulnerable, quiet. He was here for a purpose. The concentrated single-mindedness of his endeavours confirmed the existence of that purpose as clearly as its nature and the reasons for his presence remained obscure. How could she have ignored what was obvious to every-body else? Chérif could not possibly be whoever he declared himself to be. He was hiding something. *A crack in your defences, and that's enough. That's the way it shows.* He was not called Chérif at all. She saw him again, standing frozen at the bottom of her garden, the bonfire before him and the rake in his hand. He had not known his own name.

But as the night went on she became less and less certain what she wished to do with this fresh information. Karen belted off home, well after midnight, still raving about the band. Nothing was untoward or even different from usual. By now they had a routine. They watched the late news on BBC 24 at one in the morning. Chérif sat tranquil among the cushions, his eyes fixed on tanks, Land Rovers and armoured cars, zooming across the desert.

Elizabeth Webster could not sleep. What did it matter who he was? He wasn't going to blow her up. And if he does disappear it will be just as he came, the parting without farewells, the vanishing in the dark. By 3 a.m. she was quite certain that she was being both racist and ridiculous. She knew his mother, for heaven's sake. She had met some of his family. Surely all that counted for something? But the 9/11 bombers all had families, often wealthy and respectable families, none of whom could believe that their sons had done this thing. They produced videos of cheerful young boys in Western clothes dancing with ordinary girls at discos and wept before the cameras. No one appeared wearing either beards or veils. No, no, not my boy, not my son. She watched them howling and beating their breasts and she saw that the grief was real. They were confronted with a lie, a lie that sank home and destroyed the past. You were my own flesh and blood and I did not know you. The lie that could no longer be justified, explained and undone was the bitterest thing, for their children were twice lost, even the most intimate memories had become faithless and untrue. Elizabeth Webster had a distinct advantage over the wailing parents. She knew about the other lives, muffled in obscurity, that people lead and conceal, sometimes even from themselves. She realised that the stranger who had come to her would always be as strange to her as she was to him. But she felt neither resentment nor fear. And this invisible knowledge – for whom could she tell? – marked her out from all the rest.

By morning she was peacefully asleep. She had decided to write a warm encouraging letter to Saïda, telling her how well Chérif was doing at his studies and how proud of him she had the right to be.

The church at Great Blessington was always chosen as a compromise for Christmas. The faithful were not sufficiently numerous in any one of the three parishes to merit separate services at each church, but the united congregations could never have eased themselves into either of the two smaller churches at Bolt or Little Blessington. Entire families, lured by carols and sentimental handmade cards produced by desperate primary school teachers during the run-up to the feasts, turned out, replete with pushchairs and babies in red bobble hats who always started yelling during the lessons. A lukewarm love of tradition began to manifest itself among the people. The Baby Jesus launched himself once more upon the unsuspecting world in a flurry of stars, camels, shepherds and wandering kings. Chérif delighted in the camels. He also noted the proof of approaching climactic chaos in the front windows of Ottakar's, which presented a desert, much like the one where he had been born, backed by pine trees and fir cones. North and South embraced one another across the rickety crib stuffed with cotton wool.

The spending spree gathered pace and intensity. Chérif had been conned into purchasing a holly wreath, which Miss Webster now affixed to the cottage knocker in a series of red-ribboned nautical knots. She pulled on her gardening gauntlets to avoid being spiked by the greenery. Chérif ambushed the old lady with an unexpected request. 'I would like to go to church at Christmas,' he announced. And then added, 'with you.'

'Would you really? Well, that'd cause a sensation. The midnight carols? Or the early morning mass?'

Chérif didn't understand the difference. He had asserted his desire to attend in the hope of pleasing her. The only other Muslim in his seminar group was a Pakistani hippie from Peterborough, who actually wore a retro Afghan coat and who had told him that Christians had everybody on board to switch on the Christmas lights, which were a sign of hope and not specifically Christian. Everybody goes, man, women and men together, whole families, any religion, especially Jews, they love candles and call it the festival of lights, everybody all mixed up, and you don't have to believe in anything, it's cool, man.

'When do you switch on the lights?'

'Midnight. We have all the lights off. One candle comes in. Saintly little face of innocence illuminated from beneath. "Once in Royal David's City", then full boom for "O come, O come Emmanuel". You have to light each other's bloody candles. All the Christmas tree lights go pop and there we are, in a cosy glow clutching the Light of the World. Candles everywhere, and not a dry eye present on account of that odious little shit who sings soprano. Rumour has it that he strangled one of Mrs Harris's cats.'

Miss Webster scorned the midnight carols with all her vindictive angry soul. Chérif had learned to deal with the rapidity of her occasional explosions, which were beyond him linguistically, by grabbing hold of the two or three phrases that meant something. Candles. Midnight. Lights on. And one of the singers was a murderer.

'Let's go to the midnight carols,' he beamed at Miss Webster.

'OK,' she shrugged her shoulders and straightened the trailing red ribbons on the festive wreath.

And so it was that at eleven-fifteen on a Christmas night of white frost, when the grass crackled and the trees loomed spectral, edged with white, that Miss Webster and Chérif, muffled and wrapped tightly into gloves and hats, set out across the fields towards the church at Great Blessington. Miss Webster thumped ahead in her galoshes. Chérif got his feet wet. For the crisp white coating upon the path was but skin-deep, and the earth waited beneath, marshy with creeping damp.

'You should've worn those wellies I got for you at the army surplus. OK, they're a bit big, but you could have worn two pairs of socks.'

Miss Webster assumed that all men possessed enormous feet and ordered size twelve. They battled through the crunching air. The old woman had wrapped a mohair shawl around her shoulders, which made her look like a refugee from all the catastrophes of history: earthquakes, tempests, wars and rumours of wars. Chérif suddenly took note of her fragility as she negotiated the stile, and offered her his arm. This was not a habitual gesture. She accepted with a nod of surprise.

The grey flints of the church flickered and glistened in the lights of the cars pulling up down the lane. They saw its bulk floodlit, then darkening suddenly as if it were the backdrop to a *son et lumière* enacting the Christmas story. Voices were carried great distances by the still frost.

'Can we say Merry Christmas yet?'

'Oh, you should have told us you were coming. We'd have picked you both up.'

'I'm driving. Patrick's drunk.'

'We got there just in time . . .'

'Did you see the peacocks earlier?'

'She heats her shed. Can't say I'd bother.'

'Oh, good evening, Miss Webster.'

A little gust of embarrassed silence settled around them. Then everyone greeted Chérif and shook hands ostentatiously in a magnanimous burst of The Christmas Spirit. Only one person was ungenerous enough to wonder if he were a suicide bomber, well wadded with explosives, who, upon the mention of 'captive Israel' would fling himself upon the vicar, yelling 'Allah Akbar'. Good manners, that most English of rural, village instincts, asserted itself over paranoia and racism. The boy is very beautiful after all. He is the stranger in our midst. Would we turn from the black kings, the wise men following the star? No, we would shake their hands and claim kin. They knew of His coming before we did.

'Welcome to Great Blessington.'

'So nice you could come.'

'Chilly, isn't it? Aren't you brave to come out on foot?'

'Oh Miss Webster, you must both be soaked. You came across the fields.'

For behind them through the wet grass, intermittently revealed by the arriving cars, gleamed a long wake of darker green, the ploughing of the winter field, evidence of Miss Webster's leadership initiative, the pretty Arab trailing in her mighty wake. Everyone looked impressed. Then the vicar pounced.

'Aha, Chérif! What a pleasure! Thank you for escorting our Miss Webster. Hello everyone. Have you met Chérif? This is Miss Webster's lodger. He's studying at the university. Maths, isn't it? Come in, come in.'

Deck the halls with boughs of holly. Chérif had never seen a church decorated for Christmas; he therefore witnessed the Aladdin's cave of glittering tinsel for the first time. Swags of heavy sliced green, powder-puffed with fake silver glitter, shimmered in the lights. Great Blessington possessed a magnificent medieval rood screen, illuminated for festivals and reproduced in colour in all the county guide books. Here was St Barbara, holding out a miniature version of the church in her right hand, and here was St Catherine, bowling her wheel before her, like a giant hoop. Behold St George in patchy silver armour with red frills, waggling his lance at a marvellously restored monster, all fire and teeth and rolling eyes, a dragon beloved of the children, who had to be restrained from stroking him and smacked if they managed to do so. The assembled choir of saints surrounding the altar were too numerous for a monotheistic religion. You could miss the hand of God the Father in the crowd. The simple golden cross, a priceless trinket, wired up to various secret alarms, had no one nailed or roped to its shining intersections. The crucifix stood empty, the Holy Ghost masked by holly and pine cones. And so in the packed church, peopled by imperfect humanity, scuffling children and the smell of wet conifers, Chérif beheld a market scene, utterly different from the empty, carpeted spaces where he had been told the Lord was to be found.

'Sit on the edge of that pew,' rasped Miss Webster, manhandling him into the seat, 'then we can escape before the mulled wine and mince pies.'

Everyone was more or less settled as the vicar intoned the bidding prayers. The event resembled a television variety show with the vicar as master of ceremonies. Women took a leading role in the performance. Chérif gaped at this odd quirk of Western Christianity, which was very unlike the Catholic chapel near his village. The Holy Fathers were desert saints he recognised, an all-male community of simple, barefoot men of God, skilled in medicine, friends with the marabout, and expert at car mechanics. They originally came from obscure corners of France, trained in Rome and then departed to the Sahara, where they spoke little and prayed day and night. But this never seemed peculiar. Indeed, it was expected. These men were the guardians of the deep wells. They shared everything they possessed with his people and had no fear of whatever alien creed foamed and boiled in the surrounding sands. They extended their brown-flecked hands regardless and whipped the children for stealing what would have been freely given. Chérif recalled those holy men, who had been folded away in his memory, when years later, wandering in the desert, he came upon the ruins of the monastery of St Jérôme dans le Désert. For when the time came the Holy Fathers faced their martyrdom at the hands of the Islamic insurgents, fearless and stoical, their eyes lifted to the endless dunes. Even their murderers knew that they were God's servants. Yet nothing stayed their hands. For even as we bear witness to God, shall men know that our word was of God. By their works ye shall know them.

But who were these women in camel jackets with large gold buttons, who boomed with great authority, *'And there shall come forth a rod out of the stem of Jesse, and a branch shall grow out of his roots'*? The spectacle appeared increasingly bizarre. Chérif concentrated hard. *'The wolf also shall dwell with the lamb and the leopard shall lie down with the kid.'* None of this seemed at all likely. Miss Webster, meanwhile, glared at the congregation; from time to time she caught a familiar eye and bared her teeth in an unnerving smile. The midnight carols. What on earth was she doing here? She hadn't been to the midnight service since her mother died. Good God, there's Dr Brody. He looks a hundred. And his wife so much younger than he is. Perverted, really. Whose child is that kicking up blue murder? She swivelled round, intensifying her lasered gleam. Ah, don't know them. Jolly good, he's taking the thing outside. With any luck it'll freeze quietly. Miss Webster would have guarded the inn door like a savage mastiff and sent everybody packing to the stables.

The candles were being handed round. Chérif wasn't sure what to do with his and fell to sniffing it out of mild curiosity.

'And she brought forth her firstborn son and wrapped him in swaddling clothes, and laid him in a manger, because there was no room for them in the inn.'

The lights didn't go out all at once. There was a flickering, then a series of clicks; the overheads, huge orbs suspended on iron chains, gradually dimmed. The gigantic pine tree nuzzling the pulpit remained a blaze of fairy points reflected in the shiny boxes of fake, empty presents sheltered beneath the green. The choir's lead soprano, also known as Miss Webster's odious little shit, sashayed down the aisle. His cassock was a little too voluminous and he waddled slowly, already well advanced past the font before the church plunged into shadow, his candle held out before him, like a raised sword.

> *Once in royal David's city*
> *Stood a lowly cattle shed*
> *Where a mother laid her baby*
> *In a manger for his bed.*
> *Mary was that mother mild,*
> *Jesus Christ, her little child.*

The church held its breath. Miss Webster hoped that the evil-minded ten-year-old would walk up the inside of his cassock. He sometimes careered down her lane on his mountain bike, spattering her door with pebbles. She contemplated digging hidden potholes, disguised with cardboard and a thin shell of earth. It would all look like an accident. Someone was trying to catch her attention. Time to light our candles. Chérif held out his taper obediently, anxious to get it right.

'Merry Christmas, my dear,' hissed Miss Webster.

'Merry Christmas,' he whispered back. The choir rose to its collective feet and began the roar of joyous conviction.

> *And our eyes at last shall see him . . .*
> *Who is God and Lord of All.*

Not for the first time Miss Webster decided that her religion was a mystery cult followed by the half-baked and the barking mad. How on earth did one baby represent the salvation of the world? They got to 'O come, all ye faithful . . .' when she spotted two of the vicar's groupies creeping off towards the parish rooms to heat up the vats of spicy wine. *Sing, choirs of angels, Sing in exultation.* Miss Webster booted Chérif in the shins.

'Quick! Let's get out of here!'

They scuttled forth, their retreat masked by universal jubilation. When the congregation united round its festive paper cups of sweet mulled wine, received opinion was of one voice. How good to see Miss Webster back again. How far-sighted of her to bring her young man. He's a very lovely boy, isn't he? Nobody remarked that Miss Webster never came to the midnight carols, or pointed out that it was very odd to see a young Muslim in the church in the first place. They all brimmed with ecumenical conviction: we are the People of the Book, united by our faith in the one true God – but each to his own revelation. And outside in the white frost, beneath the black sky speckled with Christmas stars, their eyes raised to the glow of the city, miles away in the fold of the earth, Chérif and Miss Webster bolted for home.

5

ATTENTAT

S ometime in the early hours of New Year's Day 2003, probably between midnight and one-thirty, Chérif fell victim to Karen's mother's rum punch. The thing tasted like fruit juice: cucumbers and lemons floated on the surface, oranges stuffed with cloves circulated gently in the golden liquid, served in an enormous Italian bowl with a silver ladle. Everyone helped themselves to copious spoonfuls. No one warned him. Chérif had never taken a fanatical stand on the subject of alcohol. He downed the odd beer from time to time, but never drank spirits and in the students' union he rarely touched anything stronger than Kaliber. He was a man who genuinely preferred tea. And now, after all, given that he was entrusted with Miss Webster's car, he thought of himself as a responsible person. The first signs of something seriously awry dawned upon Karen following an outburst of wild dancing and a passionate kiss bestowed full on the lips, delivered as a postscript to the midnight rendition of 'Auld Lang Syne'. Karen was a little surprised. Unlike all her previous boyfriends, Chérif liked to take things as slowly as she did. The fact that she never had to fight him off counted greatly in his favour. He held her hand. He kissed her on both cheeks as the French do. She expected matters to warm up in the New Year, but never with such boisterous rapidity. By twelve-thirty he was dancing with anyone of either sex who would take the floor − polished boards, the rugs pulled back, all the furniture pushed against the wall. The guests yelled, 'Look at Chérif!' and 'Watch out for the Wild Man!' as he boomeranged off the bookshelves and into the American bar. Chérif took these cries of encouragement as a sign that he was not only being entertaining, but had also been fully accepted by Karen's family and friends. He flung himself into the fray, and at one-thirty, leaped the sofa, crashed into the wall, dislodging a picture, which smashed into a heap beside him, then passed out.

Karen, still afflicted with a mouth tasting of ashes and a crashing headache, rang Miss Webster at around midday on New Year's Day. Miss Webster, like many schoolteachers, proved startlingly liberal on sexual matters. When Chérif asked, yes, actually asked, if he could stay out all night on New Year's Eve and go to Karen's party, she had assumed that tonight was to be The Night of Joy for both of them.

'My dear, you're well beyond the age of consent. It's only good manners to let me know, but you don't need to ask my permission.'

Permission. Consent. Yes! She says yes. Chérif dressed himself up very carefully and pushed off at eight on New Year's Eve in Miss Webster's car. But alas, he did not return in one piece. Karen brought him home in a taxi. The rain quietly spotted the windows and the grey day never lifted its face to greet the New Year. Chérif crept into the porch, unable to speak; his face was now a very strange colour and no longer golden. A splendid black bruise, handed out by the aggressive end of the sofa, pursued its stealthy course across his left cheek and eye, darkening the bloodshot socket. He had one arm thrown around Karen's shoulders, and as they staggered through the front door they ruffled the row of upturned outdoor boots, laid out on wooden pegs like war trophies, and collapsed into the front room to a drumbeat of falling wellingtons.

'Where's my car?' demanded Miss Webster.

'In Mum's garage. It's fine. Chérif will bring it back when he can drive again.' Karen offered a row of explanations. 'He's OK really. He wasn't in a fight. He fell down behind the sofa. And that's where he spent the night.'

'I see.'

'I spent the night on the sofa,' said Karen miserably,' 'and Mum's furious. Someone was sick all over the carpet in the bathroom.'

Miss Webster's rising laughter gurgled in her throat. She passed it off as a cough and propelled them into the corridor.

'Black coffee,' she snapped. 'He can't go to bed until he's drunk some black coffee. Take him along to the downstairs shower and push him in, then bring me everything he's wearing and I'll pop it in the washing machine. Go along. Now.'

The phone rang. Chérif and Karen lurched along the passage, locked together like debutantes in the three-legged race on Parents' Day. The phone hissed and whirred; then an alien voice gabbled in French down the line.

'Meeses Webster? Ah, c'est vous! Bonne Année, Madame Webster. Prospérité, bonheur, santé, bonne santé avant tout. Ici c'est Saïda à l'appareil.'

Merde.

'Saïda! Quelle surprise. Et Bonne Année aussi. Mes meilleurs vœux . . .'

Miss Webster's command performance merited an

award. Yes, Chérif was quite well. He had just stepped out to get some fresh bread and coffee. What a charming boy! So helpful. No, of course not, I love having him here to stay. Company in the evenings. Oh yes, such marvellous results from his first semester. He studies very hard every evening. You should be proud of your handsome son. No, he has lovely friends. Yes, as far as I know he's been keeping up with the mosque. I don't ask too much about that sort of thing. But he mentioned an Asian friend from Peterborough, who is also a Muslim, and we stuck to Ramadan with passionate fanaticism. And how is the hotel? Not full for Christmas? Oh dear, that'll be the result of those awful bombings. People do take fright. Quite unreasonable really. Lightning never strikes twice. And how is Abdou? Ah yes, good . . . good. Yes, of course I'll get him to ring you. Would this evening be all right? What time? And we mustn't forget that you're an hour ahead. You see, when he gets back I'll start cooking . . .

But Miss Webster never heard the return conversation, which would, in any case, have been conducted in his own language, rather than French. Chérif claimed that he rang back on Karen's mobile, as he could not bring himself to run up a bill on Miss Webster's phone. He sank into a demoralised hangover, brought on by disgrace.

'Chérif says he can't thank you enough.' Karen slumped down at the kitchen table. 'Is his mum furious too?'

'Luckily for him,' said Miss Webster, grappling with her Italian percolator, 'she knows nothing whatsoever.'

Miss Webster rarely entered Chérif's room, except to hoover. The photograph might still be hidden there, but she never looked again. Every time she did enter the room she shuddered, appalled by the sudden explosion of pink floral horror which still coated every surface. She returned to a project abandoned nearly a year earlier: a knitted quilt in orange, red and gold squares. She found the completely mindless task of knitting three dozen squares, all exactly the same apart from the colours, marvellously soothing. She menaced the boy with the massing web of Saharan shades, which were destined to replace the unchanging floods of roses.

'It's lovely,' he said, stretching the quilt out over his knees as it grew across the sitting room. He noticed that she simply stitched the different squares together at random.

'No rhyme or reason to the whole damn thing,' said Miss Webster, turning on all the lights. 'I can't be bothered.'

'C'est comme la vie,' said Chérif, suddenly gripped by unnecessary philosophical revelation. 'You think there's a pattern, but there isn't.'

'There probably is a darker purpose,' replied Miss Webster grimly. 'We just can't see it.'

And the world news in the illuminated square before them was indeed darkening. There were desert shots of Western troops massing in the Gulf, and sinister grey ships in small convoys slicing the blue. In the last days there shall be wars and rumours of wars. Miss Webster checked her emerging bulbs. A white bank of snowdrops sheltered by the woods on the left side of the garden fluttered in full bloom. Against the dead leaves and browned grass they braved it out, facing a wretched month of wind and rain. War was coming. But the green points and clumps of daffodils, gathered in groups on her lawns, rose up in planted ranks like dragon's teeth. Nature could not wait; the growing time had come. War is not a natural thing, Miss Webster muttered to her daffodils. It can be stopped.

They sat watching archive footage of the Iraqi national flag and Saddam Hussein making defiant speeches of heroic resistance, which Chérif actually understood.

'*Great Iraqi people,*' he translated the text into a version that was significantly different from the subtitles, '*heroic people of glory, faith, jihad, sacrifice and bravery . . . Peace be upon you . . . Dear Brothers, the Zionist aggression is perpetuated by a common arrangement between the Zionist entity and the American administration . . .* He speaks classical Arabic. Like the great poets in history.'

'Really? And how do you know about these great poets?'

'From the librarian in Tamegroute. He ran a small class for us. We learned lots by heart because he wouldn't let us touch the books. It's very beautiful. Listen.' And he recited the verses in Arabic.

> *Abbas, I wish you were the shirt*
> *On my body, or I your shirt.*
>
> *Or I wish we were in a glass*
> *You as wine, I as rainwater.*

'Good heavens.' Miss Webster had no idea what he had just said; it was as mysterious and peculiar as Saddam Hussein's mad paean to the Iraqi people's love of self-sacrifice. They switched channels. Al-Jazeera broadcast the entire speech. Chérif followed the thunderous dictator, who now appeared dressed in military attire, transfixed by every modulation in the titanic rant. Miss Webster concentrated during the Koranic interludes, which were sung, like

Gregorian chant, but otherwise she sat wondering what she would do if the war came to Little Blessington. It wasn't likely, but it's just as well to be prepared.

'I'd hide you,' she assured Chérif, 'in the cupboard under the stairs. There'd be lynch mobs out, looking for foreigners.'

For the first time since he had come to England real fear flooded Chérif's face.

'Mobs?'

'Well, maybe. It's always better to expect the worst. The power would go first, of course. But we'd be OK. I'd get out the camping gas and we have the wood stove. We'd need candles and a stock of gas bottles.'

'What if the water goes off?' Chérif began to imagine disaster. Miss Webster did not live near a well. The desert people always lived near wells. But she remained unperturbed.

'We'll divert the stream in the woods. It's only twenty yards away. Water isn't a problem in the country. And we can dig latrines, like soldiers do at the front. Heating's more difficult.' She warmed to her theme. 'Masking tape. The Iraqis have the right idea.' They watched the market stalls in Baghdad loading up with brown tape and paraffin. 'Tape up the windows so that all the glass doesn't fly out and slice you up when the bombs drop.'

Chérif had never lived in a city and the house where he was born had bars and blankets across the windows.

'Why don't they just leave Baghdad?' he asked, incredulous, as they watched amazing images of people carrying on with their daily lives, negotiating the shopping, buying spices, opening up their restaurants and garages.

'They don't have the option. They can't leave. They'd be shot. Anyway, you don't want to leave everything that's familiar. Everything you own. I'd never leave the cottage. I'd rather die here.'

She looked around at her books, pictures, heavy lined green curtains, the framed photographs of landscapes in France, the new DVD player, and realised that she was speaking the truth; this was her tomb, her pyramid, the final resting place.

'We would go out into the desert if the soldiers came,' said Chérif, reflecting on his own fate.

'It's as well to have a plan,' Miss Webster declared. 'The soldiers always do come in the end.'

Newsnight began with Paxman slumped at an angle across the desk. Saddam Hussein had apparently written two novels, which were being reviewed. Miss Webster bounced on her sofa with joy, for the titles were delightful: *Zabibah and the King*, which had been published anonymously, but widely acclaimed as a work of genius, and *The Impregnable Fortress*, heralded with universal eulogy and published under his own name in 2002.

'He should have called the first one *The King and I*,' she crowed. 'When on earth did he find time to write them?'

'You don't have to do much if you're a dictator,' said Chérif. 'You seize power and then just sit there. The secret police do the rest.'

'So young and yet so cynical,' grinned Miss Webster.

'*Do these novels tell us anything useful about the inner workings of Saddam Hussein's mind?*' Paxman demanded of the unfortunate Iraqi intellectual in exile who had just read and summarised both literary productions. The scholar paused, baffled. His main area of expertise was economics.

'*No, not really,*' he said. Then he added, '*Novels don't tell you anything. They're not real. They're just stories.*'

Paxman raised his eyebrows and rearranged his expression into a sneer. *'Thank you. We'll bear that in mind.'*

And the world moved on to other things.

But no one doubted that the war was indeed coming. Too many soldiers had been moved into place. What kind of courage would be needed now to think twice and turn back? A massive anti-war demonstration took place in London. Eight coaches left from Great Blessington at six in the morning. Miss Webster and Chérif gaped at the crowds, people with dogs and children in pushchairs, battling grannies in dated red hats, entire families with similar faces – many of them had never carried a banner before in their lives. Yet house prices in their damp corner of England rose week after week, in an elegant and steady arc. As the war seeped closer people longed for stability, safety and a walled garden. It was as if two forces, the impulse to kill and the desire to purchase, had found a rising rhythm and begun to dance. Karen kept busy. Her list of appointments – viewings, surveys, valuations, estimates – filled up every day. Her mobile phone tinkled tunes incessantly as she tore from place to place, measuring up conservatories and sitting rooms, calculating every inch of habitable space, assessing flood risk, harassing solicitors, demanding sealed bids on her desk by Friday morning. Often the house she priced up was sold even before she could print off the particulars. She dropped round to visit at the cottage almost every late afternoon during February and March and sank down, exhausted, beside Chérif at the kitchen table. He fair-copied lecture notes and she wrote descriptions of bedrooms. Miss Webster supplied tea and advice.

' "Spacious landing. Access to loft with internal loft ladder." Does that make it sound as if the ladder comes down when you open the loft door?' The language of estate agents' details created a domestic code, disturbing and opaque, with financial implications.

'No. Put loft ladder fixture. Then they can't remove the thing.'

'I'd better ask them.'

' "Kitchen, 12' × 10', with slate floor to patio." '

'Nice big kitchen. Does the slate continue on to the patio? Sounds wonderful.'

'It does, but it wasn't pretty. Not to me. The particulars are just a map really. You have to see it all with your own eyes. And the floor wasn't a selling point. I thought it looked cold.'

'You can't carpet kitchens.'

'But I like your pottery tiles. They're not black and shiny.'

Chérif listened to the women talking and fluttered the pages of his textbook. He paused over the image of a stone fragment covered in unintelligible designs.

'What's that?' asked Karen.

'It's a Sumerian tablet. It was discovered in Iraq. It's still in the museum there.'

'Which will soon be blown to bits by the Americans, I expect,' said Miss Webster. They all peered at the fragile, doomed treasure. 'Can you stay to supper, Karen?'

Miss Webster cooked lamb stew with saffron rice. She had mastered just the right combination of lemon, garlic and ginger.

'Put on the second CD.'

Carmen Campbell, Best of had been a request Christmas present to Chérif. They discovered that the new DVD also played CDs and the singer's smoky, liquid voice oozed through the dining room and washed against the dresser and the kitchen cupboards. Strange, suggestive, insinuating, that voice haunted their chilly spring. Miss Webster became deeply attached to the songs, their ghostly chants and angry eruptions. No, passion never counts as crime. Carmen Campbell lined the walls of Miss Webster's mind, her uncanny presence was never questioned. She settled there, and made her home. Miss Webster could no longer imagine music that did not benefit from the anarchic attack of several thousand amplified volts. She had passed, imperceptibly, into the electronic age.

'Have you got any exams before the Easter break?' Miss Webster demanded.

'No. They're all in May.'

'Ah, good. Give me your timetable as soon as you have it.'

She winked at Karen. Miss Webster was clearly planning something.

On Monday 17 March 2003, President George Bush addressed the American people, and in passing, the rest of the world.

'*My fellow citizens, events in Iraq have now reached the final days of decision. Intelligence gathered by this and other governments leaves no doubt that the Iraqi regime continues to possess and conceal some of the most lethal weapons ever devised . . . The danger is clear: using chemical, biological or, one day, nuclear weapons obtained with the help of Iraq, the terrorists could fulfil their stated ambition and kill thousands or hundreds of thousands of innocent people in our country, or any other . . . before the day of horror can come, before it is too late to act, this danger will be removed.*'

The weapons inspectors had already left Baghdad.

Chérif's second term at university ended officially on 22 March 2003. His last bout of coursework had been handed in early, so that he could concentrate on the war. He spent the next four days in the cottage, glued to Al-Jazeera. The images were both disquieting and repetitive. Here was the skyline of Baghdad, exploding with flame, and here was a strange, gesticulating creature in battle fatigues, with a gun prominent beneath his armpit, haranguing the assembled journalists. This was Mohammed Saeed al-Sahhaf, the Iraqi Minister of Information.

'Does he say the same things in Arabic?' enquired Miss Webster. 'In English he sounds quite mad.'

At that moment al-Sahhaf declared that the Americans were all lying in a ditch with their throats cut, whereas a small inset screen above him showed a battalion of tanks speeding unopposed across the desert. Then one image arrested the attention of Miss Webster and Chérif and held them open-mouthed and staring. A tribal herdsman, muffled and swathed against the clouds of fine sand, stepped in front of his dark, low tent and his curious goats, defensive and alert, his gun ready. Behind him lurked two veiled women and a gaggle of frightened children, pointing and shrieking and running away from the convoy. The man stood, rigid and baffled, as the war rolled towards him and then away again, on the long road to Baghdad.

'Look, look,' cried Chérif, 'that's like home. That man could be one of my family.'

'Indeed. It's exactly like your desert,' agreed Miss Webster. 'What an apparition! Like a medieval figure. Or even older. Thousands of years older. And it's that way of life that will survive.'

'As long as the wells stay OK,' said Chérif.

Miss Webster found the babble of Arabic oddly soothing. She continued with her golden quilt, looking up from
time to time to see an intense and bearded man broad-
casting from Baghdad, who gave a convincing impression
of being terrified in the face of carpet bombs. Chérif
explained opinions or translated speeches from time to
time. They slithered between the BBC reports and the
terrifying footage of Al-Jazeera, but always returned to
Newsnight for their final dose of war reports. Chérif's
ravenous eyes wolfed down the images, as if he were
hunting for a coded sign, something shining clearly through
the sandstorm before the advancing tanks, something still
visible through the deep smoke of the burning oil wells, the
blazing buildings and the terrible confusion of war.

'It will go on happening even if you don't watch it, you
know,' said Miss Webster. 'Come on, supper's ready.'

Six months in England and he had never been to London.
She purchased tickets for a show and made plans for a foray
into the legendary bright lights. What could draw his
fanatical attention away from an exploding desert, thousands
of miles to the east? The garden remained un-weeded, un-
dug, and the recycling piled up beside the shed. Karen tried to
understand; in any case, she was busy making thousands in
commission fees. She sold an old coach house with a dodgy
roof and sagging gutters for £270,000, then recounted her
exploits, propping up the sink. Chérif did not listen. He
never moved from the green sofa.

'It's his people, I suppose. Being blown up.'

'Nonsense girl, where's your geography? He doesn't
come from Iraq.'

They stood side by side, worrying about Chérif.

'I've got to go, Miss Webster, but I'll take some of the
bottles down to the recycling.'

She kissed Chérif's black curls; he stroked her arm, but never lifted his eyes from the screen with the subtitles in Arabic cruising across the bottom. Once Karen had rumbled safely away down the lane, splashing through the puddles, Miss Webster took evasive action. She stepped in front of the television and turned it off. He looked up in shock.

'You can watch the highlights at eleven. Come on, Chérif. You'll make yourself ill. You've got to eat.'

Miss Webster unfolded her master plan for their night on the loose in the city.

'I asked Karen to come too of course, but she has appointments all afternoon —'

He stared at her, expressionless, uncomprehending.

'— Of course, if you'd rather not go.'

Chérif remembered his manners.

'I would be honoured to accompany you, Madame Webster. It is most kind of you to invite me.'

They stared at one another across the chasm of the kitchen table.

This ill-fated expedition to London caused the first serious difference of opinion between Miss Webster and Chérif, and the initial error, which unleashed a chain of disasters, was the decision to drive down. Miss Elizabeth Webster had not approached central London for nearly a decade. Many of the country roads had simply disappeared into fields; three-lane motorways materialised in surprising places. Her antique *AA Map of Britain* no longer charted the landscape. The earth lay all before them, as they roared through Suffolk at sixty. Miss Webster leaned over the wheel, baffled by huge green signs for the A14, which promised The Midlands and The North. The M11 was much announced, but impossible to locate. They stalled, mired in roadworks. Above them loomed the huge spring skies and sharp light. The frost melted away from the ploughed earth and the washed black outlines of the trees, still bare, but luminous, expectant, impatient for the coming green, lined their way. Chérif deduced the route by working backwards from Stansted, his original point of arrival. However, as soon as they reached the M25, he too was lost.

'Straight at 'em, sir,' cried Miss Webster and put her foot down. They shot off the motorway into Tottenham and became instantly ensnared in a wiggle of jams and lights. They lost sight of signs to the City or the West End and then finally of any signs at all.

'We'd better pull off and ask an inhabitant.' Miss Webster feared being swept round and round the North Circular with no hope of a reprieve. They turned into a side road and stopped in front of a decrepit row of terraced houses. Many were abandoned, their windows bricked up. Some looked as if they had been in a war zone for years: doorways strewn with smashed glass backed by cardboard on the front panels, abandoned rotting furniture piled in the front gardens, black plastic sacks spewing rubbish oozed on to the pavements. This decaying slum was illuminated by the same brilliant white light that accompanied their doomed trajectory down the motorway. And there, resplendent on a red plastic sofa ripped and pock-marked by cigarette burns, blocking the Clio's slow advance down the otherwise empty street, sat three black men, magnificent as kings, their dreadlocks carefully arranged, many cans of Red Stripe lined up beside their feet.

'Good God,' said Miss Webster, incredulous. She stopped the car.

'It's the Neighbourhood Watch,' said Chérif, and got out. One of the black men rose up as he sauntered towards them. Chérif was not a big man, but he stood straight and his black curls gleamed glossy in the sunshine. He shook hands with all three men. They stared at his beauty, perplexed and interested. He was the first event of their day. But none of them could understand his accent, nor he theirs. They surrounded the car, peering in at the smartly dressed old lady, the clean floor, rugs and cushions.

'Yu lost?'

The face which peered through the window at Miss Webster's London *A–Z* had two stained yellow teeth and then a large gap. He smelled of beer and cigarettes; he knew exactly where they were and how to get back to the best route. He revealed himself as the hermit, waiting at the crossroads, replete with warnings, the wise man that always accosts the wandering knights.

'Yu caan' go into central London now without a ticket,' he declared. 'Five pound. Then yu pay parkin' on top. Twenty-five pound. Yu don' pay the ticket and yu get fine. Eighty pound.'

The red plastic sofa was the tollgate warning of the Congestion Zone, which had come into being on 17 February 2003. Miss Webster had forgotten all about the Zone. She tapped her fingers on the wheel with irritation. Of course, the Inner London Congestion Zone. It had been discussed endlessly on TV and everyone said that it would never work.

'We'll find a car park and go in on the bus.' Their simple adventure now presented itself as an odyssey fraught with obstacles. The Neighbourhood Watch waved enthusiastically from the sofa as they zoomed backwards down the abandoned street.

It was midday by the time they found a Masterpark in which to abandon the Clio, and Miss Webster's temper, frazzled by hunger and outrage at the accumulating expense, could no longer be trusted. The cheerful day trip had turned into a royal progress, the road ahead lined by her diminishing stock of £20 notes. She breathed fire and slaughter at the hapless security guard entrusted with the underground car park.

'I don't fix the tariffs, lady. Take it up with the management.'

Chérif stood by, like an inexperienced flunkey, embarrassed and desperate, carrying her handbag and umbrella. They decided to eat. The nearest restaurant was vegetarian and appropriately called 'Manna in the Wilderness'. They gobbled down stuffed aubergines, £11.75 each, and then mounted a calculated assault on John Lewis. Chérif's clothes, never numerous, were becoming much-washed, faded and shabby. Miss Webster insisted on a summer wardrobe of unostentatious top quality and put it on her credit card. He protested.

'I'm an old woman, Chérif,' she argued. 'I have no children. I have never spent my money on anyone else before. Fais-moi plaisir. I'm the one who has to look at you every morning, so you may as well be easy on the eye. I don't want other people saying my lodger is dressed like an asylum seeker.'

Miss Webster's sting lodged in her tongue. She withheld as much as she gave. The shopping folly of the afternoon was a black leather jacket with an arc of red Chinese ideograms across the back.

'What does it say?' Chérif expected Miss Webster to know everything.

'Made in Hong Kong,' she said.

The wonders of London's national monuments were rapidly exhausted. Chérif was nonplussed by the Houses of Parliament – he could not see why they should be interesting – and remained reserved on the marvels of queens, and ornamental toy soldiers marching back and forth in front of their barracks. Apparently the kings of his country embarked on extensive palace building projects as soon as they ascended the throne. These massive constructions brought no obvious benefits to the populace, but due to an effective propaganda campaign and many state visits to dilapidated rural areas, the country people loved the present king nevertheless. Chérif stared gloomily at the distant ramparts of Buckingham Palace and showed no interest whatsoever. They settled down with a thermos of tea before the ducks and daffodils in St James's Park until their bums were too cold to stay put.

'Ah well,' said Miss Webster, who wasn't interested in royalty either, but who had heard they were tourist attractions, 'King Faruk was the last King of Egypt and he said that by the end of the century there would be only five kings left in the world: the King of Hearts, the King of Diamonds, the King of Clubs, the King of Spades and the King of England.'

'He was a gambler,' cried Chérif, delighted, 'and he was exiled to a casino!' A biopic of the unfortunate monarch had recently been screened on Channel 4.

'Do I gather that you are opposed to all monarchies?' Miss Webster enquired.

'What good do they bring to their people?'

They pondered the assembled ducks and floods of

daffodils, sweeping across the greening lawns. The spring day proved deceptive, for the afternoon dusk now hovered around them, masking the distances, carving deeper shadows on the buildings, lapping their naked hands with cold. And so they slipped into the National Portrait Gallery, not only bent on education and tourism, but to warm their freezing extremities. Miss Webster pulled her hat over her ears. Chérif drew his scarf across his nose. The long escalator bore them aloft to the emptying galleries on the upper floors. But here they got no further than the grandiose jewels of the Tudors: strange, flat, white faces; evil, shifty eyes and gorgeous, cunning textures worked in satins, rubies, pearls. They faced the last great Queen of England, who stood life-size before them, her feet, lopsided and unnatural, crushing the map of her country beneath her. She looked like a gigantic voodoo doll. Robes and furred gowns hide all. Around her stood the clerics and courtiers, their unstable loyalty and probable corruption written across their cheeks and foreheads. Chérif stared into the eyes of the recorded dead, which followed him across the empty floors. Beyond the first gallery stretched room after room of fixed, ageless, unlined faces.

'What is this place?' he asked.

'A memorial. Mostly to men, but there are some famous women here too, who served England, or this culture. It's a dictionary of faces.'

'That's odd. We don't make images of people except on television or in the newspapers. We don't even take photographs. No one at home has a camera.' Miss Webster looked at him sharply. She saw the shadow in the sand before her, the two smiling boys, the endless desert rolling towards eternity.

'Really? No photographs? I see.'

Shakespeare perused their faces as they hesitated before him. The lights seemed to glitter on his gold earring. He cut a strange figure: knowing, rakish and fat.

'Almost everybody here is dead,' remarked Miss Webster. 'It's a mausoleum.' They sat side by side on a bench staring at a very odd portrait of Sir Walter Raleigh, who appeared to be wearing a ballet tutu. He posed like a dancing model on the catwalk, his legs tapering, elegant, misshapen.

'Who was he?'

'A courtier, a poet. He laid down his silk cloak in the mud and puddles so Queen Elizabeth could walk without getting her feet wet. Or so the story goes.' Chérif smiled knowingly. So Sir Walter was a flatterer.

'Then Elizabeth banned him from her court for getting one of her ladies pregnant. I think I read that in Aubrey's *Brief Lives*. It's at home if you're interested. The good Sir Walter got the Queen's lady up against one of the trees in the royal park and Aubrey says she was urging him on, or begging him to stop – history doesn't make that clear – crying "Oh sweet Sir Walter, sweet Sir Walter . . ." and as the danger and the pleasure increased the cry became "Sweeserswater, sweeserswater . . ."'

Chérif fixed Miss Webster with a wicked grin. 'I saw a film on Europe 5 before I came to England that was about Queen Elizabeth. That film reminds me of you.'

'Does it indeed?' Miss Webster was very flattered. Elizabeth was not beautiful and all her hair had fallen out, but she had been very powerful in her time and had never married. An ability to make extempore speeches in Latin clearly proved useful and apart from some obvious errors in foreign policy, her royal career had been largely successful.

'Yes,' said Chérif with real affection, 'you remind me of Walsingham.' He pronounced the name 'Walseenghum'. The image of Elizabeth's ruthless spymaster loomed before Miss Webster. She got up, less flattered, but vastly amused by this tactless, if astute assessment of her character.

'Well, there he is.' She indicated the thin, discerning face, surrounded by a stiff, expensive ruff. 'He was a clever old bastard.' She paused. 'You were doing pretty well in those days if you died of natural causes in your bed and not on the scaffold or with a knife in your eye.'

Chérif looked at Walsingham with fresh respect.

'Did he kill many people?'

'Doubtless. That was his job. But he probably didn't do it himself. He hired assassins. It wasn't a question of personal revenge. He was the head of Elizabeth's intelligence services, so he was protecting the state. Or at least I suppose that's what he thought he was doing.'

They met the royal killer's cold gaze, steady but enigmatic, fearless of judgement across four hundred years. Then Chérif said something that seemed quite extraordinary to Miss Webster, simply because he had never before used the discourse splattered across the television news, the easy words with unstable meanings.

'In Islam it is considered wrong to kill for a personal reason. You can only take life when it is demanded by jihad.' The fact that he had raised the subject at all was completely out of character. The seriousness of his tone was decidedly sinister.

'And what circumstances might unleash this jihad?' Miss Webster's lips curled in a sneer. He commanded her full attention and her feet stopped hurting.

'It cannot be for personal gain,' he said firmly, 'but to protect all the community.'

Miss Webster instantly smelt something odd, and inauthentic, about these comments. Who had he been talking to? Or, worse still, to whom had he begun to listen? Well, at least he wasn't arguing for honour killings and liquidating women who disgraced the family name. She decided to go no further in this business, or at least to shelve the discussion for the present. Suddenly, she employed those very English weapons: devious good manners and a rapid change of subject.

'I think there's a café downstairs,' she said sweetly. 'Shall we take the lift?'

Chérif had never been inside a large concert hall or an opera house. The local Edwardian gem where they had supported Carmen Campbell to the last thunderous echo had been his first indoor theatre. This auditorium was constructed on an entirely different scale. He gazed about the wondrous gilt cavern in amazement. It was like a sports stadium or the huge amphitheatres built for fights where Rocky and Spiderman took on the monstrous champion. The steep pitch of the circle and the balcony above was unnerving, but dramatic. Once seated you forgot all about it as the people around you grappled with their bags and programmes and climbed past your knees. He spied on the bustle in the orchestra and watched the bassoons tuning up, fascinated. Miss Webster sank back, exhausted. At last, let someone else do the work. Bring on the dancing girls. How could she have imagined that she could spend the entire day on her feet, trekking round shops and galleries and then be in a fit state for a two-hour drive home?

'Chérif,' she hissed, preparing the future, 'do you mind driving at night?'

'No. I'll drive home,' he volunteered at once.

She nodded with relief and began to decipher the programme.

'Bugger it. I chose Bizet's *Carmen* because I thought it would be sung in French and you'd understand it easily. But it's all in English.'

'Doesn't matter.'

And it really didn't.

Miss Webster could still retrieve the process of deliberation that had led her to choose *Carmen*. The fact that it ought, at least, to be sung in French was fundamental to her decision, but like many ordinary people who rarely go to the theatre, she discovered that she was also governed by unexamined expectations. Everybody knows the tunes. A torrid tale of adultery with a toreador. And the fast piece gets her comeuppance when he stabs her in the end. Pure melodrama with lots of colourful dancing, enjoy the show and lay your brain to rest. Also, it's mercifully short. One interval, we'll be out by eleven, home by one-thirty or two at the latest, buy the early edition of the papers somewhere on the motorway, sleep it all off tomorrow.

She had forgotten that Carmen is a gypsy, and that both the play and the opera conjured up untamed female sexuality, then mounted a genuine debate as to whether said sexual energy should be allowed to rove unchecked. She had forgotten that Carmen never was married to Don José, but that she seduced him away from his duty as a soldier and the good girl of the village whom he was destined to marry. And it had escaped her completely that the final murder was Don José's last perverted, desperate gesture, to salvage his lost honour; the murder of the woman who represents uncontrolled desire and embodies his enemy within, an erotic freedom which puts all his psychic structures in question.

The ENO production turned out to be sexually explicit and even somewhat shocking. The singer playing Carmen, a voluptuous Romanian soprano with a fabulous profile and a voice that took the roof off the back of your throat, lifted her luminous, terrifying eyes to the doomed soldier. Her sexual presence, musky with excitement, exploded across the stage. Miss Webster remembered that the Opéra-Comique, where Bizet's *Carmen* received its first performance, had functioned as a marriage market for nineteenth-century bourgeois French families. You hired a box, displayed your marriageable daughters in low-cut evening gowns, and interviewed prospective suitors in the intervals, all the business conducted in a respectable fashion – public, elegant, proper and discreet. This opera contained some scenes that actually took place in bed-rooms. No wonder the whole thing had degenerated into a public scandal.

Miss Webster was not and never had been a feminist. She saw no reason to court any kind of solidarity with the abject victims of this world. And she had no time for other women who whinged about their lot. As she grew older her misanthropy darkened, until she no longer bothered to be polite to anyone, of whatever sex, who dared to say anything stupid. She was therefore disposed to like the character of Carmen, whose intelligence manifested itself as self-interest combined with uncompromising honesty. Carmen's tendency to work the crowds, and the magnificent *habanera*, her chosen method of manipulating the mob, seemed not only understandable, but even rather brilliant. That gypsy stood up for herself, whatever the opposition; the first person she knifed was another woman.

Full support on that score too, the bitch had probably asked for it; and in any case the victim then demonstrated her worthlessness by scrabbling about for the soldiers, rather than fighting back. Whatever else she had done in her life that might be counted dubious, Miss Webster had never grassed anybody up, not even her hated sister.

But Carmen presented Miss Webster with an intractable problem. Sex. Do not think that Miss Elizabeth Webster had never been pursued, for many gentlemen had come a-courting and a-calling. Indeed, fifty years ago she had dominated the Young Farmers' Club Dance, with her light step, her sharp wit and her very pretty, narrow waist, which she showed off in all its slender glory with broad white plastic belts and great swirling skirts in rainbow rings or wide stripes. Her daring taste in patterned stockings and high-heeled shoes with naked toes titillated the county gossips. If Miss Webster had ever caught her convent girls wearing some of the shoes she used to wear they would have been whisked away to the abbess before you could even gasp Hail Mary. No man ever forgot her once he had seen her dance. And whoever looked at the frumpy young-er sister when Elizabeth Webster took the floor? Old men saw her dancing and remembered their youth, women gazed at her ankles, envious of her glamour, young men composed poems too sexy to be sent to their cold muse. Why, oh why had that lovely girl never married? A dozen suitors lurked on her doorstep, daring the quick flicker of her tongue. But Elizabeth Webster had no need to pro-claim her power over others, neither men nor women. She was too self-confident and self-sufficient for that. She didn't enjoy being kissed, and she wasn't interested in sex, which seemed like an interruption of her privacy, a state she valued more highly than anyone's company. Therefore she saw no reason whatsoever to continue doing it – this odd, fumbling activity that proved to be sweaty, interminable and inconvenient, full of slimy hazards and noxious smells. Alors non, merci. And so that door closed for ever.

Miss Webster suspected that Carmen's serial passions for soldiers and toreadors revealed a primitive desire to finger forbidden goods, to pull a prize that other women wanted. Her character proved infantile and naïve, and the woman no better than an uncontrolled child in a sweet shop. I'll have that, and that, and that – simply because I can. Miss Webster had never known the passion that flames and dies. She could credit neither its integrity, nor its force.

Chérif had, unfortunately, grasped both sides of the debate. He heard and understood the wretchedness of the abandoned Don José. Behold a man who has sold his honour for too cheap and transient a bargain. Miss Webster purchased the bilingual text of the opera in a pocket edition on sale in the foyer. She worried that Chérif might not understand the plot. But alas, this story was all too appropriate to the questions the boy asked himself, as his life unfolded in unexpected ways; he inhabited an entire landscape of ethical dilemmas about which Miss Elizabeth Webster knew nothing. Does a man have the right to desert his family and his duty for the sake of an illicit love? Surely he cannot cast aside a woman once he has chosen her? Does he have the right to do so should she prove unfaithful? If riches are spread freely at your feet, it is wrong, surely it must be wrong, to trample upon them? For the eternal ironies of art and its meanings, often so radically different for each one of us, sitting side by side in the dark, jostled dangerously between the old woman and the boy. The stage audience watching *The Most Lamentable Comedy and Most Cruel Death of Pyramus and Thisby* mocked a very different play from the one viewed by the audience in the stalls, who had just seen the jeering aristocrats snatched, by a hair's breadth, from a similar fate. How easy it is to mistake a bear for a bush.

Chérif peered at the words in the hushed gloom of the circle. He could just about make out the French.

L'amour est un oiseau rebelle
Que nul ne peut apprivoiser
Et c'est bien en vain qu'on l'appelle
S'il lui convient de refuser.

Love is a rebellious bird
Who cannot be tamed,
And you call to him in vain
If it suits him to say no.

Indeed, some of the ninth-century Arabic poets at the court of the Caliph, whose work he had once learned by heart, had said much the same thing. Chérif remembered the first scene, where the gypsy danced around the soldier, as he witnessed the last, the murderer circling the woman. How had it come to this? Don José had been warned.

L'amour est enfant de bohème,
Il n'a jamais, jamais connu de loi
Si tu ne m'aimes pas, je t'aime,
Si je t'aime, prends garde à toi.

Love is the gypsy's child
Who has never known the law
If you don't love me, I will love you
If I love you, be on your guard.

Here were the stated terms of engagement. Why could he not resist temptation? And yet, and yet. When can lies, treachery, betrayal, deception ever be justified? Herein lay Carmen's strength; she was treacherous and unfaithful, but she did not lie. If you are a servant of God then you must also be bound to the Truth, for all Truth is of God and is God. Therefore you must walk in the light of Truth. But what course of action should you take if Truth and duty part company, never to embrace again? What if you are party to a lie, and become that lie in your own flesh? How can you ever retrieve the Truth and the Light, as the world grows dark around you? Chérif sat mesmerised by the erotic opera, caught up in the drama, and the horror of this lesson, which remains one of the oldest commonplaces in every system of ethics that exists on earth. Strait is the gate and narrow is the way. One step aside and you aren't in the shit up to your knees, but to your neck.

He watched Don José fall off the path to righteousness with a mighty crash. But he also perceived, quite clearly, the magnetic power of the temptation in the gypsy's fabulous breasts and stamping feet. The Romanian soprano had trained hard at the Sevillanas, for as she led the women of the cast cavorting across the disordered tables, the serpent sex uncoiled its savage length and loosed its jaws. A suggestive *frisson* of applause rustled through the auditorium. The stage shook with their vibrating shouts, their skirts swirled, but only a glimpse of black-gartered stockings with a tiny rose tucked above the knee appeared, disappeared, as their block heels hit the boards in perfect time. One single glimpse was enough.

Chérif and Miss Webster were, even before they spoke, utterly divided concerning the moral of this opera, performed more often than any other in the world. Miss

Webster reconfigured Chérif's passionate internal debate between duty and desire as a battle between order and chaos, enlightenment and revolution. She felt the gypsy's power, but being able to resist it herself, with no difficulty whatsoever, did not recognise the need for anyone else to struggle like a madman caught in a noose. Elizabeth Webster had no sympathy with weakness or indecision. Choose the right. Do it. Only men who were idiotic and irrational loved unreliable women. And this one even admitted that she wasn't to be trusted. Carmen represented one of the *marginaux*, the parasites on the edge of society; she associated with contraband criminals and lived in caves. People like that never settle down in houses. But that doesn't give this soldier the right to stab her in the heart. She wasn't a hypocrite. She had warned her hapless lover; she told him the truth. *Si je t'aime, prends garde à toi.* That Don José, he was clearly useless as a soldier since he'd allowed her to escape in the first place. And someone stab-happy with a knife clearly had no business peddling a rifle. *Basta!* Case closed. She gathered up her programme and handbag and gave Chérif the plastic numbers for their coats and shopping.

'What a bloodbath! Let's run for it.'

Out in the cold air they escaped the crowds and turned up St Martin's Lane. They needed a taxi going north. London exhaled an evil, suffocating damp. Miss Webster put up her brolly and Chérif carried the bags. All the taxis had either disappeared or were already taken. They strode up towards Long Acre and Covent Garden, by which time the rain was streaming off Miss Webster's black umbrella. Water glossed the pavements; everything around them speeded up, hurrying for home. They stood on a street corner in the drizzle, weighed down by shopping bags, gazing to left and right. Exhausted irritation had taken hold of Miss Webster, who was beginning to niggle at the bit.

'What a dreadful melodrama, don't you think? Were we supposed to feel sorry for that drivelling soldier?'

Chérif had identified completely with Don José. He tried to discriminate, to judge carefully, as Miss Webster herself had taught him to do.

'He was wrong to kill her out of jealousy. She was not his wife.'

'And he'd have been right to kill her if she was?' This came out more sharply than Miss Webster had intended.

'He would have had more justice on his side.'

'Really? So if a man thinks he owns a woman he can slit her gullet with impunity? Is that what you learned in the mosque?'

Chérif tensed, pale with tiredness. His lips tightened.

'I didn't say that. No, we don't learn that.'

'But it's what you all think, isn't it?'

She was addressing a political system, which stretched across all continents, cultures and religions, and back through centuries of lost time. He was thinking of his own family and a small community of men and women who negotiated a precarious existence on the edge of the greatest desert in the world. But it was this hammering together of all Muslim men into an undifferentiated lump that cut Chérif to the quick. He knew plenty of men in his village who believed they had the right to beat their wives senseless if they so desired, on more or less any occasion. He also knew women capable of handing back every blow they received with interest. He knew men who adored their wives and called them 'la gazelle', and he knew one man who dreamed of his wife's face, her slim wrists, her huge widening eyes, whenever he was apart from her. He had seen that man brave the censure of the entire village and all his extended family for the love of a woman who was not of their people, and pass up all hope of blessings, paternal and maternal. He conjured up Fatima and Saïda, both women who owned land and property, and heard them laying down the law, criticising their husbands and their children, matriarchs in their own families. His respect for Miss Webster was undiminished, and he was appalled to realise that, for no reason he could grasp, he had forfeited her good opinion.

Miss Webster had lived in the kingdom of this world for nearly seven decades. She was a battle-scarred veteran of the sex wars, fought mostly in the workplace. Chérif had scarcely even begun to grasp the fact that he lived in a war zone, for all his life he had been protected by the armour of his identity as the eldest, indeed the only, son. The little that his family had was his by right. But, as in the case of Don José, and as Chérif himself well knew, with privilege came responsibility. He now feared that his judgement was unstable and his moral sense radically at fault. One night at the opera had made every bold decision – the entire discourse of passion, daring, sacrifice – appear not only foolhardy, but potentially fatal. The cards which foretold Carmen's death now seemed, in his paranoid imagination, to predict a cruel, even-handed destiny that would be his as well.

'If you wait here, I'll find a taxi,' said Chérif, his face blank. He propped the bags up against the wall beside her and walked away into the swaying darkness. Miss Webster bit her tongue and watched him go.

Now, Miss Webster wore glasses for reading only. Her long distance vision was perfect. She saw exactly what happened and was able to make a detailed statement to the police. Chérif was striding fast, directly into the rain. He was aiming for the lighted two-way street up ahead. The alleyway down which he marched was dark and narrow, no cars could pass there, no bright shops or bars illuminated the wet pavements, there were only deserted offices and locked metal shutters. But it was not pitch-black. Up ahead gleamed the streetlights, and overall the ubiquitous orange glare. She saw three men, two wearing anoraks with the hoods pulled up so that their faces were obscure, but the third, a black man, possibly of West Indian or African origins, was not wearing a hood, and he was the first to stop and address Chérif. They were too far away for her to hear what they were saying. The black man had his hand raised, pointing. The other two were white. She was utterly certain. They were not wearing gloves and she saw their naked white hands. One was smaller, fatter than the other, but they were both white men. The black man was the leader. They were all young, twenties maybe, no older. Their jackets were dark, dark blue or black, and one was a waterproof, because it shone slick in the rain. The black man's anorak had a white strip at chest height all round the jacket, and that glowed slightly yellow in the dark. One of the white men grabbed hold of Chérif and pushed him back so that he stumbled in the gutter and fell.

Then all three set upon him like a pack of dogs. Chérif lashed out at their legs, but was rapidly overwhelmed. One was kicking him in the kidneys and he curled shut like a seashell to avoid the blows. The scene unfolded in silence and slow motion. The boys tried to rip off his new jacket, his new black leather jacket with the Bruce Lee kung fu writing on the back. Miss Webster abandoned the shopping, cast the umbrella aside and pounded down the alleyway with the agility and panache of a woman half her age. She was wearing Hush Puppies, and the hiss of the traffic on the wet streets masked her approach. They didn't hear her coming until she fell upon them. She pitched into the fray, her handbag whirling like a cat-o'-nine-tails and caught one of the hoods a nasty crack across the cheekbone and the side of the face. The rapidity and ferocity of her attack was so unexpected that two of them sprang back, alarmed. Her short white hair and smart green coat with gold buttons seemed an unusual outfit for a street vigilante. Even more horrid and startling, a terrible squeaky yell resounded around the empty buildings as she joined battle.

'Get off him, you stupid bullies!'

The black man thumped her in the stomach and she collapsed, like a winded doll. Chérif had wrapped his arms around his head, but was struggling to get up. The stakes had suddenly evened up, if only slightly. Neither of them saw which of the three men produced the knife. He clearly intended to slice the whirling handbag free from Miss Webster's manic clutch, but failed and stabbed her arm instead, cutting into the green tweed, through the cardigan and silk blouse and deep into the thinning flesh beneath. She let out a screech, then a howl – but she would not let go.

'How dare you stab me!' She sat up, embracing the green leather bag, her best, the one with the gold clasp, as if it were a long lost child, and accused her assailant of those most fearsome crimes, dreadful to witness òn the streets of England: insolence and bad manners. 'Who on earth do you think you are? How dare you! Now piss off.'

And amazingly, like Banquo's murderers, they did, flying away into the rainy night. Chérif's face was masked with blood, a red curtain falling across his cheek and running down under his chin. A deep cut above his left eye furrowed into his black curls, which hung ugly and lank, plastered with blood and rain. Blood trickled round his left ear. They sat absolutely still in the gutter for a moment. The old lady spoke first, clutching her gouged arm.

'Oh dear. I've left all the shopping on the street corner. And my umbrella. Your face looks bad.'

And then they just sat there, side by side in the gutter, for many minutes, without saying anything, drenched by the thickening rain. Chérif clutched his head and lifted himself on to the edge of the pavement, the blood running over his fingers. Miss Webster remained in the gutter, where the water making for the drain had to find a path around her and flowed forth beneath her bent legs. Both stockings were ripped at the knees; through the shredded holes loomed a pair of nasty scraped cuts. She had been dragged forwards when she fell.

Then a man walked past them on the other side of the narrow street. He was so close they could have grabbed the edge of his raincoat, but he almost walked straight past them. People have a right to sit bleeding in gutters if that is what they wish to do. But something about the odd combination of the Arab boy and the respectable old lady did not look quite right. The stranger paused, stared, doubled back and crossed over to their side. He addressed Miss Webster.

'Excuse me. Are you all right?'

'No. I'm not all right. I've been stabbed. Would you be so kind as to call an ambulance and the police?'

Both Miss Webster and Chérif continued to sit there in the gutter, puzzled and shocked, frozen like the miraculous statues of silent saints who have just begun bleeding copiously to the Glory of God the Father. The stranger

drew away from them, pulled out his mobile phone and
began to summon the emergency services.

'Do you think that we can ask him to go and fetch our
shopping and my umbrella if they're still there?' whispered
Miss Webster.

'No. He's busy,' murmured Chérif. 'I'll go.'

Chérif had staggered halfway down the street before the
stranger began shouting. But neither Chérif nor Miss
Webster could understand what he was trying to say.
The rain fell heavily now, and they could not decipher
complex meanings, or make sense of what was said to them.
The world drifted away into the great desert distances,
upon a sea of blood. A miracle! The shopping, astonishing
to behold, leaned saturated against the wall, but bearing up
well inside its posh carriers. Chérif could no longer locate
Miss Webster's black umbrella, which had taken wing and
bowled away towards Leicester Square. The traffic surged
back and forth and people pushed past him, ignoring the
wreckage of his appearance. He set off back towards her,
aware that he could neither walk nor see straight, but not
yet fully conscious of the hammering pain that surrounded
his head like a helmet of wasps, waiting for the signal to
close in.

The emergency services were arriving just as he returned.
Miss Webster, still propped up in the gutter, was now
encircled by paramedics in luminous yellow jackets with
reflecting white bands. She could neither turn her head, nor
move, but his return did not go unremarked. The Good
Samaritan pointed straight at him. A moment later the
police surrounded him and grabbed all the shopping. He
yelped with pain as a blue man bent his arms into unnatural
positions.

'That's him.'

'Got him!'

'Well done, Missus, you clearly landed quite a blow.'

Chérif realised that he was being arrested just before he collapsed. His chief worry centred on the shopping. Where were they taking Miss Webster's new suit and towels? What about the shirts and trousers she had bought for him? The last thing he heard was Miss Webster taking on the Metropolitan Police with the same energy and venom with which she had despatched the unfortunate Mrs Harris.

'That's my lodger, you incompetent idiots. And take your hands off my shopping.'

Miss Webster's voice was the last thing he heard before the world closed down and the lights went out with a snap. It was also the first thing he heard, even before he dared to look up at the shabby green screens surrounding his trolley in Accident and Emergency.

'Oh good, you've come round. I told them that you'd lost a lot of blood. Can you see anything out of your left eye? It's practically closed over. We're in Casualty. I've had fourteen stitches. My knife wound is spectacular, but I think your injuries are actually worse.'

Miss Webster had switched to information overdrive, like an accelerating car. Chérif could not speak, or even acknowledge the fragile old woman perched beside him in a green plastic armchair. She wore one of the new shirts they had bought for him, a chunky tartan lumberjack pattern in brushed cotton. It sagged over her narrow shoulders. Miss Webster, bent on explanations, talked nineteen to the dozen.

'Do you realise that they tried to arrest you? They actually accused you of mugging me! Now, is that likely?

Surely if you'd fled the crime scene you wouldn't come back carrying the victim's shopping? Sorry about nicking your new shirt. Those swine wrecked my cardigan and my blouse was a dustbin job too. They nearly cut all your clothes off you, while you were out for the count. But I stopped them. Did the bastards get your wallet? Not the doctors, the muggers. Your new jacket's on the chair there. I've sponged off all the blood, otherwise it stains. I can't reach it. I won't be able to lift anything substantial with my right arm for at least two months. Dreadful. How are you feeling?

'You've got severe concussion. You'll have to lie quietly in a darkened room. Pity about the lights in here. Hospitals are always lit up like film sets. You haven't had any stitches and they didn't think you needed a transfusion. Apparently head wounds often look much worse than they are. You've had a brain scan. You were whisked off to X-ray while I was being stitched up. Your bruises are dreadful. And you won't be so beautiful for quite a while. But they patched you up with sticky tape. Your eyebrow looks like a quilt . . .'

'Thank you, Madame,' whispered Chérif. She leaned closer.

'What?'

'Thank you.'

'Whatever for? We didn't come out of that fracas particularly well, let me tell you. We should take a self-defence class. Did you see which one knifed me? The police will need you to make a statement. Several statements I expect . . .'

A white coat topped by a young face appeared in the booth, and gazed tenderly down at Chérif.

'Ah, welcome back to the world. Miss Webster, Chérif

must rest now. I'm going to give him something to help with the pain. And you can have a bit of a rest next door.' He helped her to her feet. 'Now, is anyone expecting you back tonight?'

'Not much night left, is there? And I've got my car running up a gigantic bill in Masterpark.'

'It's four-thirty. We've just cleared the backlog. Can I ring someone for you?'

Miss Webster made a swift set of decisions, demonstrating the fact that she was still in possession of all her marbles.

'We'll ring Chérif's girlfriend in the morning. If he's fit to travel she'll come down on the train and then she can drive us both back home in my car. I must get it out of that car park.' She turned to the doctor, her spiky hair flattened and dank, her face still smudged with blood, and bowed like a guest at a country-house party. 'I do hope that we haven't overstayed our welcome.'

The young doctor supported her down the corridor. He smiled.

'Actually you have friends in high places. One of the consultants in Cardiology came down to ask after you both. You were having your stitches done, but he spent quite some time with Chérif. He checked all the scans himself and he dealt with the police. I can't remember his name, I don't think I've seen him before. But he said you were one of his patients. He has very strange, damaged hands, very disturbing to look at and he doesn't wear gloves in the ordinary way. But he must do for surgery.'

'That's Dr Broadhurst!' cried Miss Webster, genuinely startled. 'So he runs a London practice too.'

'I don't know him. You'd remember those hands. I was told that he was over in Cardiology. He wasn't worried about you at all. He said you'd got through the worst, even though you were the one who'd actually been stabbed. And he didn't go to see you, but he sat with Chérif for ages, holding his hand like a father and looking very concerned. He gave us lots of instructions about Chérif and told the police to clear off. They'll be back in the morning.'

The doctor's buzzer vibrated gently.

'I have to go. Nurse, can you settle Miss Webster in the upstairs ward?'

'I want to clean my teeth and take out my bridge,' Miss Webster demanded.

But before the sound-proofed square of her hospital window lightened, and before she fell fast and deeply asleep, despite being confined to her back and left side, Miss Webster pondered the mysterious reappearance of the doctor with the ravaged hands. What an extraordinary coincidence! Miss Webster did not believe in coincidence. How could he possibly know who Chérif was? Why had he taken them under his wing? But, upon reflection, everything the strange doctor bearing chocolates from Switzerland had said to her seemed so odd, she began to suspect him of espionage. He had sent her off on that wild goose chase across the desert, when she clearly wasn't well enough to travel, and had practically caused her early death by terrorist attack. And now here he was, in this very hospital, minimising her stab wounds and having fits about Chérif's headache. She prepared a few contemptuous sentences with which to despatch the doctor should he reappear, and then sank back into blessedness and oblivion.

She was very much the worse for wear the next morning, her remaining teeth rattled and her tongue tasted bitter and dry, as if she had spent a week drinking. She felt for her handbag, which was carefully stowed under her pillow. It was Saturday. One of the assistant kitchen staff menaced her with orange juice and scrambled eggs. She looked at the watery offering, which came perched on soggy white toast, then wolfed the lot. A different set of nurses in green appeared to check her pulse, temperature, blood pressure and heart rate. They perused her notes, examined her bandages and delivered their opinions on stabbings and muggings.

'Why is it so silent?' she asked. Surely if they were in Accident and Emergency it should be all go – sirens and stretchers and transfusion sacs of evil red blood racing past on metal wheels.

'Everything happens downstairs,' smiled the nurse, 'you're up in the ward.' She pulled back the curtains.

Miss Webster found herself in a big square room. The patients along one wall were all wired up to machines that printed their heart rates into huge computers. Along the other wall lay a row of silent bodies, eerie and still, some bandaged, all motionless. A sealed glass box, staffed by white coats, projected out into the middle of the square, as if they were all taking part in some illegal experiment and the scientists feared contagion. She searched for Chérif and could not find him. A large black woman appeared and offered to help her wash. Miss Webster gratefully accepted the vast, outstretched arm. They set off down the ward.

'Who are these people?' Miss Webster glared at the row of calcified mummies.

'Those are the heart attacks,' explained the black woman, indicating the cyberbodies attached to the machines, 'and these are the suicides. Road accidents downstairs.'

Miss Webster scanned the rows of overdose coma cases; some sported bandaged limbs, just as she did. 'Why am I in with the suicides? I haven't killed myself. I was attacked.'

'But you weren't attacked by a car.' The black woman's laughing bellow echoed round the shower. There was still no sign of Chérif.

The hospital provided the basics: toothbrush, soap and flannel, even down to a pair of disposable knickers. Miss Webster returned clutching a plastic bag of bloody clothes and a row of swanky, fluffed towels with the John Lewis barcodes still firmly attached. The right sleeve of her green coat had been slashed to shreds. Did she want it back? Yes, she did. Miss Webster decided to convert the coat into a laundry-basket lining. Her jewellery – one gold chain, one gold watch, one gold ring, her father's wedding ring – was all stashed in a sealed plastic envelope down in Casualty, awaiting her signature for its release. She had never let go of her handbag and still clutched the thing to her chest like a pilgrim's offering. The green leather bore a few speckles of splashed water from the shower. Still no sign of Chérif.

Miss Webster re-emerged on the ward shortly after 8.30 a.m., compos mentis, perfectly clean, clear-headed, if a little bleary with painkillers, and prepared to join battle with all comers. She came upon Karen, standing over her disordered bed and staring round at the immobile coma cases and the fabulous machines with the leaping green dots. Karen wore her Biggles jacket and white airman's scarf. Her face, filled with alarm and misgiving at the strangeness of the ward, exploded into joy when she saw Miss Webster. She bounded forwards, then stopped in mid-embrace when she noticed the plastered arm.

'Oh no,' she gasped, 'the doctor said that you were OK and that Chérif was in the dreadful state. But you've broken your arm.'

'My dear girl,' Miss Webster cut to the chase, 'how did you get here? I haven't rung you yet. And I haven't broken my arm. I've been stabbed.'

'But you sent the doctor. He rang me on my mobile and picked me up at six o'clock this morning in his dirty great Merc. We came whizzing down in two hours flat. Mum's really worried. She wanted to come too, but the doctor said no, just me. And I'm to drive you both home if Chérif is fit to travel.'

'Who is this doctor?'

'He says he's your doctor. He's ever so nice and he filled me full of chocolates. I shouldn't say this − Mum says you mustn't make personal comments − but he's done something horrible to his hands. Like an acid bath or a fire.'

The ubiquitous Dr Broadhurst. Her life was being fingered in strange ways. Someone had interfered with her arrangements, anticipating the freedom of her decisions. She was not pleased.

'Have you seen his car? De luxe!' Karen wanted to talk about fitted CD players and real leather upholstery.

'Help me pack up my things, dear. Some of the shopping is still a little damp. There's a present for you in there. Oh no, we can't go yet. Here come the police.'

In the end Chérif came back to the cottage in an ambulance, his head wrapped in swaddling bands. He carried a box full of medicines; reading and television were both prohibited. And so it came to pass that Chérif missed most of the assault on Baghdad. Miss Webster gave him the radio and *From Our Own Correspondent* became electric listening. He metamorphosed overnight into a radio news junkie. Karen sat on his bed and read the foreign news sections of the newspapers and the polemical editorials, for and against, aloud to him. Karen's Mum came round with fruitcakes and marmalade. The church sent flowers and a huge card addressed to both of them, signed by some people Miss Webster had never heard of. Did they really all live in the village? I've been here thirty years and I've never heard of them. They've never spoken to me. How do they know who I am? Would you send a card to any old woman who'd been mugged?

On the nights of 27 and 28 March 2003, US forces devastated the centre of Baghdad. Miss Webster read out the reports from the last Western journalists lurking in the stricken city. The planes hurled down missiles known as bunker-busters, gigantic precision bombs which burrowed deep into the earth before exploding, rocking the buildings and sending huge sheets of glass cascading down the stairwells and into the streets. The two women surrounded Chérif with their comfort and their love, and read aloud together these *Arabian Nights* tales of slaughter and ruin. He cowered in the bed, spattered with half-healed cuts, looking like the victim of a shrapnel catastrophe.

When a tale is read aloud it hollows out an echo in the air that remains even after the reader falls silent. The word has been spoken; it is no longer elusive and imagined, as it always is in writing. It blossoms with the authority of being heard; the spoken word is greeted, witnessed. Miss Webster folded the paper when she finished describing the scenes in the Al Noor hospital, whence the dead had been carried from the place known as Al Sho'la. The hospital swelled with the sound of the women screaming out the names of their loved dead and beating their breasts in the formal gesture of grief. Their lament filled the small bedroom, thousands of miles away, where three were gathered together, and thundered across the damp English gardens, the woodlands, the rising meadows. Their voices careered against the hedgerows, the phone box, the bus shelter. Their cry disturbed the chickens in their wire pens, the cows brooding in their stalls and the dog fox, who paused, his brush lifted, in his furtive patrol round the edge of the copse. The rooks gathered in the great bare trees heard the women's cry, and flooded the spring sky with their dark reply and the gaunt flutter of their wings. Karen sat, white-faced, her back wedged against the wall, her stockinged feet hanging over the bed. Miss Webster, whose voice had remained carefully neutral and impassive, fell silent.

'Allah karim,' whispered Chérif.

'Will it come here?' Karen pleaded with the old woman to keep the war at a great distance, away from her mother and father, her little sister, her friends at work, the cottage on the edge of the woods and her beautiful Arab boy. But Miss Webster had no comfortable words for her to hear.

'War will always be with us in one of its several shapes. But it may not pass directly through Bolt or Little Blessington.'

And if it did?

Miss Webster imagined a medieval dance of death, the bishop and the king leading the knight and the merchant hand in hand past the church and the village shop, following the grisly black silhouette of the skeleton cut out of darkness, armed with the scythe and the hourglass. Karen pictured her new office transformed into a heap of glass and metal, the board with NEW INSTRUCTIONS reduced to a shredded mass of green baize and painted beading, the burning photographs of desirable residences curling at the tips in flame. Chérif saw the market square of Al Sho'la, the stalls, cars and people blown to bits, and then he saw the market at Tinnazit and his uncle buying rice. He saw the old scales, carefully polished scoops of brass and the row of different weights that the vendor wrapped in paper before packing them away at the end of his working day. He saw the brown paper bags in which the rice was sold. Behind the stall he saw the donkeys tied to wooden stakes, the smoke rising from the outdoor restaurants, which amounted to a row of benches and stones facing the baked hills. He heard the boys singing and saw them chasing one another in the dust. Everything was safe and ordinary, the market conducted its business to a noisy accompaniment of taped dance music and exasperated shouts. He smelt the hot wind from the desert. Then he clasped his hands before him on the sheets and looked up at Miss Webster.

'I know,' the old woman smiled, 'you want to go home.'

The weather turned warm. The apple tree blossomed and filled the garden with a dense, pink scent. The hedges and beds unfolded like a clenched fist, as if the earth, suddenly convinced that it is better to be generous, squandered her gifts. Chérif reclined on the somewhat mouldy sun-lounger and listened to tales of bombs descending on men and women shopping for flour and cooking oil, far away, in another world. On 3 April 2003 the Americans destroyed the electricity power grid which supplied Baghdad and the city fell into darkness. The marines captured the airport and were inside the perimeter within days. Chaos overwhelmed the city. The giant metal statue of Saddam Hussein buckled and fell into the midst of spitting, cheering crowds. The siege was almost over and the looting began.

★

A plain-clothes officer materialised upon the cottage door-step at around 11 a.m. about a month after the attack in London. He flashed a plastic card in a little leather wallet. She didn't have time to read the name, but suspicion flared in her stomach.

'Miss Elizabeth Webster?'

'Yes. What do you want?'

'We're following up the incident in London. I hope you're quite recovered.'

'I've had the stitches taken out of my stab wounds if that's what you mean.'

'Well, are you busy? May I come in? It won't take long.'

She stood aside and drilled the back of his light coat with her malevolent glare, then sat him down at the kitchen table and looked him over. He was about forty with calm, still features and he carried a battered foolscap folder which he laid out on the table before him. The stillness alarmed her. Never trust people who don't fidget. They are preparing to strike. She stood before the sink, refused to offer coffee as a bribe and said nothing. He gazed back, very calm, very settled. Probably a trained killer, thought Miss Webster and assessed the distance between her hand and the kitchen knives, nestled in the wooden block. She knew what it felt like to be stabbed. What would it take to stab someone else? He opened the file.

'And Mr Chérif Al Faraj, your lodger, how is he now?'

'He's at college.'

Who wants to know? All the hair on the back of her neck bristled and rose up beside the raised white spikes.

'I have your earlier statement to the Met. Here. Were you present at all times when Mr Al Faraj spoke to the investigating officers?'

'No. He speaks English perfectly well. He doesn't need me.'

'And is it your view, Miss Webster, that this assault in London was a simple attempt at robbery?'

'What are you getting at? They wanted his coat and my handbag. Isn't that robbery?'

This meddling intruder had invaded her territory. She should have felt more secure standing over him, but she didn't. Neither spoke. Neither moved. His stillness enveloped the kitchen.

'Miss Webster. Did you suspect or did you have any inkling that Chérif Al Faraj may have known his attackers?'

That took the biscuit and Miss Webster began a low rising growl.

'What are you accusing him of? Beating himself up? Egging them on? Damaging his own kidneys? Asking for it?'

Silence.

'Well?'

The visitor spread out his fingers, very pale, very steady, across the folder.

'I'll be frank with you, Miss Webster. Since 9/11 and the terrorist attacks against our embassies we are investigating all foreign students who originate from volatile states. Mr Al Faraj has been involved in a very odd incident —'

'Are muggings odd in central London?'

He shrugged.

'You say that he spoke to his attackers.'

'Yes, he did. He probably didn't understand them. It takes him a moment sometimes to get hold of someone's accent. But I saw what they were doing. They caught him off guard. They wanted his jacket.'

The officer changed tack.

'And has he any other friends here? Arab boys his age?'

'I'm not his keeper. He has an English girlfriend.'

'And does he attend the local mosque regularly?'

'If you'd done your research you'd know that there isn't one,' snapped Miss Webster. 'And for your information we fasted for Ramadan together. I'm not a spy and I don't like answering questions about my lodger when he's not here to defend himself. If you want to know more about Chérif, ask him.'

She folded her arms and set her jaw like an angry mastiff. The officer nodded and stood up. As he stepped out of the porch he asked one last question.

'Has Mr Al Faraj ever mentioned a woman named Carmen Campbell?'

The final question. They always withhold the most important question until they are almost gone. You're off your guard, relaxed. The interview is over. But this is the javelin they have come to throw. This is the thing they really want from their hapless informants. This is the moment of betrayal.

A poster on a theatre wall rose up before Miss Webster. She expected to see the singer, gleaming in her second skin of cobalt blue, but instead a terrified child, her head a mass of decorated dreads, glared, aghast, menaced, out of an inner dark. Carmen. Is it a crime to be passionate? Is it a crime to care? Is it a crime to love someone, no matter what she has done or what the law says she deserves? The glittering eyes of the fugitive begged Miss Webster not to speak.

'Carmen Campbell? Never heard of her,' lied Miss Webster with ferocious conviction, 'and no, he hasn't ever mentioned the name.'

She arranged her face into a fixed, unsmiling mask and

stared him down. He climbed back into his nondescript blue Ford, which was blocking the lane, without thanking her or taking any kind of formal leave, and drove off. He had not looked at her again. As she backed into the cottage her eye rested on the CD, perched on the television set, the spare and elegant face of the outlaw jazz singer met her with a half-smile of gratitude. And there in gleaming italic script she saw the name, *Carmen Campbell, Best of*. The plain-clothes officer could have been looking past her straight into the singer's eyes. Miss Webster took a hefty swig from the sherry bottle without bothering to find a glass, her knees and hands suddenly unstable and twitching. Anger had a galvanising effect on Elizabeth Webster, who always stood four square in a rage. She never trembled with fury. This was fear.

Chérif had lost a lot of weight and Karen voiced her worries. 'Should we take him to see Dr Brody or Dr Humphreys?'

'Nonsense,' said Miss Webster, 'he'll put it on again. Anyway, think of the Duchess of Windsor. She said you could never be too thin or too rich.'

Karen had never heard of the Duchess of Windsor. Miss Webster grinned.

'Don't worry, my dear. She was a naughty American lady who came to no good – living proof that you can be too stupid and too fascist. I think that we have to get Chérif out of this unhealthy country for a while. His exams end on 12 May and I've got tickets for the 14th. Don't tell him yet. It's a surprise. I want you to send an e-mail to Abdou, asking him to meet the flight. I'm hoping that you'll come next time when the house-buying boom is over.'

'I'd love to see where he lives. He doesn't talk about it much. He hasn't invited me.' Karen clearly brooded on Chérif's evasiveness. 'What's his mum like?'

'Tough, glamorous, ambitious. All good qualities in a woman, my dear. Cultivate them.'

Karen straightened her miniskirt in the dining-room mirror, which hung above the pine cabinet with the drinks and glasses. The mirror tilted forwards, thus giving her a rather splendid cleavage.

'That's right, you'll do nicely,' said Miss Webster. She had not mentioned the officer's visit to anyone else. She kept this troubling development to herself.

On 1 May 2003 George Bush declared that major hostilities in Iraq were at an end. They sat watching the looters destroying the offices of Saddam's administration. A cheerful man in a dirty T-shirt pushed a television away in a wheelbarrow. He made a V-sign to the cameras. Behind him huge coils of black smoke boiled out of the ravaged blank windows. Broken glass and wrecked vehicles littered the roadways. A masked gunman retreated behind a garden wall, then ducked down, his gun still visible, the single eye of the barrel pointed at the audience. The whole world held its breath as this new beast, its hour come round at last, reared its back on the streets of Baghdad. Miss Webster pursed her lips grimly and Chérif covered his face.

'It's not over, is it?' said Karen, desperate to hear the comfort of her own voice, sounding through the calm of an English evening in late spring.

'No,' said Miss Webster, 'it's not over.'

★

She was excited as they began their descent into Casablanca and peered out of the window at the approaching white lights. But Chérif appeared to hold his breath, ready for a plunge into the abyss. He sat braced for impact, his eyes tight shut. Faced with three thugs, all far larger than he was, and an inevitable bloody doom, Chérif fought back, clearly courageous to the point of being foolhardy. She diagnosed fear of flying, with possible added indigestion, and offered him a honey pastille. He refused.

'We'll have to change planes. It'll mean taking off again.' Chérif took the sweet. He didn't open his eyes, but sucked hard. The wheels bucked down on to the runway in a series of alarming bangs and one of the overhead lockers flew open. A few passengers grunted in alarm, but Chérif never flinched, as if gathering all his strength for some terrible trial that was awaiting him in the *salle d'attente*. His replies shrank to alarming monosyllables; his colour drained away.

'Are you sick?' Elizabeth Webster leaned over, genuinely worried on his behalf. Her own stomach, apparently made of tin, and trained on school dinners, never rumbled or wobbled, whatever the circumstances. Fearlessness defined her character, the danger of terrorism never entered her head, and as for planes – she no longer cared if they dropped from the sky in droves, like dead pigeons.

'Yes. A bit.'

'What are you afraid of?'

He turned to look at her, but said nothing. The flashing lights on the wingtips gleamed across the cabin windows. She returned his gaze, astonished by the upheaval in his eyes: fear, regret, anguish, tears. This last look bore the shadows of a leave-taking, an unmistakable farewell.

'Chérif! What is the matter?'

A babble of Arabic thanked them for choosing Royal Air

Maroc and everyone leaped out of their seats and dragged coats out of lockers. A baby began to wail, slightly off-key and at intervals filled with splutters, then he pitched his yells an octave lower, deepening to a terrifying rhythmic howl. Chérif got up and grabbed her hand luggage.

'Please, Madame Webster. I will carry that.'

She was in two minds whether to stop him in his tracks and demand an answer or to let it all go; but people pushing behind him down the narrow aisles, struggling into jackets and cardigans, grappling with enormous packets, nudged the moment aside. They were swept asunder until well inside the tunnel leading to the airport.

'Are you ill?'

He had recovered his colour a little. She relaxed, reassured.

'Well, I suppose you've only ever flown once before. Had you ever been in a plane before you flew to England?'

Chérif didn't appear to be interested in the question. He bought her a small plastic glass of freshly squeezed orange juice and then sat quietly beside her, silent and preoccupied. Elizabeth Webster was not a woman to plague other people when they were troubled by moods, but she did think it was peculiar that he seemed so uninterested in his own country. He had been gone for eight months. Why wasn't he excited to be coming home? The Moroccan immigration boys stared enviously and at length at his student visa. They even held it upside down. No one raised an eyebrow at his elderly female companion with the British passport. Miss Webster surveyed the dawdling groups around her, seized with an uncanny sense of déjà vu. I have sat here, at this very table, with an unknown black man before me and a newspaper spread out upon this spangled plastic top: CRIME OF PASSION KILLER

GOES FREE. She looked at Chérif. *What had he done?* She tried one more question.

'Are you missing Karen?'

He nodded.

'But you'll see her again.'

He shrugged.

Elizabeth gave up and dug out her airport thriller. The plot shifted around the question of doubles. One of the twins was a murderer. But which one? Only when they were climbing the steps on to a smaller jet, bound for the Sahara, and Chérif gave her his hand to help her aboard, did she notice that his flesh felt grotesquely cold. The air breathed warm and dry around them, the night perfectly clear. Far above, barely visible, a faint torrent of stars fluttered. The smaller transfer plane across the Atlas Mountains bulged full of travellers, and they found themselves wedged in between some chattering Spaniards, the only other Europeans.

'Chérif.' She gave him a prod. 'Is there something you aren't telling me?'

He shrank down into his Bruce Lee leather jacket, but did not speak.

'Are you in trouble?'

He nodded.

'Have you done something wrong?'

He raised his head and looked her straight in the eye, the grim film of guilt clearing away from his face. The truth tasted like fresh water on his tongue.

'Yes, Madame Webster. I have done something terribly wrong.'

'And are you going to tell me what it is?'

'*Mesdames! Messieurs! Attachez vos ceintures.*'

The flight lasted thirty-five minutes. Her ears ached. The

Spaniards gabbled. Chérif said absolutely nothing, but sat there rigid, like a man condemned, sentenced and awaiting the last walk towards the post against the wall and the firing squad. Elizabeth Webster's patience dissolved, her temper mounted alongside her increasing irritation. By the time the plane had cleared the Atlas Mountains, she was bubbling with rage. She hadn't brought him home to make him wretched, but to give him pleasure. Her anger simmered at his remote refusal to confide in her or to ask for her help. It never occurred to her to worry about what he might have done. In her experience young people generated crises of their own that expanded into mountains of potential horror, but which resulted in no lasting consequences. She was hot, tired, hungry. Her ankles had swollen. She wanted a shower, clean pyjamas and a bed sprinkled with rose petals. She guessed which one of the twins was the murderer and lost interest in her book. She gazed at the long line of runway lights far beneath them and prayed that Abdou had checked his e-mail. If he's not there, then that's the last straw and I'll end up giving this young man a clout round the chops. She glowered at the abject boy. The air hostess packed the Spaniards into their seats and removed their sticky apéritifs.

'Come on, Chérif,' she snapped – this too came out sharper than she had intended – 'let's face the music. Whatever it is. You can't sit on the plane for ever.'

They stepped into a different world, palm trees loomed out of the dark; she could smell water pouring on to the gardens in the hot night and stretched out her aching knees, delighted to feel the difference in her stride as she marched across the tarmac. Nine months ago I couldn't have carried a shoulder bag. Watch me now.

The first person she saw was Abdou, dressed in a

spanking new kaftan; his white turban swirled behind him as he dashed towards her.

'Madame!'

He arrived like a cartwheel, all teeth and arms and smiles. She noticed that his lopsided grin had been fixed.

'C'est grâce à vous, Madame.' He bared his fangs like an angry camel. 'Look! New teeth. First class work.' He actually kissed her hand.

Chérif was fishing their bags off the conveyor belt. Abdou hadn't seen him.

'Wait a moment. I'll get Chérif.'

'I'll get the taxi.'

They ran off in opposite directions. Chérif stood there, resolute at last, hung about with bags.

'Bon, je suis prêt,' he said, clear-eyed and calm.

'Well, thank God for that.'

She gave him a huge smile, turned around, and blundered into the open arms of a woman she hardly recognised. It was Saïda, done up like a wedding cake with her hair in a sparkling mound. Her eyelids were very black and her lips were very red. But as she reached out to embrace Elizabeth Webster, her face, at first glowing with recognition and joy, suddenly froze. She bellowed something in a language which sounded neither like Berber nor Arabic, sprang past Miss Webster, and flung herself upon Chérif in a lunge worthy of an army-trained, anti-terrorist security guard. She almost brought him down. Then she savaged his shoulders and began shaking him, screaming desperately all the time and giving him no chance to reply. He dropped all the bags. Saïda began to drag him towards the automatic doors, yelling. All the airport officials turned round to stare. An incident! Abdou reappeared in the gaping exit and let out a terrible shriek. The guards tapped their guns and began to approach the domestic brawl in case they were needed.

Elizabeth Webster gawped at the confusion and then retrieved the abandoned bags, which lay scuffed and over-turned upon the marble floor.

'Will someone please tell me what is going on?'

One of the security police marched up to Saïda and tried to stop her beating Chérif about the head with her handbag. She turned up the volume and the pitch. Her diatribe became a screech. Abdou joined in, echoing the main theme with a bass line. A crowd, which included the armed security guards, gathered around them all, peering and staring with fascinated concentration, as if they were following one of the storytellers in Djamma el Fnaa who had reached an exciting moment. Everybody ignored Elizabeth. It was as much pique at being linguistically excluded as baffled shock at this peculiar welcome which led her to mount her attack in booming colonial French.

'Mais arrêtez! Stop this at once!' She grappled with Saïda's hairdo. 'Abdou! Taisez-vous! Saïda, control your-self! Chérif, will you please tell me what on earth is going on.'

But before he could reply Saïda thrust her distorted face close to Elizabeth, her mouth open and screaming, her breath hot.

'This is not Chérif,' she roared. '*This is not my son.*'

6

DESERT

M iss Webster awoke the next morning beneath the anticipated flood of scented petals. The bed had not been turned down, as it would have been nine months before. Nor had the curtains been drawn. The small brass lamp covered in jewels and mirrors, subtly placed before the silk drapes, had not been lit to signal her welcome. Dust coated the shade. The invisible worm had entered the rose.

Miss Webster awoke in a rage. She had been abandoned at the airport. Chérif had vanished. Abdou had vanished. Saïda rushed forth into the night, her wails trailing in the air behind her like floating scarves. And so Elizabeth Webster was left to fend for herself. She found a wobbling trolley and rescued the suitcases. The boy had flung down his bag and never returned to reclaim his possessions or offer his assistance. The arriving airport crowds gathered to stare at her. Miss Webster did not like being the centre of invidious and disagreeable attention. Nor did she like joining the ordinary taxi queue and being leered at by a stranger, who offered to take her to a cheaper hotel that was just as good, but run by his friends. She did not like being forced to heave her own suitcases through gates and up steps. And she was alarmed and displeased by the cavernous sound of her own heels upon the marble squares as she staggered into the once scented and exotic halls of the silent hotel. The flunkeys no longer stood ready to wheedle and bow. A scruffy night porter handed her the key and left her to find her own way up in the darkness.

The world had changed in frightening and uncomfortable ways. Why should she suffer the change when she was not culpable? None of this emotional chaos was of her making. How could she be responsible for all this mayhem and disaster? And so she awoke upon the following day with the conviction that she had been dreadfully imposed upon and fearfully misused. Moreover she was now being held to account for villainy of which she was not guilty.

Miss Webster rang reception without preparing a speech. She was ready to overflow with lurid threats and righteous demands. She was not prepared to lie there in modified and diminishing luxury, fretting, enraged. Nine months ago Saïda's voice would have purred dedication, comfort, reassurance. Now the phone sounded in the void; the hollow chambers of marble and alabaster with decorated iron grilles across the arched windows, the small, low tables inlaid with mother-of-pearl, the fountains in which the mosaics glimmered and rippled, all crouched beneath her, empty and neglected. There was no one shaking cocktails in the Desert Rendezvous, no one watering the gardens, no one busy in the kitchens. No one answered her early calls for recognition and acceptance. The hotel had entered that long sleep which descends upon temples of tourism after the advent of the bombs.

Reception simply did not respond. Miss Webster's fury mounted and amplified like a tropical storm. She counted out her cotton shirts, plain colours, no frills. Were there enough for three weeks if the hotel laundry service had collapsed completely? Evidently not. She glared at Chérif's offending suitcase, one of her old ones, dedicated to the cause and filled with presents for all his family and friends. The thing cowered in the lee of the door, shrinking beneath Miss Webster's glare. He had packed his books and notes, reading for the summer, and all his new clothes. Where was he now? Or, more to the point, who had he become?

There is a thread of privacy in the English character. The best of us develop the habit of leaving well enough alone, of not interfering with our neighbours and inserting a handsome get-out clause to all our enquiries. A comment such as 'Off out, are you?' does not entail a demand as to where we are going. A cheery wave will do as a response, if you have no intention of revealing your destination. Miss Webster now realised how cleverly Chérif had played the game of evasion. He had never appeared to be secretive or underhand. He had never refused to answer direct questions, but his cheerful, good-natured politeness had exploited her determination never to pry. He had indeed spoken of his mother, and of Saïda, but always in such terms that left the doors open. They could have been two separate people. And now it was clear that they were. He's related to Saïda, thought Miss Webster, striding towards the staircase. She knew him as a child. Or she wouldn't have dared to box his ears.

The curving marble stairs emerged gloomy and obscure from the bowels of the foyer, despite the wash of gold light flooding the courtyard. The globes that were always aglow on the balustrades were now eclipsed by the half dark. Clearly the hotel was economising on electricity. The same hollow void she had encountered on arrival repeated her steps as she descended into emptiness. No lights shimmered in reception. The tall blue vase, which in more prosperous times always overflowed with lilies and gladioli, now stood stricken and empty; the computers' screens cowered, blank and dark. Miss Webster realised at that moment that she was the only person staying in the hotel. The world had been closed down around her.

'It's the war, isn't it? And the bombs.' She addressed the mass of keys with their heavy tags attached, hanging in the empty pigeonholes, with fearless contempt. Miss Webster's fatalism would never allow her to cancel her voyages, even if her journey took her into the heart of a civil war. She asserted her right to travel, one of those terrifying tourists who carry on with their sightseeing even as the streets explode into dust just behind them.

'Bonjour, Madame.'

Before her stood a young girl, dark-skinned, anxious, wearing a faded blue dress and sandals. Her hair was covered with a long black veil, tiny silver medallions stitched into the fringe. These tinkled softly when she moved. She smiled at Miss Webster, clearly wishing to please and to help, but uncertain of her welcome. The child could not have been more than twelve or thirteen, her breasts looked quite flat. The old lady replied in slow careful French.

'Good morning, my dear. Do you know where Saïda is?'

'Oui, Madame. Elle est partie.'

'Partie? Gone where?'

'To the desert, Madame. To see her sister.'

That's it. Miss Webster's deductions snapped into place. She's his aunt. Saïda is Chérif's mother's sister. So they are related.

'Was she very angry when she left?'

'Oui, Madame. Quelqu'un a volé tout son argent.'

'Aha!' cried Miss Webster with great satisfaction. So, Saïda has been robbed. And I know whom she has accused of theft. There was a pause. The girl stared at her, less nervous now, but wary.

'Est-ce que vous voulez prendre le petit déjeuner, Madame?'

'Yes, my dear. I would like that very much indeed.'

But Miss Webster was not prepared for the confrontation with the shrouded tables in the abandoned dining room. The scene of emptiness and desolation appeared yet more horrible because of the gleaming brightness of the morning on the terrace outside. The garden tables and chairs were stacked and covered with blue plastic sheets. It had actually rained a little in the night and the ragged lawns shone and bristled. The jasmine was still flowering, still fragrant, and a torrent of undisciplined plumbago, blue and white, surged down before the French windows. Miss Webster flung open the doors, chasing out the foetid, stale smells of old food and damp floors. She stepped forth into the bright day and placed one of the indoor tables in the long wedge of sun. She used a stray napkin to polish the grimy surface and installed herself before the windows. The gardens had been watered, but not clipped. She noted the ragged little lines of box and the red sand blown into a smeared tide line across the flagstones. The hibiscus loomed purple, scarlet and white, the torrid wash of colour masking the signs of deterioration and neglect. Miss Webster knew, without going to look, that the swimming pool was empty. She missed the low drone of the chlorinating unit. Beyond the florid row of fig trees with their huge leaves like deep green outstretched hands, the sky rose, gigantic, filled with the promise of morning. The green world of the garden, flowering out of control, reproached her depressed indecision. What is to be done? To whom should I complain? Miss Webster turned her back on the miraculous garden, blossoming in the desert, and stared into her empty coffee cup.

The little girl was standing beside her.

'Papa has gone to get the bread, Madame.' She offered fresh orange juice as a pallid excuse for failing in hospitality.

'Who is your papa?' demanded Miss Webster, but the child did not understand the question and stood before her, disconcerted and afraid.

'What does your papa do in the hotel? Apart from fetching the bread?'

'Oh,' her face cleared. 'Il est jardinier.'

He's the gardener. Miss Webster sank down before her orange juice, fearing a long wait for coffee, croissant, bread and sweet cakes. Here a huge buffet once towered up, on several levels and across many tables, a theatre of breakfast tended by white-uniformed actors with golden polished buttons. A woman devoted to fresh pancakes cooked them for her waiting plate. There lay sliced fruit resting in beds of ice, white roses everywhere, palms and banana leaves laid out with brioche, jams and sweetbreads, rosettes of fine charcuterie, folded ham arranged in patterns, and rondelets of goats' cheeses for the Germans, cakes of all sizes, glistening with icing sugar, topped with crushed nuts and almonds. Miss Webster contemplated the barren tables and the departed feast. She fished another book out of her red rucksack. This was not the airport novel, which she had, appropriately enough, abandoned at the airport, without investigating the conclusion.

Miss Webster was now reading a satirical novel entitled *Das Parfum* about an eighteenth-century murderer. She read very little modern German writing and had always preferred teaching French classics at the school. But *Das*

Parfum fulfilled a different, stranger need. It had been a huge European bestseller during the 1980s. Miss Webster always ignored bestsellers until they were nearly twenty years past their best before, sell-by date. Her logic was this: if the tale survived the hardest test – that of immediate contemporary time, and was still there re-jacketed, garlanded with quotations of praise and decorated with red stick-on medals, 300,000 copies sold, then the effort would probably be repaid. Yet anger and disappointment usually awaited her, and this odd quirk became a trial of her temper and patience. She read on, in irritated discontent. What had seemed clever and slick to an audience ravished by capitalism and greed, a moral tale of fatuous mass hallucination, no longer intrigued and beguiled. Malicious cunning and scented duplicity seemed cold and out of place in the world transformed since 9/11, a world where the smiling outsider embodied the new threat, those smooth and handsome Arabs with their plausible stories and their faultless manners. Miss Webster gripped the book more firmly. The threat might stroll through your door, late one autumn night, pretending to be other than he is. Why fear the hunched mass of immigrants, waiting outside housing offices, cringing and alarmed? Or the hook-handed mullahs preaching up a storm in the leafy London streets? Their game is clear enough. And why read this long-winded, outdated bestseller that warns us all about self-delusion and unhinged desire? Why blather on about surface scents and naked virgins? The world we know is melting in explosions and black flame from the burning oil rigs. The tale in her hands seemed self-indulgent, misogynist and old-fashioned.

And yet.

It is a rare thing that has come to pass if a book fails utterly to speak.

The little girl offered a small plate of cakes and dried apricots. The coffee proved disgusting. Miss Webster ignored the empty dining room and went on reading.

Amidst the otiose and florid prose lingered one passage where the creature, Grenouille, the frog, his very name a lazy and irritating joke, wandered the Cantal Mountains in search of unpolluted air. He withdrew from all society and hunkered down on his bed of straw in the deepest bowels of a cave. Miss Webster suddenly saw herself again, as she had been just over a year ago, subdued and inconspicuous, locked away at the end of a green lane, swathed in roses and honeysuckle, her body rigid with resentment, clamped fast within the English dream. She had come to a dead halt many years before her heart, dying of cold and isolation, had flared its own warning and ceased to beat. That's right, sighed Miss Webster, if you care for no one you can never be betrayed.

She swallowed her bile and her orange juice and laid her novel down. She had ventured too far into the Garden of Allah to turn back now.

'I must go out.' She addressed the empty tables. 'I must find Abdou and go out into the desert.'

'Vous désirez, Madame?' The young girl appeared again at her elbow, wielding a coffee-pot that looked like a medieval siege engine.

'Is that thing full?'

'Oui, Madame.'

'Then you'd better give me some more. With no chicory in it tomorrow morning. Do you understand?'

'Oui, Madame,' stammered the hapless maiden. She sensed, correctly, that Miss Webster was back on the warpath.

★

217

'*Ici les Grands Taxis du Désert. Je suis absent pour l'instant. Veuillez laisser un message après le bip sonore.*'

'Abdou. This is Elizabeth Webster. Please ring me at the hotel as soon as you get this message.'

Miss Webster sat upon her bed upstairs, changing her shoes; then the shouting began. At first the gardens slumbered, filled with silence, harbouring nothing but birdsong and a light wind. The morning cool slowly burned off the jasmine and the watered grass. She unpacked her yellow hat and scarves, hesitated over her suncreams. Someone rang the porter's bell at the gate. She remembered that bell, clanging in the hot night, when she had first come to the desert. It had been a signal for the dozing children to pounce upon their next victim. There was a pause. She waited. She listened. Then a dreadful stream of unintelligible invective poured out across the distant gardens. Miss Webster stepped on to her balcony to get a better look, but could not see the gates. Above the seven palm trees at the edge of the old walls she could see the rocky frontier of the desert, where all green and living things ceased to be. She felt the sudden quick breath of hot wind upon her face. The shouting rose half an octave.

It was a fight between a man and a woman, possibly in not quite the same language. The exchange of insults became ever more furious. Miss Webster was puzzled. This was not a country where women spoke their minds in public. As if in answer to her question, a young voice, high and clear, yelled in perfect English:

'And fuck you too, you shitty Islamic git!'

Once more, and the implications were not lost upon her, she heard an English voice. Miss Webster snatched up her

hat and raced downstairs. But by the time she reached the
hotel entrance the battle of the gateway was over. A man
she had never seen before stormed through the gardens, still
fulminating, his nostrils dilated and his face purple.

'C'était qui à la porte?' demanded Miss Webster. The
man, whom she guessed must be the gardener, was wearing
a baseball hat that was slightly too small for his bald head.
His skin swelled and glistened beneath the elastic. A vein
throbbed in his throat.

'J'ai mes ordres, Madame,' he bellowed. 'I've been told
not to let the Black Witch into the hotel. Not under any
circumstances. Ever. The woman is accursed.'

'The Black Witch?'

Events had taken an unexpected supernatural turn. Miss
Webster surveyed the enraged gardener. He was probably
younger than he looked, but in the huge O of his mouth
the incisors were blackened and many teeth were gone. His
tattered blue jacket vibrated with aggression.

'Does the Black Witch come from England?' she enquired politely.

'She comes from hell,' roared the gardener.

'Well, that may be where she's going, but it cannot be
her country of origin.' Miss Webster delivered this reflection in perfect measured French. The gardener stopped in
his tracks, confused. His eyes bulged.

'She wants you!' This final explosion proved too much
for him. He fell silent and stood biting his lip.

'So this young English girl asked for me and you refused
to let her in?'

He immediately began raving once more.

'She is a witch. Une sorcière, je vous dis! She will
ensorcellate your eyes and steal away all your money, so
that you have pains in every limb.'

Miss Webster had never heard of a financial loss that resulted in osteoarthritis, and decided that the oddness of this exchange was due to a lack of linguistic expertise on both sides. The gardener made a perfunctory bow and stormed off in the direction of the kitchens. Miss Webster peered through the iron gates. There was no one waiting outside. The gates were now padlocked. No one could get in. She had become a prisoner.

She returned to the gates at midday and gazed out into the gathered heat. Adbou was still stubbornly silent, his mobile switched off, and she had already filled up the tape on his home answering machine with pleading and threats. There were the seven palms, steady and rustling in the hot wind. There lay the desert, outstretched before her, shimmering ochre and red, the heat haze gently veiling the shelf of rocks. At her feet were little pools of sand swirled into whirlwinds by the desert's breath. A gaggle of ragged cacti peppered with black plastic sacks fluttered on the rim of the dirt roadway. No one loitered beneath the walls. The Black Witch, whoever she was, had left no trace upon the sand. The begging children, once hidden in the shadow of the oleanders, had also abandoned their posts. The vast eerie silence, which spread like a stain through the dusty air, swept over her. She leaned against the gate and accepted the great stillness. The silence was almost solid. The wind brushed past her like a great cloak, rimmed by the blue heavens. Rock, scrub, dust and wind lined the silence and emptiness. The great silence presented itself neither as frightening, nor comforting; it was simply there, endless, present, shouldering against the old walls of the kasbahs, the green minaret of the fourteenth-century mosque, and the white block buildings of the old colonial town. Here, clasped in the desert's embrace, the town wavered and shimmered in the rising heat. Miss Webster decided to act.

She drew forth her new mobile phone and began, carefully, laboriously, just as Chérif had taught her, to compose a text message. ABDOU PICK UP HOTEL TOUT DE SUITE. DEPART DESERT. TOP FEES PAID. WEBSTER. His mobile number was already in her directory. Select. Send. TOP FEES. That'll get him here faster than rubbing a lamp three times. If there aren't any more tourists, he'll be back. Miss Webster decided to ignore his defection at the airport. This is a crisis situation, but I'll get to the bottom of it all. She strode back towards the hotel. Hardly had her feet touched the first step leading from the cupola into the hallway, when a trumpet fart from behind the walls and a dim roar shook the iron grilles. A cloud of red dust and a thump announced the arrival of a battered, unmarked black Citroën. The windsurf boards with bottle caps, which had proved their salvation on the night of the bombs, were still there on the roof rack, tackled up like spare masts. As the dust cleared Miss Webster beheld Abdou, who surged forth from his taxi, still wearing the exotic white kaftan of last night's debacle, and commenced a desperate clamour at the gates. He managed to sound like a crowd intent on riot.

'A miracle,' she murmured.

'Madame Webster,' shrieked Abdou, who had spotted her on the steps, 'come away to the desert. Very urgent!'

As she settled among the shiny orange cushions clutching her bags, hats and veils, Elizabeth Webster realised that she had nothing whatsoever left to lose. Chérif's suitcase lurked behind her, safely stowed in the boot. If Saïda accused her of conspiracy to defraud and deceive, Miss Webster's incorruptible innocence would withstand any amount of interrogation. Now she really had undertaken the classic task of the detective, finding out not only who done it and why, but what they had done in the first place. Beneath her shuddered the unsteady diesel roar of the taxi, and before her, the immense expanse of space and time, the great wilderness of eternity. What profit a man − or indeed a woman − if she lose her life, a life passed in pique, irritation and defensiveness, and die with no heirs and a great deal of money in the bank? Stride forward into the light; get to the bottom of things.

'Thank you for answering my text message so promptly, Abdou.' He must have been parked in the palm grove.

'What text?' snarled Abdou. 'I didn't get any text. I've been sent to fetch you. The English woman wants to speak to you and the hotel won't let her in.'

'Ha! The Black Witch!' Miss Webster produced her trump card. She was already making discoveries. Abdou actually turned round in his seat, taking his eyes off the potholes, and gave Miss Webster a flashing tour of his new teeth.

'Don't call her that,' he growled, 'that's a bad name. She's a good woman. As good as you. As good as anyone. Just not as rich.' He turned up the pounding music.

Miss Webster held her tongue. She was captive amidst the cushions and Abdou's response gave her pause for thought. Clearly there were two sides to the affair and the dramatis personae of the desert town had placed their bets. The gardener had lined up alongside the hotel, Abdou had pitched in with the witch. They lurched past the last shacks outside the walls and rumbled away into the hot, windy spaces. The rock cliffs rose up about them and the red earth paled in the glare. It was the time of day when travel is inadvisable. Miss Webster cradled her survival supplies: two large bottles of still mineral water and two packets of dates. She pulled out her map to determine their route, steadied her dark glasses and arranged her white veil across her face to avoid breathing red dust. When Abdou glanced at her in the mirror she looked like *The Mummy Returns*, in the monster's initial gruesome phase, before he gains enough power from his victims to regenerate completely and to take on human shape.

She gazed out across the massif. This resembled a lunar terrain: huge blocks of hulking stone flanked the battered road. The earth had been reworked in ochres, reds and golds, but the heat drew the colours together into a shimmering watery curtain that hung before them, sheathing both the desert and the road. They lumbered round a high hairpin bend to the roll of 1970s disco music. Miss Webster looked out into the shining, unstable landscape before them and saw, far below, the immense empty space into which unfurled the giant palm groves that marked the valley of the Drâa, a long snake of green in the lost world of red dust and dark rock.

'It rained,' shouted Abdou, repenting of his over-hasty rebuke and implied defence of sorcery. He had just noticed that his text message promised TOP FEES. 'The date palms are growing green again. This is the first time we have real rain in six years!'

'Really!' Miss Webster shouted back. Peace and unanimity were re-established in the taxi.

For here in the austere waste of dark sand and red rock was proof of life, the promise of prosperity, the massive palms, the flood of green. Miss Webster wanted to give thanks out loud, but restrained herself. They swooped down the mountain road and at every turn she saw the long scarf of green draped across the land. They had been driving for three hours. She had drunk both litres of water and eaten one packet of dates, but lunch had simply never happened. Miss Webster rocked inside that light-headed feeling that she had left all ports astern and was now facing the ravaged beauty of a world in which all frontiers had disappeared. Anything could happen and probably would.

'Shouldn't we eat something, Abdou?' she roared above the music.

'Soon, soon, soon,' came the cry from the taxi driver as they pounded onwards.

As she had no idea where they were going she remained uncertain as to whether they had actually arrived when they turned down a narrow earth road between mud walls. On the rocks above the palm groves she saw the whitewashed dome of a saint's tomb – the defunct local marabout.

'This is Amazrou,' said Abdou. Small vegetable gardens flourished beneath and between the date palms. On either side were little gullies filled with rushing water which smelled fresh and strong in the heat. She noticed a heron rising between the palm trees in a slick flash of white and grey. They came out where the river should have been, but no longer flowed. A wadi of rounded stone and fine sand crumbled beneath the taxi, which negotiated a bumpy descent into the dry riverbed, then a perilous climb up the opposite side through loose sand. Abdou urged the car on with the same wild noises he used for the camels.

They crunched to a halt before a small blockhouse built of stone with blue shutters, but no windows. The roar of the engine died and Miss Webster became aware of the wind tugging at the taxi's rattling frame, licking sand against the doors, pulling her veil tight against her face like a death mask. The violent light slowly eased against the earth, and the white shroud of heat mellowed into gold. Miss Webster climbed stiffly out of the taxi. A child carrying a baby hovered in the open doorway, staring. Infant and child were both encircled by large black flies. Around the house a broken-down wall enclosed some gnawed acacia tees and browning rushes with depleted feathery crests. Behind the building, inside the derelict walls facing the desert, stood a giant barrage of date palms, which acted as a windbreak. There were chickens ruffled up against the persistent rushing gusts, nestling against the hot stones. An intrepid band of goats cantered loose in the scrub; they all paused from foraging to stare at the strangers, their eyes blank and golden in the changing light.

'C'est ici,' said Abdou, offering his arm. Her sensible flat shoes sank into the sand. Abdou harangued the child for a moment in a version of the southern Berber dialect. Miss Webster knew how to say no, yes, please, thank you, and I want that done now, in Tashelhaït, but was incapable of following Abdou any further than the greetings.

'They are out with the camels. I put the car in the palm grove and ring them on the mobile. You sit down and wait.'

He placed a chair for her in the shade of the overhanging terrace, which ran alongside the length of the house. The floor was made of mud tiles. A worn bench hugged the wall beneath the shuttered windows. Then Miss Webster looked up. Above the main door, gazing outwards into the desert, hung the only object that wasn't functional, the only thing that could be described as decorative, and therefore redundant. The fixed mad eyes, which in her own sitting room always sought her own, looked past her, outwards, into the endless void of blown sand and giant rocks. It was the green man. The girl with the baby took up her post to study Miss Webster's every move. She too gazed up at the strange, displaced image from the Gothic vault of a medieval English cathedral. For here the icon seemed undomesticated, savage, his original power restored. Miss Webster inspected the children; neither was terribly clean, but they had no immediate signs of ringworm, jiggers or lice. They were dark-skinned, with the same vast brown eyes. The baby, of uncertain sex and very tiny, wore a nappy tied at both hips, and was draped in soft cotton folds which resembled swathes of bandages. It sucked at a grimy bottle, filled with a murky fluid. The girl ignored the flies and nibbled her middle finger, expectant.

'Bonjour,' said Miss Webster and lowered her veil for added privacy.

The child did not reply, but continued to stare at Miss Webster's clothes, veils, shoes, bags, hat. She placed the baby in a rush basket. The thing gurgled and kicked, but did not cry, just stared at Miss Webster. They all settled down to wait. Miss Webster now felt safely sheltered from the hot wind and began to measure and assess her surroundings. Palms, trees with thorns, an old wall in need of repair, a well. That must be a well. It is a round font built of stone with a wooden crossbar and a chain that dips out of sight. She noticed the iron pump and the wheel. That's why they live here. Water. There is water. She looked up at the rustling palms with the scabbed trunks and then out towards the desert. There, beyond the farm wall, the great ocean of silence rolled in, the sand breaking like spray against the stones. At first she saw nothing but the rocky slopes marking the river's death, but beyond that, now becoming clear as the light deepened against shadow, were the changing, endless dunes. The child scrabbled in the dust at her feet, patient, uncomplaining. The baby dozed, its feet still twitching. Miss Webster slumped down in her chair. The silence and emptiness that leaned against the rocks and palms hollowed out the sky, cradled their bodies against its vast indifference. She sensed the stealthy, breathing thing, animate, gigantic, which overflowed the great spaces of the desert, nuzzling against the dilapidated walls. It was tangible, so close, that she could touch it, were she to raise her palm and press against the air. With a sigh she closed her eyes and shuddered, confronting the immensity of absence and soundlessness. The silence folded round her and the waste spaces of sand and rock slid open to receive one more.

When she opened her eyes again she was aware of someone close, present, attentive. The children had disappeared, but someone was standing behind her. She looked down into the sand at her feet and saw the shadowed outline of a woman. There was the *foulard*, blowing sideways in the gentler evening wind, the sharp waist and wide skirts; there was the image sketched clearly in the sand before her. She looked up and expected to see the two young men, Moha and Chérif, with their arms around one another, standing under the palm trees on the edge of the desert. She was looking at the photograph. She sat up straight and turned around.

Before her stood a young black woman wearing the traditional layered costume of the desert people. The top of her head and her ears were covered by her veil, but a heavy mass of dreadlocks hung over her shoulders. Small seashells were stitched into them so that they rustled and shifted with

227

a life of their own. Miss Webster looked carefully at the dreadlocks. The cowry shells were held in place by strange glass beads and tiny silver death's heads. No wonder she was called the Black Witch. The woman was out of breath.

'I ran all the way back,' she gulped, 'as soon as I got Abdou's call. I've got a message for you from the boy you know as Chérif. He says he's really, really sorry.'

The voice was pure South London, but Miss Webster only recognised its origins from sitcoms on the television. No one was black in Little Blessington and the only black girls who had ever attended the convent were two Nigerian princesses who could afford silk underwear. This encounter was therefore an unusual occasion for Miss Webster. She made herself more comfortable in her chair, did not offer to get up or shake hands, eyed her hostess suspiciously, and then said, 'Perhaps you could begin by explaining who he actually is.'

The woman squatted down on an upturned blue bucket.

'My name's Carmen,' she said.

'I'm well aware of that,' snapped Miss Webster, whose heavy guns were now loaded and aimed. 'Your name is Carmen Campbell and if I'm not mistaken you're wanted for murder.'

'Oh,' said Carmen, and gave a huge shrug of incredible relief. 'I don't have to explain. You already know. Is my picture up everywhere?'

Both of them imagined a WANTED poster, with a desperate black and white image ringed by slogans. Have you seen this woman? Huge Reward. Dead or Alive.

'No,' said Miss Webster, ice cool, 'don't flatter yourself. It isn't up everywhere, but I spent an evening staring at your face last year. At a fund-raising benefit concert. To pay for your defence.' Her tone was scandalised and incredulous.

How could she have spent an entire evening listening to unsuitable music in support of this dissolute wastrel, who lived in a desert and bumped off her boyfriends?

Carmen beamed, inordinately pleased. The fans were rallying round after all.

'Do you want to hear my side of things?'

'No. It's your business, not mine. I want to know who Chérif Al Faraj actually is. And then I want to visit the Alimentation Générale and the Hôtel des Voyageurs in Tinnazit. Perhaps you can help me on both counts by being quite frank and then calling Abdou back again.'

Carmen gazed at Miss Webster, astonished and a little annoyed. She did not like Miss Webster's insinuation that being a murderer was not especially interesting or that she was marginal to the affair in hand. She shrugged.

'Oh, well. It's all easily explained. Chérif and Mohammed are cousins. Chérif is Saïda's son and Moha's parents run the store and the Hôtel des Voyageurs in Tinnazit. I'm married to Chérif and that's why he didn't want to go to England. Saïda doesn't like me. She thinks I've ruined his life. One of the reasons she wants to send him away is to separate him from me. But we've got a baby now. And work. Moha did want to go and study in England. So he went instead. That's it.'

'That's it? That's it?' Miss Webster lifted her veils and rose up like a resurrected Ouija queen. 'What do you mean, that's it? You stole money from Saïda, tricked her into squandering all her savings on her sister's son, imposed upon me with a pack of lies – and you think that you can solve the whole thing by telling me they just changed places? It's illegal immigration, although that's not important. You told lies. All of you. A pack of lies, with intent to deceive! Do you realise what you've done?'

Carmen clearly didn't. The implications of the affair escaped her entirely. She crouched on the bucket, staring at Miss Webster, baffled by her rage. Then she thought how wonderful it was to be talking proper English with someone else from England, even if they were having a row. The fact that they had lied seemed to her to be the least of it. The money, she had to admit, was a bit of a problem. But it wasn't exactly stolen, just recycled. They had divided the funds. Half of it went to Mohammed to fend for himself in the white North, and the other half had been the down payment on the farm, which now gave them a living and a home. Chérif, the real Chérif, ran a string of eight camels and two 4 × 4 white jeeps. He was building up a highly successful safari business. He was the only desert bivouac service in their sector that had survived the bombs, and now he employed everybody else. His trans-Sahara caravans carried precious products other than tourists, but when they travelled, armed to the teeth like real bandits, they used the tourists' protection and security as a handy excuse. So far no one had been killed in any shoot-outs.

'I'm really sorry we upset you,' said Carmen with uncomprehending but unfeigned sincerity. 'So is Mohammed. So is Chérif. You may not have known you were doing so, but you've been a huge help to us. You've made all the difference.'

Miss Webster failed to grasp the fact that Chérif was not one, but two people. Nevertheless, she heard the genuine regret in the apology and her heart softened.

Why is it that a lie in which we have believed, or passionately wished to believe, so disturbs us when it is revealed to be untrue? We build our worlds around the truths, however small, that we exchange with one another. We act according to the information in hand. If we tell one another that we care and will not be party to anyone else's bitchiness or abandonment, then we trust that it is true. We believe that those whom we love will not betray us. Miss Webster's life had been transformed by her visitor. She confronted illness and despair, her defences breached at last, and then a stranger came out of the night, not to help her, but asking for help. Her energy, wit and sharp tongue had been needed again, marshalled in his defence. She had someone else's battles to fight. She could not afford to lay down her arms and stretch out in sculptured stone upon her tomb. She had been called up to fight. She had gained a friend. If someone offers us his name, we make that leap of faith, and believe that he is who he claims to be, and that we are no longer strangers. He had named himself Chérif. The lie disturbed Miss Webster to the roots of her being, but not because this revelation was unexpected. She had known that Chérif could not, or would not, tell her everything about himself, but she had wished him to be real and the story to be true.

'Well, it's all over now,' said Carmen. 'He can't go back and finish his studies in England and we're in financial shit up to our ears.'

'So is Saïda,' retorted Miss Webster. 'How much of her money did you purloin for your own purposes?'

'Well . . . ten grand. It was at least that much in the end. But we weren't to know that the tourists would vanish overnight out of fright.'

'Dozens of people were blown to bits last September.'

'Yes, but we didn't do it. I didn't do it.'

'You did for one man, however.' Miss Webster sniffed at Carmen's slightly too earnest righteousness.

'I think it's better to kill someone you know,' said Carmen. She leaped up from the bucket and stalked in a dusty circle, her dreadlocks shaking, the light deepening around her. The jingling clink that accompanied her every move disturbed Miss Webster. She watched the shifting image in the poster come to life at last.

'It's not right to kill anyone at all,' returned Miss Webster, 'for any reason.'

But she wondered – in spite of herself. How many would die in this war, this needless cruel war, the invasion that opened the gates, so that every man's hand was against his brother? In whose name was the war being fought? And for whose benefit? In a world of random murder was it more dreadful to kill 3,000 people and then oneself, like the 9/11 bombers, or just one person, the man you had once loved, as Carmen had done? The widow of a man who had died in the plane that crashed into the second tower had said of his killers, 'I think they were very brave men. I don't share their beliefs and they have taken the man I loved most in the whole world, but they were brave men. They were prepared to die for what they believed.' Miss Webster said none of this aloud and so her subsequent outburst was very startling.

'May God preserve us from madmen and their intimate convictions. Every time we turned on the television in the last six months we were presented with a maniac muttering, *it is the cause, it is the cause, my soul. Let me not name it to you, you chaste stars.* If a man is prepared to kill and die – or send other men to their deaths – for some dotty principle, it tells you nothing whatever about the worth of his cause, only how deluded he is on the strength of his feelings.'

Carmen couldn't be bothered to make sense of this. They didn't have electricity in the desert and never watched the television. She just pursued her own line of argument.

'The man I killed was the one with the feelings. I didn't plan to kill him. It wasn't premeditated or in cold blood or all that. I just knew he would threaten me and that he meant it – so I thought I'd be ready for him.' Miss Webster contemplated the ethics of slaughter on a world scale and Carmen rehearsed a scene she relived day after day.

'He said I was trash. He accused me of fucking other men.'

'And did you?'

Carmen then realised that she was on trial. Miss Webster, like cunning Old Fury, was both jury and judge. She was already considering her verdict on the case.

'What's that to you? That didn't give him the right to knife me.'

'So you aren't any better than you ought to be,' sneered Miss Webster.

There was an awful pause. Carmen stared at the empty desert and the lowering sun. The heat had gone out of the day and the wind had dropped. The great silence lapped against them. Miss Webster followed Carmen's gaze. A faint tower of dust swelled in the distance. The colours of the dead riverbed darkened from ochre into red. They both felt the shift in the dying wind. Neither of them said anything.

'I was knifed recently,' said Miss Webster, who now regretted the severity of her earlier tone. The experience of being knifed was an unusual topic for polite conversation, but seemed to be the only thing they had in common. She pulled up her sleeve and revealed the long white scar on her forearm. The edges were still red. Carmen inspected the damage.

'Nasty. At least my murderer didn't actually get me. He lunged. But I had a gun and I shot him.'

233

'Were there any witnesses?'

'Dozens. It was in a café.'

'Then my girl, why on earth haven't you defended yourself in a court of law? That's self-defence. It probably wouldn't even count as an excessive use of force.'

'He worked in military intelligence. I'd never have gotten away with it.'

Miss Webster now expected another pack of lies and immediately smelt something odd about Carmen's tale. Why, if she could clap eyes on Carmen so easily, were the massed ranks of the British specialist forces unable to do so? Why had that still presence of a man sitting in her kitchen, the man she had been wise enough to fear, mentioned Carmen Campbell, in passing, over his shoulder, on the way out?

'They know you're here, don't they?'

Carmen fixed her miserably.

'I told them you'd know. I told them. I told them that you used to be a private detective and that you find everything out in the end.'

'What on earth are you doing here? Working for them?'

'I'm in cold storage. Deep cold after this little fiasco.' Carmen made it sound like a tragic destiny. 'I have to work for them. Or I'll be sent to prison. It was their price. Are you going to tell them I've cracked and told you?'

'My dear girl, who would I tell? I don't know them. Or even who they are. And the only one I've ever met was a plain-clothes officer so frightening I flung him out of my house as quickly as I could.' Miss Webster reflected for a moment. Carmen Campbell really was trapped between the devil and the deep blue sea. 'You'd better watch it here. You'll end up decapitated. Saïda's probably hired a dozen contract killers to hunt you down. She sported a vindictive

234

glint, or so it seemed to me. You'd better be careful. These people aren't civilised. They're mired in the Middle Ages.'

This speech disturbed both of them. Miss Webster stared at the house, which had neither electricity nor indoor sanitation.

Carmen waited a moment and then replied, 'That's not true, Miss Webster. I came here to find sanctuary and they took me in. No one has ever judged me for what I did. I work hard. I try to repay the debt. It's very difficult for me. I had to learn the languages. I only know English. And I've never lived outside all the time before. Goats and camels are hard work and it means you have to be outside no matter how awful the wind feels. I'm a jazz singer. I come from London.'

They stared at the Sahara Desert and imagined England. The old woman from the country of dark soil and big skies and the black girl from a nice suburban neighbourhood and a church-going family found themselves thinking of strangely linked, yet different things. Carmen remembered *EastEnders* going out up to three times a week and the theme tune from *Thunderbirds Are Go*. Miss Webster remembered frost on the lawns in the mornings and her Michaelmas daisies, pale purple against the red-brick walls of her vegetable garden. Carmen recalled the sweaty smell of the Northern Line and the CDs packed under the bathroom sink in Pepper's flat. Miss Webster saw her potting shed and Chérif's dark curls shining through the glass, as he planted out the seedlings. Carmen saw her name in huge blocks of red neon scudding across the forthcoming events electronic notice-board at the Royal Festival Hall, and remembered pounding the floor of the taxi in triumph with her high heels. Miss Webster relived the great recycling wheelie bin debate, which took place on the gravel in front of the village shop. Carmen heard her mother's voice calling down the staircase and imagined the smell of chillies and onions cooking up together. Miss Webster recognised the trees beyond her cottage, swaying in the autumn storms.

'You should go back, go home.'

'I can't.' Carmen turned to face Miss Webster, who now saw that the young woman's huge brown eyes were awash with tears. Without any hesitation Elizabeth Webster held out her handkerchief and opened her arms.

'You poor girl, you poor wretched girl.'

They walked silently to and fro in the riverbed, Carmen crying uncontrollably, Miss Webster supporting her, speechless and moved. She realised that this was not repentance or regret, but homesickness, the most terrible longing that can ever seize our hearts. We are called home. Our desire to return, to go back to the place we recognise as our source, our first beginning, arises from our bitter rage against the old enemies, our only common foes: time, age, death. We long to burst over the threshold and find the dead still present, waiting for us with their arms outstretched. We must believe that we will find our welcome assured and the world unchanged. Carmen tasted the full measure of her loss. She would never, ever be able to go back or go home. They sat down at the edge of the palm groves in the shadow of a cracked mud wall. The sound of water rushed behind them. The late afternoon light brushed their faces.

'I don't usually break down like this. I'm not weak and feeble. I'll be all right in a minute.' Carmen sniffed and wiped her nose on the back of her hand. 'You know, it's great being able to talk English again. To someone English.'

Miss Webster nodded. 'Use the handkerchief.'

'You wouldn't grass me up, would you?'

'No, my dear. It had never occurred to me to grass you up,' she replied in stately tones. And indeed it hadn't.

'Miss Webster? Can I ask you to do something for me? To post a letter? In England. So that it won't have foreign stamps.'

'Yes, of course.'

Carmen dashed back across the wadi into the house and returned with a large smudged white envelope sealed up with wide brown tape. Miss Webster took out her glasses and looked at the name and the address. Percival Leroy Jones.

'But I know this man,' she exclaimed.

'Everybody knows him. He's very famous. He's always on telly,' crowed Carmen, full of pride.

'But I know him personally. He was at the airport last year. In Casablanca. Looking for you.'

'For me? Looking for me?' Carmen's childlike tone registered pleasure, gratitude and alarm.

'He said he didn't think he'd find you and he obviously hasn't. But he came. He was here.'

'Send him my letter.'

'Is he your father?'

'No,' said Carmen, as if she was scoring a crucial point in the argument, 'he was my manager. And he's my friend.'

She pronounced the word *friend* as if should be spoken only by princes, as if it was the one thing that was faithful and infinite, a loyalty and a passion that surpassed all other bonds, forgave all things, and knew no betrayal.

★

They became aware of a figure on the far horizon, coming out of the desert, a small cloud of dust rising behind him. He was still a long way off, walking slowly across the stony crest beyond the dunes. He carried a tall stick with which he flicked the battered scrub bushes. Carmen waved, but he did not respond. The sun was behind him. He may not have seen them.

'He spent the night crying. We got very fed up,' said Carmen.

Elizabeth Webster gazed at the hunched silhouette of the person who became steadily more unknowable, even as his familiar shadow stretched behind him, lengthening against the gold. The boy she knew was translated into a stranger. He reached a rock in the wadi twenty yards away and then stopped. Miss Webster was not prepared to put up with any more emotional scenes.

'Come here, young man. Sit down in the shade of these palms and start talking. You have some explaining to do.'

The boy wove an erratic trail across the space between them, avoiding her eye. Carmen got up, her beads and skulls rattling.

'I'd better go and leave you to it.'

She swished away down the mud tracks into the palm grove and vanished. The boy obeyed and sat down in her place beside Miss Webster, staring at his hands, clutching his stick. They were no more than four feet apart, and yet the distance seemed impossible to breach. The palms above them rustled and stirred. A little tornado of sand whipped down the wadi between the stones; then the wind dropped completely. The gigantic silence leached all emotion out of the space between them and the sky lifted a little, darkening at the core. She could hear the birds' wittering, far away in the fronds of the great rushes that marked the end of the river that had perished in the dust. Behind all things there lurked a silence so huge that it sucked the breath from her chest back into the austere and endless waste of rock and sand. Before her lay nothing, nothing but an indifferent ferocity that stretched away across the earth, harrowing and infinite. She looked at Chérif, or whatever his name was, crouching before her, making himself smaller and smaller, clutching the smooth grey dip of the rocks.

'Well? Speak.' Elizabeth Webster took no prisoners.

'Madame Webster, you can never forgive me.'

'That's up to me, whether I intend to forgive you or not. We haven't got that far yet. I actually need to know what you've done. And how you did it.'

There was a grim and dreadful pause. Then Chérif began his confession, speaking very softly. Elizabeth had to lean forward to catch every hesitant word.

'We changed passports. My cousin gave me all his documents – his student visa and his immigration papers. I practised his signature. We paid someone in Casa to change the photographs. He's a Kenyan. He also specialises in British documents. You have to pay a lot in Euros. It wasn't hard to do. Everyone knows us here, but no one does in the city.'

'But your letters home? You sent weekly e-mails. Saïda told me that you were very conscientious.'

'I told my cousin all about my course. I would anyway. He wrote the e-mails in the Hôtel des Voyageurs. They've got electricity and Internet access. He sent them to me. I tidied up the French and sent them back home from the Fac. So he did write to her every week.'

Yes, thought Elizabeth, with a concocted pack of lies. The dimensions of their duplicity astounded her. If someone willingly hands you their identity and their life, even

239

the life chosen for them by someone else, you cannot be said to be an impersonator or a charlatan. Chérif had become two people. The crunch came with the cash. Miss Webster went on to the offensive.

'You took Saïda's money.'

The boy shrank down into the rock.

'I will pay back every centime.'

'You'll have to.'

The vast silence clamped a band across Miss Webster's mouth. The cruel words she had prepared in the taxi drained away into sand. The light drew the shadows out across the golden dunes. Two camels appeared in the wadi, apparently free, nibbling the scrub. She watched each step, stately and deliberate, as the creatures belched and grunted their way down into the muddy puddles in the gulch. They raised their noses towards the palm grove and stared at Miss Webster. The light deepened and gleamed. She looked out into the vast arching blue. And after all, what mattered most to her? His company? Having someone else in the house? Speaking French in the mornings? Becoming addicted to very sweet *thé à la menthe* at ten o'clock every night? Taking an interest in the world again? In fact, who he actually was had never really mattered. She had never known who he was. She had accepted him nevertheless.

'By the way, what is your real name?' she asked gently, in a spirit of cautious enquiry.

'I am Mohammed ben Yacoub. Chérif calls me Moha. Everybody calls me Moha.'

Elizabeth Webster suddenly smiled.

'I think I might have to go on calling you Chérif.'

He looked at her, doubtful, but encouraged that she intended to continue speaking to him and might therefore have a use for his name. He had fully expected a bevy of *gendarmes* to emerge from the date palms and arrest him for fraud. Saïda would hardly accuse her own son. The role he had to play was therefore that of both villain and scapegoat. It was useless to argue that the idea had not been his, or at least not in the beginning. Besides, he had no real regrets. They had swapped lives for the sake of chemistry, mathematics and the love of a woman. The trick had been a daring risk, and they had pulled it off.

Miss Webster sensed this little rush of pride and stared him down.

'You must have known you would be found out.'

'Yes, but we thought that Saïda would come round. We thought that she would accept Carmen in the end. Especially when she saw the baby. She loves her son and that's her first grandchild. My cousin doesn't want to leave the desert. He hated being at university. He's happy now. The desert is his home.'

'And where, young man, do you imagine your home is?'

He had no answer to that. This boy, she realised, had never lied to her. Here he was, still exactly as he had always been: complex, reserved, ambitious, anxious to succeed in his studies and increase his chances in life, a boy who wanted to work and who would always, like a responsible son, send money home to his family.

'Who else knew about this deception, Chérif? Apart from your criminal Kenyan?'

He did not flinch at the borrowed name. He had adopted his cousin's name as part of an alternative identity. The spliced graft had taken. He loved the name. It had been upon his lips as soon as he could speak.

'Carmen of course. No one else at first. Maman and Papa found out at the end of Ramadan last year. They wanted to tell Saïda then, but the hotel was going badly and she'd had lots of bookings cancelled. And my parents were frightened about the money. Saïda can be very extreme. Maman had quarrelled with Saïda anyway – about her cruelty to Carmen, because she refused to see the baby. And then they weren't speaking to each other. So she would have to ring up and say, "My son had tricked you. Your son is still here in the desert and he has married the Black English Witch." And Ma just couldn't face it, so my parents didn't do anything.'

'Did you even think what the consequences could have been?'

Chérif looked blank. Then he spoke the pure truth.

'I wanted to go to England to study. My cousin didn't. He is in love with the desert and his new wife. We did this because it was the only solution to our lives. The only way out.' This was wishful thinking after the event, but at that moment it seemed to Elizabeth that it had indeed been the only possible solution. And the right one. The messenger with mutilated hands had sent her to the desert. And she was now convinced that her purpose was to bring back Chérif.

The giant silence lapped against her face. Chérif sat gazing at the last light on the golden dunes. The camels had strolled away, out of sight, and all across the domed earth a deep blue light flooded the night sky. Here was the first star. Abdou was still out there, somewhere in the grove of still palms, dozing in his taxi. A terrible stillness engulfed the world. This must be put right. And I can now make a decision that will ensure all manner of things shall be well. She stood up. Chérif picked up his stick and stood beside her. He spoke from the heart.

'Before we take our leave, Madame Webster, I beg you to forgive me. I have betrayed your trust.'

'There is nothing more to forgive, Chérif. The person who needs to forgive you is your aunt. You owe her a lot of money. You never pretended to be someone other than you are. You took your cousin's name. That's all. I loved having you to stay at the cottage. I even enjoyed watching the endless news.'

'You have been more than a mother to me, Madame. You have been my friend.'

Elizabeth looked at the boy's heartbreakingly beautiful face. Her lip curled. She bit back the ironic response that had risen to the back of her tongue. This was not the moment to cut the boy's feet from under him; instead she patted his dusty elbow. His jacket stank of goats.

'Of course we are friends, Chérif. We will always be friends. Now listen to me carefully. Come round to the hotel on Sunday at the end of the day. Get Abdou to send me a text and I'll come out to meet you. Don't try to get in. The gardener is probably programmed to shoot you.

'I'm going to see your parents and your aunt. You all owe her nearly £10,000. I'll find out how much she paid for the visa and the plane tickets. I think it's best if I buy her out now. Then she hasn't got a weapon against your cousin and Carmen. You'd be amazed at how rapidly angry people calm down at the sight of vast sums. We'll settle up later.

'You'll have to re-register at college under your real name or your cousin will be awarded your degree. I'll put my mind to it. And you'd better visit everyone you know. We've only got until the end of the month. After that we're going home.'

Chérif stared at her, dumbfounded.

Suddenly he saw the old woman with disturbing distinctness. What had she meant to him? In the beginning she had been an eccentric curiosity, a convenience, a house and a television set. But her tart and subtle tongue became a drawn sword in his defence. He had never negotiated the alien world alone; he had been accompanied every step of the way. The hot wind lifted and fixed her spiky white hair, which now stood up all around her head. The light washed her lined face with gold. She stood before him, transfigured. She was studying him with amusement and interest, as if he were a recent archaeological discovery of questionable provenance but great beauty. Respect is a powerful element in the connecting web we build between us and it is closely threaded with authority. The power of the old woman startled him into seeing her, as if for the first time.

'Mais qui êtes-vous?' he demanded. She had never looked so arresting, or so strange.

'I'm the messenger,' she said, and laughed out loud at his surprise. The darkness rushed across the desert towards them. 'Till tomorrow then.'

She strode off down the dusty path into the irrigated network of palm trees and gardens. Dim lights were coming on in the houses. He watched her go until she disappeared from sight into the shadows of the red earth walls and the giant date palms.

ACKNOWLEDGEMENTS

All the places and persons described in this novel, apart from Dr Broadhurst, who plays himself, are entirely fictional and any resemblance to an actual town or person is coincidental. My main source of technical information concerning the Sahara Desert was Marq de Villiers and Sheila Hirtle, *Sahara: The Life of the Great Desert* (HarperCollins, 2003). My greatest debt is to my guides, Fettah and Yussef, who showed me the desert where they live and were unfailingly helpful, courteous and funny when everything went wrong.

I would like to thank the following people for their help, encouragement and support: Barbara Carson, Sheila Duncker, Peter Lambert, Jacqueline Martel, Michèle Roberts, and Janet Thomas. Thank you to my editor Alexandra Pringle, the team at Bloomsbury, especially Victoria Millar, and to Kate Jones and everyone at ICM. Thank you to Claude Châtelard for her French expertise. Needless to say, all the remaining errors are my own.

I wrote a substantial part of this book while I was one of the writers in residence at the Château de Lavigny in Switzerland, run by the Ledig-Rowohlt Foundation, and I would like to thank the Committee for their hospitality. I am grateful to all the other writers who were there with me for their good company.

This book would not have been possible without the women behind Miss Webster, who are Miss Joyce Caiger-Smith, Miss Rachel Cary Field, Miss Kathleen Cusack, Miss Persis Freer, Miss Barbara Wetherall, and Violet D'Oyen Fitchett, known as Miss Vi.

A NOTE ON THE AUTHOR

Patricia Duncker is the author of three novels,
Hallucinating Foucault (1996), *James Miranda
Barry* (1999), *The Deadly Space Between* (2002),
and two collections of short fiction, *Monsieur
Shoushana's Lemon Trees* (1997) and *Seven Tales of
Sex and Death* (2003), all of which have been
widely translated. Her critical work includes *Sisters
and Strangers: An Introduction to Contemporary Feminist
Fiction* (Blackwell, 1992) and a collection of essays
on writing and contemporary literature, *Writing
on the Wall: Selected Essays* (Rivers Oram, 2002).
She is Professor of Creative Writing at the
University of East Anglia.

RHODES, philip